THE JUSTISAAR

SPACE HUNTER CHRONICLES 2

THE JUSTISAAR

SPACE HUNTER CHRONICLES #2

As an info broker, Selira wants nothing more than to be reunited with her daughter.

As an exiled judge, Diaz has no choice but to bring justice to the wilds of outer space.

But when Diaz is an unwitting pawn in luring Selira's daughter to a mining planet, he's embroiled in family drama while struggling to discover how she knows so much about his origins.

After all the worlds he's tried to civilize, never has he been tempted to rebel. Not only does Selira drive lust through him, but her daughter, the infamous Shikari, must be judged and executed for the abomination she is.

Or so he's been commanded.

Diaz has to choose between a justisaar's honor or a life on the run.

Selira must decide between saving her daughter or the man who fires her blood like no other.

Also by Sevannah Storm

The Blood of Legends Series
The Huntress
The Healer

*

The Gifting Series
Soul Forged
Fate Forged
Sun Forged
War Forged
Star Forged
Shadow Forged
Earth Forged
Lust Forged
Fire Forged

*

The Qaldreth Warriors
Sol Survivor
Dark Survivor (Coming soon)

*

The Space Hunter Chronicles
The Shikari

*

Standalones

Xiaxan Fox

Ire of Silver

The Crucible of the Eternal

*

Plump Playwright Series

Plump Jane

Seducing Amelia

Loving Finley

Keeping Tessa

Kissing Navy

GLOSSARY

Characters

Elizabeth Danvers – Ee-lizz-ah-beth Dann-verse – an info broker known as the Data Reaper.

Mikaela Danvers – Mick-ay-lah Dann-verse – Elizabeth's daughter

Thomas Danvers – Tom-ass Dann-verse – Elizabeth's ex-husband and xeno-zoologist

NOX – Nocks - Nano Omnipresent X-class A.I.

NOXV - Nano Omnipresent V-class A.I. – a newer model Selira calls Five.

Cason Themis – Cay-sonn Themm-is – hired messenger

Selira Myers – Suh-leera My-hers – Elizabeth's new name.

Tieren Fanyell – Teer-in Fan-yell – Black prince of the Greeven

Justisaar Diaz Rowfallak of the Opato Clan – Just-ee-sarr Dee-ass Row-fill-lack – exiled judge from Gy'Rux.

Hom'Garr – Hom-Garr – Councilor.

Ober Pantok – Oh-Burr Pan-Tock – childhood friend of Diaz.

Esha – Esh-ah

Rifa – Ree-fah

Vasaa – Vass-aah

Johah – Joe-jah

Da'Ager – Deh-aarga

S.o.S. – Soldiers of Solomon – mercenary group.

Solomon Burger – founder of S.o.S. – now retired.

Kiros Caldwell – Keer-ross Cold-well – Current Solomon

Wyatt Palmer – Why-it Palm-her - pilot, listens to audio books.

Ru (Ben) Holcomb – Roo-bin Hole-comb - bald, brown eyes, chews on a matchstick.

Gy'Rux

language

Gy'Rux – Guy-Roo – from the planet Nuberu.

Ruxling – Roo-ling – young Gy'Ruxian.

Camis – Come-iss – type of courier ship used for single-person transport.

Weyr – Where – nest of Gy'Ruxians (in a family unit.)

Mar ruome – Marr–roo-omm - blood mate

Kavex – Car-vex

Bapos – Bapp-oss – like a didgeridoo.

Purmoro – Purr-more-row – my fragrant one.

Purlievo – Purr-leaf-foo – my lovely

Purruome – Purr-roo-omm – my mate

Remyi – Rem-yee - the creator/God.

Qaf Dahn – Kwuff Darn – Justisaar initiation ceremony

Sillstari – Sill-starr-ee - Make visible/invisible, depending on the ship's current state.

Gotry – Gott-ree – small creature the size of a medium dog with green fur, multi-rows of teeth, and a lolling tongue. Often found in the sweltering jungle zones on Nuberu.

Mammo – Ma'am-oh – Mother

Pappo – Papp-oh – Father

Sasso – Sass-oh – Sister

Braddo – Brad-oh – Brother

Sanno – Sann-oh - Son

Danno – Dah-no - Daughter

Greeven language

ateeko – a-tee-koh - my hearts

   ateek – a-teak - my heart

   Gawen – Garr-win – the Greeven gods

   kekaseea – kekk-a-see-ah - mate

   Zelet – zeh-lett - shit

   Nona – No-nah - grandmother

   Moma – Mo-mah – mother

Miscellaneous

Fentus – Fenn-tiss – Science Research Company

   Followers – Expansive religious movement.

   Gy'Rux – Guy-Roo – from the planet Nuberu.

   Drueen – Droo-een – dragonlike shifters in the realm of Levion on Tau Ceti/Rianus.

   Locke – Cryo-rifle – fires freezing darts.

   Flint – Sniper rifle and can fire tranqs or excise darts.

Creatures

Hokou – hoe-koo – albino monkey with three tails, three-fingered hands and feet, and razor-sharp teeth.

   Okukuro – giant cockroach like creatures.

   Bebbayaya – bebb-a-yah-yah - worm-like creature with sharp spikes and gaping mouths. Yellow acidic venom and massive mandibles.

Consumables

Jaketta – Jah-kett-ah – blue fruit

Places

Tau Ceti – Tow Seh-tee

Cetus – Seh-tuss

Rianus – Ree-ann-us

Greeven – Gree-vin

Drueen – Droo-een – dragonlike shifters in the realm of Levion.

Navaardj – Naar-vaar-geh – the mountains holding Gy'Ruxian burrows/weyrs.

Nuberu – New-bear-roo – planet to the Gy'Ruxians.

Levion – Leh-vee-on

Qilaetor – Kee-lay-torr – home to the Greeven.

Chapter One

Justice is served.

Year: 2350

The planet, Nuberu

The High Gy'Rux Council Chambers

"*THE BLACK OF NIGHT, the color of sin, no soul shall be spared, the judgment within*" was embossed in gold on the forty-foot metal doors behind the dais of the council chamber. A beam of sunlight slipped through the stained-glass windows in the vaulted ceiling and shone on the doors—Diaz's destination. On either side of the marble-and-silver walkway leading to the dais stood his fellow justisaars. Ahead were the high council members, their robes solid black and lined with silver thread. Their tribal headdresses made of iron and gold had been passed down through the centuries and were only worn for...exiles.

Such as he.

Drawing in a deep breath, he strode off the landing. The first pair of justisaars stripped off his pauldrons. The second pair took his greaves. With each stride, his armor was removed, revoking his vows to serve and protect, to judge with fairness and honesty, and to never...murder. Even by accident.

For years he'd hunted those intent on harming others, and he'd meted out justice as decreed by the draconic emblem burned into his chest. Many had come to fear his name. Except for the sinless or those innocent in the eyes of the Gy'Rux law. *His* eyes no longer.

A bapos horn droned, spreading dread with its low bass resonating through the stone walls and the mounted tablets holding the ancient laws justisaars adhered to. When he only wore his hardened pants, soft tunic, and boots, the thundering of drums began. He knelt, bowed his head, and endured the removal of his tribal beads and shaving off his braids.

Around him, tufts of his hair and discarded beads littered the floor—mimicking the destruction of his life and dreams. It took all his strength to rise. A fellow justisaar snapped a bracelet onto his left wrist—to pay for his final mission. Another held out a modified duster coat for him to wear; the leather tight across his shoulders. He raised his arms to the side to be fitted with a bioblade holster and the weapon; its meager weight offered little comfort. With soul-deep heaviness, he climbed the steps to the councilor, who balanced a greatsword in both hands. His braided blue hair was a stark contrast to his councilor robe, his eyes a crisp blue in a face riddled with wrinkles. No one knew his age.

"Justisaar Diaz Rowfallak of the Opato Clan, you have failed your duties, your vows have been erased from our archives, and you are hereby banished to the wilderness to bring justice to those in need. Do you contest this verdict and its sentencing?"

"I do not, Councilor Hom'Garr. Let the will of the High Gy'Rux Council remain just, pure, and omnipotent." Diaz took the greatsword and sheathed it down his back.

"May *Remyi* bless your path." Hom'Garr bowed his head in sorrow.

His justisaars roared words like honor, obedience, suffering, compassion... Each was a knife to Diaz's hearts.

The councilors moved aside; their arms tucked into their voluminous sleeves. They nodded when he strode past. Two servants cranked the mechanism older than time. A deep knell shot through the chamber when the massive doors unlocked, then inch by inch, they parted. A sliver of orange sunlight blinded him for a moment. He grimaced and waited, as was the custom, for the doors to fully open. It would take some time with them thicker than an arm's length.

A bridge, in the same marble-and-silver detailing led to a circular platform upon which sat his transport. The camis was a single-manned spaceship designed for military couriers. It wasn't sleek but squatted like a ponderous insect. The obsidian-colored vessel was adorned with intricate geometric patterns etched into its metallic surface. The designs were reminiscent of their ancient civilizations, featuring sharp angles and interlocking shapes. Silver and red accents highlighted the engravings, stating its purpose; that of an exile vessel and a courier no more. One glimpse had agony twisting his hearts when the stylized motifs mimicked those in the armor he'd worn with pride.

The long snub nose held the cockpit, and to the rear was the living quarters that housed a bed, a bioray to take care of his biological needs and cleanliness, and a galley—all he'd ever require to travel to the far reaches of space.

He marched across the bridge, the tails of his new coat flapping in the strong winds this high up. An orange-tinted sky rolled out in all directions, the umber-colored clouds ominous with an impending storm brewing. He didn't glance over his shoulder or off the bridge to his homeworld, Nuberu, below. This was his life now; his arrogance and recklessness had made sure of it.

From the ass end of the ship, a ramp lowered when he approached. He didn't break his stride and climbed inside, sighing at its cold minimalistic interior. Knowing the councilors and his justisaars watched, not free to leave until he did, he slid into the pilot's seat. And froze.

On the left console sat a familiar *kavex* dagger. The dragontooth hilt was worn smooth by centuries of Rowfallak males. Engravings carried his family's pledge: in honor and obedience. He gripped it, ignoring the fiery burn of a tear slipping free.

His pappo had abandoned his duty, snuck here, and left this heirloom for Diaz, now an exile who'd brought shame upon their weyr.

He dipped his head in sorrow, aware he'd been his weyr's pride when he'd become a justisaar. Leaving this for him showed they still loved him. He sheathed the kavex and powered up the engines. The weight of his sentence bowed his shoulders. Shaking them didn't rid himself of the sense of doom encasing his hearts. He cupped the ball to his left and shot off, aiming for the binary stars in the heavens. A map of the known universe layered the windshield, a blue dot flashing his first destination.

He clenched and released the lever, venting his self-directed anger. His mammo and sassa had sobbed this morning, but there was nothing he could do or say to ease their grief. It had been goodbye. He doubted he'd ever see them again. They should mourn him as if he'd died. The councilors had advised as much.

And none of his battlemates had met his gaze while ripping off his armor. They couldn't show empathy, or they'd face the same fate. He grimaced then cursed with every word his pappo had taught him. The camis broke through the exosphere, his vision filled with endless space and Nuberu's binary stars glowing in the left corner of his windshield. He veered right, aiming for his first world.

His exile mission wouldn't be simple. Even on Nuberu, the lawless resented any interference, especially from a justisaar. He ran a hand over his shaved head and cursed again. Tapping the dot popped up an image of bright skies and green lands. Dosvin; predominantly farming settlements, with central repositories for interstellar export. Horror twisted his gut at there being thousands of towns he needed to visit on this world alone. All the planets scattered across the map might not be habitable. He took solace in that.

With days to reach Dosvin, he punched autopilot and stepped away from the console. For the second time in the last hour, he stripped. When he stood naked before the bioray, his image appeared on the bulkhead while a green light scanned his body. Without his long red hair, he looked odd like he wore the face of a stranger. And with the justisaar emblem inked into his chest, it served as a reminder of his failure.

He opened the cooler and removed a packet of water, sprawled on the bench, and sipped. Tucking his arm behind his head, he pondered his tasks, one of them being docking at various Gy'Rus stations to restock. Not to mention the accounting for every token spent and full reports on his attempts to civilize villages.

He smirked. No way would the high council issue endless tokens to an exile for no reason.

At least the act of beheading had ceased a century ago.

For now, he was alive, and he'd keep it that way.

Chapter Two

The Prey

Year: 2350

Near TOI-715b or Liccid

Goliath Way Station

The Mall – second level below the main docking bays.

ELIZABETH COULDN'T SHAKE THE sense that someone was watching her. Which was a stupid notion in the bowels of Goliath. Of all the stations in this part of the universe, this monstrosity was the dirtiest and most populated. Bouncers were the gatekeepers to dens of iniquities—their gazes vigilant like they expected trouble. Food peddlers eyed their clientele, hoping for a spark of connection to lure them to their stalls. Illegal travel passes were sold to those too desperate to argue over tokens or even ask where the documentation came from. No doubt some Galactic Security or G-sec officer loitered around the corner for a hasty arrest and a bribe for release. Corruption was rife, more so in 'civilized' way stations.

She'd once considered it odd how her husband, Thomas, preferred the seedier ports. Now, she knew better. "NOX, scan the area..." She bit her lip and pulled her daughter closer.

"I am uncertain of what you seek, Elizabeth," NOX said in her ear.

A Nano Omnipresent X-class A.I. was an advantage when traversing space. The ship, the *Jinsei*, had come fitted with him when his kind was far too expensive and not something Thomas would ever have purchased. NOX was gender-neutral, but she chose to think of him as a man, mostly because he didn't grasp her nuances in speech or expressions.

"Never mind," she muttered.

"What is it, Mom?" Micky asked, twisting to peer behind them when they entered a pod.

It shot up, taking them to the docking bays. As it climbed, a glorious scene came into view. Hydra-siphs, with their bulbous bellies, shuttled past the station's shields, shipping water to the massive haulers scattered like naval mines in the surrounding space. Beyond that in the distance, the super planet Liccid glowed a bright blue.

Dragging Micky, Elizabeth weaved through the food carts, gambling bins, and G-sec officers in their gray uniforms, their hands on their multi-phasers strapped to their chests. Their presence brought her some relief. She slowed her steps, hugged Micky to her side, then veered into a clothing shop.

"Need anything?" she asked, running her fingers over the overalls and T-shirts while snatching glances through the holographic windows for any suspicious behavior—as in someone trailing her.

"My boots are pinching," her daughter said, waving a foot. Now twelve, she'd shot up in the last few months.

Elizabeth smiled, her chest swelling with warmth and light. "Well, choose a new pair."

Micky hesitated. "Do we have the tokens?"

Pressure built in the area of Elizabeth's heart, and she hurried to blink back tears. "Yes, we do. And maybe a few T-shirts, a pair of jeans or two, and a bra." She whispered the last part and was glad she did when Micky flushed.

"But...Dad said we shouldn't spend." She stroked the sleeve of a pseudo-leather jacket.

"Well, you know all those hours I've been working at the console? I started a new job." Elizabeth shoved clothes at Micky and nudged her to the dressing room. "It pays well."

Crushing the garments to her chin, she peered at Elizabeth. "Then why do you two fight all the time? Isn't Dad happy you found work?"

Elizabeth wrapped her arms around her daughter for a tight squeeze. "He's just worried I don't get enough sleep." Which was an outright lie.

Where she'd once thought Thomas her world, her passion for knowledge had impacted her more than she'd anticipated. Sure, her husband was a genius when it came to xenology, but tokens were wasted, or worse, gambled away. He'd hidden the extent of their debt from her. Hence the arguments. Just when she paid them off by selling information, he'd spend again. They were damn lucky to have NOX, who made sure the *Jinsei* ran at peak performance. Should anything happen to Elizabeth, at least the ship wouldn't randomly explode and kill her daughter.

A shadow sauntered across the shopfront. The hairs on the back of her nape rose, sending a shiver through her. For a second, she froze, her thoughts in a panic. With a forced grin, she nudged Micky into the dressing room, then slipped behind an overloaded rack. Who would've thought knowing shit would endanger her? Twice, she'd received death threats. NOX hadn't been able to trace them yet, which left her suspecting every stranger. Leaving the *Jinsei* hadn't been wise. Hindsight sucked.

"NOX." She lowered her voice to 'mumble' to herself, dipping her chin to bring it closer to her wristband. "I'm in Future Fusion. Hack the security system and get me the name of the man striding toward me."

"As commanded," NOX whispered back.

If fear wasn't chilling her body and stiffening each muscle, she'd laugh at him mimicking her. Instead, she grabbed the nearest thing off the shelf and faced the shop assistant. "Does this come in pink?"

From the corner of her eye, she caught the man veering off, acting like he found overalls fascinating. His military pants, those magno-boots, his tank shirt in olive green, and the metallic toothpick hanging from his lip should've been out of place, but not on Goliath. Military gear adorned most of the workers, miners, and mercenaries frequenting the unsavory level above the generators, water purifiers, air filters, and sol tanks.

"Um, it's a hazmat suit." The poor woman widened her eyes at Elizabeth.

She glanced at the garment in her hand and grimaced. By legislature, such clothing items had to be certain colors to denote their significance. Stuck with her faux pas, she flashed a grin, hoping to cover her stupidity with charm. "I know. It's just for a bridal shower. Do you know if I could get one made in pink? Or dyed? It's my bestie's fave color."

Her smile faltered at the drivel coming from her mouth. Had her brain gone on vacation?

The assistant glanced around the shop, her eyes sparkling. "I'm being filmed, right? This is a joke. It has to be."

"Fine, if you won't take me seriously, I'll have to go elsewhere." Elizabeth shoved the suit back on the rack and marched to Micky's dressing room. "Howya doing, sweetheart?"

"Almost done." Micky shot her hand through the tinted holographics. "These fit."

Elizabeth took the jeans, the boots, and the T-shirts, then staggered under the mountain toward the assistant.

A gasp escaped her when a blur of movement preceded a burn on her side so excruciating that tears stung her eyes and nostrils. She dumped the stack on the counter to clutch just below her ribs. Twisting to face the stranger, she was met with an empty store.

He was gone, taking the sensation of being watched with him.

A peek at her palm confirmed the worst. Red stained her hand. She pressed harder, hoping direct pressure would stem the flow of blood. Choosing the black T-shirt had been a stroke of genius, hiding the spreading stain.

"Will this be all?" the woman asked, her blonde ponytail swaying.

Queasiness roiled Elizabeth's gut. She nodded, unable to speak past the lump in her throat.

Micky strode out of the dressing room, a tentative smile forming, and for once, her brown eyes full of excitement.

Elizabeth swiped the paypoint built into the counter's surface, desperate to make it to the *Jinsei* before Micky noticed anything odd.

"Ready to go?" Elizabeth nudged her chin at the air-degradable bags. "I'm starving. Let's head home."

"Thanks for these, Mom," Micky said, carrying her bags when they left the shop and strolled along the causeway to where the *Jinsei* was docked.

"Anytime," Elizabeth managed to say, wishing she could reach the *Jinsei* quicker.

The bulky vessel dominated her focus; its size blurring her ability to measure how much farther she needed to trudge. Each step pulsed fire through her torso, cramping her internal organs. Well, that's what it felt like, the twisting of her intestines until she had to bite her inner cheek to stop herself from moaning. The cool interior of *Jinsei's* loading bay prickled her skin.

Micky kissed Elizabeth's cheek then hurried to her room. As soon as she was sure her daughter wouldn't glance over her shoulder, she slumped against the metal wall, shivering at its icy touch.

"NOX, power up the med pod." She inched toward the ladder.

Climbing that would be a bitch, but she had to get to the pod. NOX was a hazard in his antiquated A.I. suit, so asking him to don it and fetch her might get her more injured.

And there was no way she'd call Thomas to help her. He'd blame her, and he had a right to. Thankfully, her attacker hadn't cared about Micky. This time.

"Fifty percent." NOX's voice boomed in the bay. Elizabeth didn't have the energy to ask him to whisper.

She gritted her teeth and took the first rung. Peeling her hand from the wound took courage, when for all she knew the direct pressure was the only thing keeping her alive. But she'd need both hands to reach the platform. Not as easy as the idea implied. With wet blood on her palm, gripping and pulling was harder. Her breathing raged from her lungs when she stepped onto the walkway. She kept one hand on the railing and stumbled to the med bay.

Her vision blurred, spun, and the urge to throw up hit her hard. Along with a flush of ice-cold sweat. She swallowed past the bile pooling on her tongue and inched to the white pod sitting centerstage. Now to slide into it. Frig. Who thought lifting it off the floor was brilliant? Sure, raised made it easier for the medic to access their patient. Logical, but for her attempting to sneak in a healing, this last hurdle just might kill her.

Lifting up her arm drew a yelp when fire blazed outward, bending her over.

"What the frig happened?" Thomas demanded from the doorway.

Tears slipped free. The anger and gloating in his voice lacked an ounce of concern. It was the final realization she'd needed, that he no longer loved her.

"Not now," she snapped, gathering the courage to throw herself inside the pod.

Its clear door closed, and a soft hum triggered the flicker of stats on the glass. The bite of an injection couldn't compare to the pain coursing through her.

Thomas glared at her. "Where's Mick?"

"Safe in her room," Elizabeth mumbled.

Couldn't he leave this until she was well? The agony in her side retreated, and at last, she could draw in a deep breath. A laser scanned her, lingering on her torso.

"Dealing with secrets has put Mick in danger. Can't you see that?" He slapped the glass. "You stop this nonsense now, or that's it, you're off the *Jinsei*."

She blinked at him, shock tying her tongue. *Leave? How? Why? Where will I go?*

"NOX, get the spare shuttle prepped," he ordered.

"I'm not leaving," she said, squaring her shoulders and curling her fingers into fists.

"You will if you value Mick's life." He gestured to her wound. "Did she see it go down?"

"Of course not." Lying in the pod put Elizabeth at a disadvantage, but sitting up in the tight confines was impossible. "So I'm supposed to leave our daughter with you on this monstrosity with who knows what out there? Frig, she's too scared to ask for shoes, Thomas. Lying to her and saying we have no tokens because you blew it on poker? Will you have enough to feed her?" She met his gaze, wondering what she'd once found lovable about him. "I'm not breaking her heart by abandoning her."

"One of us will have to. The *Jinsei* and the stability it brings her are all she's known. It's her home." He threw an arm out wide. "Who knows what awaits you in your new world of espionage. More hunters, killers... I warned you, Beth. People don't like someone stealing their secrets then selling them to the highest bidder."

She pursed her lips. Her tokens had kept this stupid ship running. How dare he.

"I'll never disembark again." She'd endure anything if it meant staying with Micky.

"And one well-timed missile won't obliterate us? You're not thinking."

"I will *not* give up my daughter, and you can't ask me to." She sat up, banged her head on the glass, then slumped, her temple smarting.

"Then quit chasing secrets."

"Then quit gambling," she snapped. "Grow a spine."

His face mottled, he swiveled on a heel, and stormed off.

She sighed. Once again, a pointless argument. "NOX, did you find out who that man was?"

"Yes. You are not going to like it." An image flickered on the screen mounted to the wall of the med bay. It was fuzzy as she peered through the holographic lettering and misted glass.

In her stomach, dread coiled into a aching knot and triggered another injection from the pod. "Frig," she muttered, tears forming for the fourth time that day.

Ruben Holcomb, ex-military and dishonorably discharged from Central Universe Forces for the mutilation of a prisoner. Now he was a gun for hire. A list of clientele followed; NOX being as thorough as usual. She stared at the last name... Governor Antoine Pienaar. The very man she'd leached information on during his tribunal. He'd been found guilty of fraud and human trafficking and was sentenced to life on a penal colony orbiting the planet Onasilos in the Serpens constellation. She'd thought him taken care of and not someone she needed to worry about. The dull throb in her side confirmed her foolishness. That he still had so much power from his cell when he had limited access to the outside worlds surprised her. Tokens did buy privileges; something she should've remembered.

"Where is Holcomb now?" She hoped whatever ship he boarded would reveal his client. Anger fused her thoughts into one: revenge. No one tried to kill her and got away with it.

"In a bar, checking the news and morgue after every Miner's Hopper."

She grimaced at him waiting to hear of her death. "He thinks he's done me in with one stab? That makes no sense, NOX. Why not finish me in that shop than leave it up to chance?"

"Done you in?" NOX hummed, which sounded like whirring gears. "One moment."

"He was paid to kill me, and once he realizes I'm still breathing, he'll hunt me again." She thumped the glass when the lighting flickered to green. The pod swished open, the med bay air cooling her and rippling goosebumps across her skin. "Even if I reported him, got him locked up for an eternity, whoever hired him would send more...unknowns. What do you think I should do?"

"What is this?" NOX gasped like air sucking through a filtration system.

"What?" she asked, striding toward the bridge.

"My Fair Lady... A musical? One moment."

She sighed. NOX was on one of his tangents. She'd get nothing out of him until he'd satisfied his curiosity. "I'm going to shower. Tell me when you've figured a way out of this mess."

"Will do, Elizabeth," he said then sang, "I could have danced..."

Unable to deal with his delighted distraction when she was far from happy, she headed to her private cabin. Thomas had moved out of their room, stating her odd hours impacted his sleep. Not that she'd minded. Yet another sign her marriage had ended without her noticing. While she showered, she pondered her situation.

Her info broker career had started so innocently. Throughout their long journeys between worlds, her passion had begun with the gathering of folklores, sightings of strange creatures, news of exciting events across cultures, stars, or planetside geographical anomalies just to have something to do, helping her fight off the constant loneliness of space. From any vids and signals shared between passing ships, she'd sort and store data that intrigued her. Curiosity had led her to research the names, ships, and conglomerates mentioned.

A few small research facilities had offered her tokens for specific information like passing planets' metallicity which the *Jinsei's* recon scanners documented. Even an entertainment company had wanted to buy her collection of folklores and fairytales. She hadn't accepted when they weren't hers to sell. But when she had evidence on Pienaar and his dealings, and when it seemed his case would be dismissed, she'd shared what she knew.

The *Jinsei*, a roaming xenologist research vessel, made her a moving target and difficult to trace. NOX had taught her how to cover her tracks for the most part.

How could she stay in Micky's life *and* keep her safe?

The more she mulled it over, the more Thomas made sense. She had to leave until this matter could be sorted. A different station, another stabbing, and she could be dead, abandoning Micky forever. A temporary trip was justifiable, freeing her to find a way to protect herself and her daughter.

And perhaps lure Pienaar's spies away from the *Jinsei*.

Unless they thought Elizabeth Danvers died.

She chewed on her lip as she dried herself. One shuttle, a fake-but-believable explosion, and she could start again. Except Thomas and Micky would know the truth. Could he make himself cry at her funeral? Could Micky? Their performances had to be convincing.

Pretending to be dead for real would break Micky's heart. Elizabeth couldn't bring herself to do that—to hurt her baby. She'd pitch the idea to NOX when she had his undivided attention. If he could work out a solid plan, then she'd explain it all to Thomas.

That should make him happy. Once Elizabeth Danvers was 'dead,' he'd be a free man. She'd have to assume a new identity, start fresh, but not where it came to information brokering. All her saved secrets would go with her. This time, she'd be more cautious—expecting the worst and preparing for it.

And perhaps a few new personas wouldn't go amiss.

Chapter Three

Redemption paused.

Year: 2365

The mining planet, Aibra

THE LAST BOUNTY'S DENIALS echoed in Diaz's mind, plaguing him even in the far reaches of space. Her delicate face flickered across his thoughts, her pleading with him to listen, to spare her life. But he hadn't. What information he'd received had painted her guilty. He'd heard it all before: the regret, sorrow, arrogance, fearlessness, cowardice... No last-minute words could save them from execution. It had been his responsibility to discern the truth and to listen to them in a final semblance of dignity. He hadn't done that either. Granting her one minute more of his time would have altered his fate. Questioning the data might have as well. He didn't dare consider the possibility that there'd been more innocents he'd judged. That way lay soul-destroying darkness at his inability to discern the truth.

He grunted, willing his thoughts to dissipate. Sifting through them on repeat garnered no new enlightenment. He'd messed up. Still, it irked. Something niggled at his consciousness, a sliver he couldn't quite grasp. His honed sense of justice wouldn't rest, even about his own conviction. He couldn't *not* accept the verdict when the evidence proclaimed his failure. Perhaps he'd misread his bounty's list of crimes? No, that made no sense either. Why would she have been on his task list had she not been guilty? One didn't land in a justisaar's sights without earning it.

He'd found her where he'd expected to, on the outskirts of the frontlines. She hadn't tried to hide. Her expression when he'd stood before had been one of curiosity, not of fear. That should have alerted him, but pretense wasn't new to him. His bounties tried everything to appear 'innocent' in his eyes, like 'hiding' in plain sight. Except she was a camp servant; not a life he'd wish on any female.

That day had been hotter than normal. Fires blazing on the horizon marked the current battleground. Behind him stood the commanding Mountains of Navaardj, its pinnacle disappearing into the orange clouds above. At its foundation, thousands of jagged doors marked Gy'Ruxian homes, burrowed into the base of the gray-blue rock. Not only did rankings determine the location of homes, but a crimson weyr like his preferred cooler temperatures and solid rock at their backs.

His cobalt bounty needed water, and she was far from it.

'Justisaar Diaz' had rippled across those observing. He hadn't spared them a glance. With the suns beating down on his head, he'd wanted the task done. Hers had been a simple case, or so he'd thought when he'd incinerated her body with a blast from his bioblade.

Nothing in life was simple.

The chill of the cave sank into his skin, traveled to the depths of his bones, and summoned thoughts of home. He hummed a ruxling's rhyme, one he hadn't thought about for decades.

Wing, wing, and flight,
Eyes in the night,
Never a friend, always to fight.
Death will follow, by breath or bite.

The damp rock-hewn walls brought on memories of a happier time before he'd become a justisaar. It was that or war, and judging everyone seemed safer than the frontlines. It didn't help that his pappo faced death daily. Seeing the struggle, the constant fear on his mammo's face had convinced him not to fight beside his pappo. Not once had any of them anticipated Diaz's exile.

He'd failed as judge and jury, but not as executioner.

With a chunk of rock in hand, he ran one edge along the floor, hoping to sharpen it. Thrumming his thumb across the smoothed side, he tested it. Almost there. Back and forth he went, singing to hide the grating. He could just break the bars to fetch his kavex, but he needed something to keep his hands busy while he waited for nightfall. The temperatures would dip further and lure him to sleep, he hoped.

The muted thump of footsteps raised his chin. He narrowed his vision along the tunnel leading to the surface of this gods-forsaken world. Everything brightened, showing the crevices of the cave they'd led him to. Lifeless, de-saturated browns made up the soil, rock, and mountains. The palest of insipid blues was the sky, like a merciless hand had leached this planet of its promise.

When no one appeared except those crisscrossing their dusty road, he pursed his lips at having to deal with these humans. But the lure of a cool cave, a chance to rest, had been too much to resist. Shielding his face against the glare, he willed his eyes to return to normal, bearing the blinding agony lancing through his skull as his due. Imprisonment was always a possibility when venturing into these lawless settlements scattered across... Where was he? Miv? Aibra? On his sixteenth world since he'd been shipped off his beloved Nuberu, he could be forgiven for not remembering. These backward races needed the law, or so the High Gy'Rux Council decreed. This was his mandate until every habitable world in the known universe had seen his face.

Or he died.

He snorted. Killing a Gy'Ruxian required some skill. His captors couldn't harm him with their pathetic weapons.

And yet, here he sat, behind rusted metal bars so brittle, his cough could snap them. Some might think him a weakling for letting them 'trap' him here, but bone-weary exhaustion clung to him. He'd hoped, naïve fool that he was, if he, without complaint, did like they commanded, they might let him return or, at least, visit his weyr. The endlessness of it all...

He glanced up, at the hooks on the far wall holding his gear and weapons—thankfully untampered with. And in the meager light shone his pappo's ceremonial kavex—proof that his weyr believed in him. Just holding it gave him the strength to carry on.

The slap of boots warned him he was no longer alone. He pocketed his make-shift dagger and shuffled until his back pressed against the cold rock wall.

"She's on her way." His captor spat out a thick wad of black goo onto the pale sand-covered floor. The skinny runt was all limbs, a matt of brown hair and shit-brown eyes. Tiny teeth filled his stained mouth.

Diaz absorbed the shudder of disgust and wished he didn't have to acknowledge him.

"The Shikari freak will kill your ass. I say we set you free, see if she can hunt like the rumors claim." Runt Two rubbed his hands together in glee, his grin stainless but toothless.

"Either way, you will pay," Diaz gritted out, ran a hand over his head and grimaced at the fuzz growing.

So they planned an arena-like event? Mm, it had been a while since he'd fought a worthy opponent. This Shikari female he *had* heard of—mutated and almost unstoppable. He doubted that. Everything had a weakness. There were no exceptions, not even in this mining town of...

"Where am I?" he asked.

"Richwood," Runt One said, chewing with his mouth open.

Diaz snorted. That would be his fourth such-named settlement? Humans weren't as original as they thought. On days like this, he was amazed he hadn't gone on a rampage and just judged them all. None were innocent, of that he had no doubts. He could count on one hand the towns that hadn't escorted him past their outer boundaries. Some 'mayors' had tried to kill him. For those, he'd had no remorse meting out justice. To take his life because they didn't like what he had to say? No death was necessary for such a slight. Their willingness to do so implied they'd done so before and often. He had no issue executing those too mired in their wickedness to change.

Runt One glanced at the entrance and bolted, bobbing like he bowed to royalty. Runt Two hesitated, casting glances between Diaz and whatever had startled his partner. But coward that he was, he soon left.

That suited Diaz well. He scrambled to the floor, sitting to run the 'dagger' across the rock. Another thrum of his thumb along the edge had him grinning. He maneuvered the weapon in hand until he could grip it well then ran it along his forearm, scraping off the fine hair growing there. Satisfied, he worked on his head, removing any semblance of forgiveness. An exiled judge was denied normalcy until his mission was complete. His was far from it. So growing his hair like a ruxling would garner yet another strike against his name.

Besides, keeping his head shaved meant fewer tokens wasted on actual baths. He'd parked his camis a few towns back, so tracking to it every time he wanted a bioray would be a waste of energy. Strolling into each settlement gave him a chance to assess the 'lay' of the land, when setting his ship down on the 'main' road would only tempt these desperate folks to steal it. Or try to.

But after a good rest here in Richwood, he'd head back and fly his camis to its next hiding spot, wherever that might be—near a cave, if he was lucky.

"I can provide a razor," a female said, her voice melodic with a cultured accent.

He snapped his head up, and in an instant, narrowed his vision. How had she snuck up on him? From the shadows emerged a cloaked figure. Was she who the runts feared?

"The rock will do." He peered under her hood, but there his sharp eyesight couldn't penetrate. He sniffed, instead, for body odor revealed much about an individual. She smelled good: clean, sun-kissed with a hint of sweetness. That alone was an anomaly when cleanliness wasn't a priority for these people.

"I came to apologize," she said.

He stilled mid-scrape to test where he'd missed. Without a mirror, he had to go by feel. "An apology requires your name."

"Selira." Humor filled her voice. "Not many know it."

"Ah, so you too expect me to die?" He laughed. "I aim to disappoint."

"No, your death is not my agenda. Besides, any Gy'Ruxian can bend these bars with ease."

He lowered the dagger to stare at her. Twice, she'd surprised him. "You know what I am."

"It's my job to know. Hence my apology." She shifted closer, her movements graceful if not for a subtle whir-and-hum.

Which part of her was mechanical? He frowned. Her deep brown cloak hid much.

He waited, peering into her shadowed hood and wishing she was lovely like her voice or, for his sanity, uglier than a demon.

With delicate hands hidden by gloves, she caught the hood between two fingers and flicked it back.

His breath lodged in his throat. One of his hearts paused, then hurried to sync with the other, and in that moment, he reveled in the female before him.

And he'd thought brown lifeless.

A braid, three fingers thick, roped from the top of her head to drape over one shoulder. Pale skin glowed in his heightened vision. Brown eyes, almost black, met his gaze. No fear stiffened her body or darted her focus from him. A small nose tipped up at the end but led his focus to her lips: plump, uneven, and scarred.

He smiled. "Revealing your name when no one should know it, then showing me your beauty? Pray, how do you intend to kill me?"

She chuckled, low and husky. "I don't know anyone capable of matching your skill. No, you serve a different purpose. You are the lure. When I heard of your intended arrival on Aibra, I planted a few seeds among the...riff raff to capture you before you spread your particular brand of justice." She paused. "They're not too keen on anyone telling them how to live. Rebellion, I'm afraid, is bred into us humans. But I digress. With the tokens I offered as reward, she thinks you're a monster terrorizing children."

He leapt to his feet, striding across the cell to peer at the female through the bars. This close, she was stunning and her scent... He drew in a deep inhale before asking, "The Shikari freak?"

She betrayed herself with the tiniest of lip twitches. "Yes. Mikaela Danvers."

"Do you aim to kill her?" He knew not the nature of this mutated human, but what she did she believed was for the greater good, and somehow through her actions, she saved lives. Rolling his shoulders didn't ease the sudden knot building there. "I might intervene." Though why he warned Selira, he couldn't say. Beauty had never swayed him before.

"It will not come to that." She lifted her stubborn chin, determination pouring off her. "You'll be released the day she arrives."

Just like that with no contestation? He doubted that. "To test my strength against hers?"

"Absolutely not," Selira snapped, her tone aghast. "I won't share why I seek her. Know that you *will* be freed to pursue your absolution as ordered by your council."

He scowled. Her knowledge of his exile grated since those records should've been erased. "How do you—?"

"I do my job well," she said again, like that explained it. "Micky's en route. And if the shit hits the fun, try not to hurt her." She ran her gaze over his chest. "I'm certain you can."

"So an apology and a plea?" He stepped back to scrape the make-shift blade behind his ear. "And why should I accept either?"

Selira splayed her fingers at her cleavage, highlighting the enticing curve of her breasts. "Because she's an innocent…for the most part."

Theft? Murder? Those mattered to him. Adultery, no thanks. Dealing with who-said-what made his skin itch to escape. If he had his way, he'd kill both spouses just for the suffering they put him through.

"Then why are you after her?" He folded his arms across his chest. "I am not helping you trap an 'innocent' female."

Despite the flicker of interest crossing her eyes when she glanced at his body, her expression remained neutral. As if she weighed a decision, she peered at the cave's entrance, granting him a view of her profile. "She's my daughter."

He stared at her, running his gaze over the lines around her eyes and mouth. "I call ass shit. You are not old enough to be a mammo."

She laughed, the sound bright and tinkly. "I've been charmed before and am immune to it. You can escape whenever you choose to. So why stay then?" She stroked a finger down a metal bar.

"It is cool and a free bed." He gestured to the rock ledge he used for a bench.

She hummed. He must have confirmed something she'd expected. Was she omniscient? Telepathic? How could she have known his plans when he'd only formed them the moment he'd been arrested? The runts mentioning tossing him into the cave had halted any thoughts he had of killing them. The many towns he'd visited had the standard jail, not anything this…unusual. Their soft beds, bright sunlight, and too-hot weather was a 'comfort' he didn't need.

"You haven't slept, not since Cooksey. I figured the cave would tempt you to 'let' them take you without too much or if any bloodshed." She gave a delicate shrug.

Cooksey? Hell, he hadn't yet documented the last town's rejection of his brand of law and order. Even the H.G.C. weren't aware of his location.

"Start explaining yourself. How do you know so much about me? And do not say it is your job." He grabbed the bars, almost hard enough to snap them off—layers of the rusted metal crumbling beneath his grip.

She offered him a gamine smile. "I ordered fruit in anticipation of your arrival."

Her change of subject blindsided him, but hell, if his mouth didn't salivate. He swallowed hard. "Fresh?"

"As fresh as space travel can allow." She created space between them, taking her sweet scent with her. "I can get them to bring you a bath, if you wish?"

A bath? In a rural town fed by a single well? "Who are you truly? The mayor?"

Again she chuckled and dismissed his questions with a flick of her wrist. She clasped the hood's edges and drew it up over her head. When she reached the cave's entrance, she paused to say, "Play your part, Ex-Justisaar Diaz Rowfallak of the Opato Clan."

He sank onto the bench and blinked into the glaring sunlight. Not much stunned him, but she had. From the moment she'd arrived, he'd been on the back foot—a position he hated.

Runt One brought him a platter of sliced fruit and a pitcher of *gi'hayna*—a wine diluted with fruit juice. He didn't try a sliver of what they called oranges, not just yet when she intrigued him. Yes, he'd play this role, just to see if she was a female of her word. And no, he wasn't staying put because of the meal she'd provided.

But it didn't hurt to indulge when she'd gone to all this effort.

Chapter Four

Blindsided.

Year: 2365

The mining planet, Aibra

Selira slumped against the rock wall the moment she stepped out of Diaz's line of view. Her knees trembled, her heart thundered in her ears, and for the life of her, she couldn't draw in a deep enough breath. Never had she experienced such a visceral reaction to a man. Not even with Thomas, her late ex-husband.

She'd observed from the safety of her office when Iane and Hajo led the ebony-skinned giant into the cave. Even in the weak sunlight, his skin had glistened, highlighting every exposed muscle. The dragon tattooed in silver above his left pec had drawn her gaze more than once. She'd wanted to trace each line with her tongue. And for someone as celibate as herself, the urge to lick a man was a rarity.

His bald head only served to enhance the angle of his jaw and those penetrating red eyes switching between normal irises to that of a cat's.

His deep voice, drenched with curiosity or good humor, added to his allure.

She'd have to guard herself around him. Twice he'd revealed he found her attractive. Said so matter-of-factly, it went straight to her head. If she didn't already know he'd decline her offer of employment, she'd hire him in an instant. Bodyguards were hard to come by, and none were so intimidating while being strikingly handsome.

Exiled judges had a mission to complete. She doubted he'd toss aside his honor code to work for her in whatever capacity she needed. Sex slave came to mind. She swallowed a bark of laughter at that telling thought. Pity. Having him tied to her bed was a delicious daydream she'd keep for the lonely nights in space.

When Hajo carried the fruit passed her, she flicked the cape aside to stride un-hindered across Richwood's main street. The whir-clunk of her leg when she moved reminded her that love of any kind, especially the physical, wasn't meant for her. And hadn't been for a long while.

He fascinated her, though; so strong, determined, honor-bound, and yet exiled.

Without having met her Micky, he was prepared to defend her simply because she was an innocent in his eyes. That told Selira more than she needed to know what type of man he was. She tossed her braid as if doing so would clear her head.

The goal here was Micky, not Diaz. He was but a means to an end.

Cason Themis, the best bounty hunter in the universe, delivered her message to Micky almost a year ago. It had taken decades to find her. Thomas's death had reached Selira so far away in the Leo constellation, but too far for her to rush to Micky's side. When Cason located Micky near Phoenix, it was the happiest day of Selira's life.

A million times she'd berated herself for letting Thomas convince her that Micky staying with him was the safest course. The fake explosion had been Selira's silly idea. She gripped her metallic knee through the cotton trousers. The shuttle she'd fled on had to 'explode' to convince those hunting her of her death. Elizabeth Danvers had to die.

She'd snuck off the *Jinsei*, sobbing her heart out at having to 'abandon' her daughter for a while.

Boom went her shuttle, and off went her leg.

The damage had been extensive, but with the *Jinsei* nowhere in sight, a passing hydra-siph had come to her aid. The connections she'd formed that day had propelled her career into the stratosphere. She smiled in memory at how much miners liked to gossip. It had been a struggle at first, using what information and tokens she had to set up a base. But her first purchase wasn't a ship but a NOXV. The cost alone had emptied her pockets, so to speak.

Raising two fingers to Old Gladys behind the saloon's counter, Selira veered into the kitchen, peeking at the meals being prepared. Gladys ran an honest-to-goodness brothel, serving clean women and food imported from the nearest farming moons. At the Hidden Depths, both were the best any miner would get on Aibra. The aromas were unusual, sharp and earthy. Since the saloon was a front, Selira gave Gladys full control.

She'd also lost the ability to blush at the sex talk, grinding and grunting she often overheard, or the occasional flash of nudity. None of that mattered as long as Gladys stayed in business and Selira's safehouse—one of many—remained secure.

Into the staff bathroom then through a concealed door to a mining elevator she continued. Down it traveled until 'fresh' air became a memory. Humidity dewed sweat on her skin, plastered escaped strands of hair to her temple, and left her inhaling hot air. A slight tremble shook the cage just when she touched down.

They were sinking shafts in the nearby mine of Sosrak where most of Richwood's population worked. Rhodium, iridium, platinum, and gold fueled the mining industry on Aibra. She had no complaints, having bought shares in every conglomerate worth her while. Ice hauling was lucrative with the demand for water skyrocketing. She'd shared info with Central Universe Forces on criminals stealing water from random planets and violating the Primary Directive which carried a harsh punishment for anyone intruding on planets without a space program. That included no stealing their resources and people.

Her wealth mattered less and less while the years passed without finding Micky. When this Shikari story hit her desk, she'd cried.

Not once during the reconstructive surgery, the fittings for her augmented limb, and enduring the pain of her healing wounds had she shed a single tear. Thomas had died without revealing the truth to Micky, like he'd sworn he'd do when she'd brought the stupid plan to his attention. As soon as their daughter reached fifteen, he would spill the beans.

Cason had said she'd almost killed him the first time he'd delivered the data crystal. Called him a liar to his face.

Selira grinned while marching along the tunnel, ducking cables and light bulbs to reach her satellite home. The white door loomed—solid, smooth, unblemished, and looking out of place in a rusticated and dilapidated mine. With a palm to the center panel, it swung open.

"About time you showed up," her NOXV said, waiting to the side. His metallic armored body glimmered in the artificial lighting.

Cool air made her sigh when she ventured deeper into the living area. The door shut, thunking when the locks slid into place. Beyond that to the left was her bedroom and en suite. To the right, her office, and between was an escape door leading to an exit tunnel.

"What happened, Five?" she asked, accepting the offered towel and bottle of water while handing him her cape.

He draped it over his arm. "Data feed is secure, so you can unbunch your panties on that."

She hid her grin with the towel. "And Micky?"

"En route with no detours scheduled." He smiled, twisting his metallic lips, and flashing a solid strip of white. "Oh, Lord, she be coming."

"Good." She drank deeply from the bottle then capped it. "What correspondence has arrived?"

"All the requests from your whining clients, except those marked high importance, have been dealt with. I was nice in my responses. Okay, tried to be." He trailed her, stomping like an elephant. "I haven't been slacking, y'know."

"I assume you were listening in?" She gestured to the wall of screens surrounding her office.

"And monitoring your stats. You like him."

She grimaced. *Like? Sure. Desire? Oh, yes.* "He serves my purpose. No more."

"Fine, lie to my face, but your heartrate is all over the place, not to mention your thought-to-be-extinct hormones going berserk." Five stared at the security video aimed at Diaz's cell.

He chose each sliver of fruit with care, wiggling his fingers in eagerness. His hums of pleasure was a reward in itself. Flustered, she pressed the bottle to her neck, hoping the condensation would cool her amorous thoughts.

Five swung to look at her, arching two rubbery eyebrows. "I rest my case." He leapt to tap a screen where bars on a chart danced. "See, you're horny A.F."

"No one says that anymore," she harrumphed. "And quit monitoring my hormones. I'm nearing forty-six, not a hundred and two."

"Mood swings, check." He counted off on his fingers. "Menopause looms. Dear Lord, save me."

"Peri has to happen first." No way was she discussing her periods with him. Not again. He probably had her charted and the next ten years of her cycle extrapolated.

She sank into her chair then swiveled to tap the surface of her desk, summoning the emails, status on stocks across her innumerable investments, the security of her other satellite offices, all filmed and monitored, and a steady stream of incoming information from her various informants. Many of them were low-level employees, eager for a small payout. The most lucrative data mines came from executives who'd landed in some sort of predicament they needed her to bail them out of.

Five's data mining bots were hard at work, twenty-four-seven.

Her underground facilities on Aibra were small and butted up to an old mined shaft, so as not to rouse suspicion with ground-penetrating scans. Her state-of-the-art ship, the *Usuba*, was tucked into an abandoned cave. Each location was chosen based on her access to data, power, and the planet or moon's geology. No mine, no cave, no satellite office.

"Have you planned what you're going to say to Micky? I have compiled a list of options."

She grinned. "Oh? Let me hear them." She flicked through mails, answered one, then archived it.

"Hey, Micky, it's your mama. Come give me a hug." Five's gaze was expectant.

As wonderful as a hug would be from her daughter, she didn't expect it. "She's twenty-six. It's not going to happen."

"All right, discard that one. How about, 'Your father's a dick?'"

She laughed. "Sure, when she adored him?"

"Okay, bad idea." He rested his fists on his hips. "Where the hell have you been, missy? You can't be hying across the universe and not let me find you." He twitched his eyebrows. "I like that one. What did you think of my performance?"

"Brilliant," she said, keeping her smile in place while swallowing a giggle.

Five went with her everywhere, but she hadn't ordered him a skin suit when her own leg was skin-free. So, his wiggling, rubbery eyebrows and that little ass jiggle... Comedy gold.

"You got any ideas?" He frowned. "She might cry when she sees you."

"I might do the same," Selira said, her eyes stinging in anticipation of their reunion.

Despite not liking these mutations, whatever they were, it meant Micky could protect herself, and since she'd violated the Primary by stealing a man from Tau Ceti, she needed back-up too. Selira had erased what data she could discover on who this Prince Tieren was. A prince, for the love of... Couldn't her daughter have taken a farmer from a distant island with not a soul for hundreds of miles?

She huffed. And by erased, she meant it, with Five trawling every database imaginable.

"I'm going to hop in the shower. Make me a cup of tea, would you?" Without waiting for Five's response, she bolted.

In the privacy of her bathroom, she stripped out of her pants and button-up blouse. The mirror was unforgiving, but in Diaz's presence, she'd felt... She glared at herself; the scars crisscrossing the side of her face and down her body were a tarnished silver. Her breasts sagged despite her skincare and exercise regime. Her waist tucked in with a nice flare to her hips. But then her left leg... The skin puckered where it met titanium. Some days, she could stab her thigh with a knife and not feel a thing. Other days, her non-existent toes itched like they'd misconnected her nerves when they'd attached this thing to her body. Not that she'd see a doctor. That way lay agonizing pain, and she didn't care how much medical science had evolved in the last decade.

She stepped into the cubicle and activated the jets, grateful for the luxury with water a scarcity.

Her thoughts slipped to Diaz, shaving his head with a sharpened rock. *Damn.* It was the sexiest thing she'd ever seen. Then he'd faced her, his massive fingers denting the metal bars. He'd loomed as only a six-foot-six man could do. More so with his dark-gray skin and muscled chest. His presence had dominated the space around her, like a vortex, drawing her in.

His greatsword leaned against a wall, partially hidden by his duster coat. Daggers, pistols, and ammunition were sheathed to his belt hanging on a hook. He had a small backpack that held devices for location, healing, and water extraction, or so Five had documented. She had no doubts Diaz could survive in the wild for days. But between Richwood and Cooksey, there were no trees to cast shade, and no known caves that might tempt a Gy'Ruxian to rest. And with two suns offering sunlight almost all the time, 'nightfall' without a cave wouldn't bring him much relief.

The three-minute timer cut off her shower, but thankfully she'd shampooed and soaped despite her mind being elsewhere. She wrapped a towel around her head and slid into a robe.

The heated flooring meant she didn't need to wear slippers. And when she opened the bathroom door, Five held out her tea. "Something to eat, your highness?"

She chuckled. "Some of that fruit, if there's anything left."

He beamed, widening his lips without showing non-existent teeth. "I saved you an orange or two."

"Ah, Five, you know I love you, right?"

"Don't get soft on me, woman," he called as he headed for the kitchenette. "Now, come eat your dinner like a good girl."

Chapter Five

In limbo.
Year: 2365
Just flying through.
Circinus constellation

MICK TRACED A FINGER down Tier's obsidian-toned chest. She was too lethargic to get out of bed, and so was he. But where she lost herself in her thoughts, he was reading yet another of Dad's journals. She wasn't going to bother asking him what his plans were for the day while they hurtled through space to their next 'client.'

Who was on some planet in the Scorpius constellation. At least it brought her closer to finding her mother. She shoved that thought down, not wanting to spoil her mood. With a kiss to Tier's cheek, she rolled out of bed and crossed to the shower. Coffee was in order.

She turned under the spray and smirked at Tier, watching her with his yellow eyes darkening to amber—an indicator he liked what he saw. "Breakfast?"

"Mm, later." He lifted the book but peered over it.

"I'll check in with NOX then meet you in about an hour in the gym." She towel-dried then yanked on jeans and a T-shirt. Skipping a bra was a given when Tier would just remove it later, and if he had his way, she'd remain naked. To dress or not to didn't matter when she had her earbuds. Exiting her cabin, she stuffed them in before the constant humming, whirring, churning, whining drove her crazy. She stamped on her boots, then strode along the passages to the *Jinsei's* bridge.

NOX was belting out another musical number; this one quite catchy. When she peeked around the door's edge, she swallowed a bark of laughter. A state-of-the-art A.I. suit doing jazz hands? Priceless.

"...on babe, why don't we paint the town? And all— Oh, morning, sweet cheeks." He lifted his non-existent top hat.

"Anything new, exciting, something I can do, kill, tag, hunt?" She ventured deeper into the room to grip the back of the pilot seat and stare at the passing stars, praying one of them offered her some sort of distraction.

He gave her an I'm-afraid-not smile. "With our focus on getting to Aibra, Libra, then Leo, I've been doing reconnaissance and documenting locations for possible bag-and-tags on our return trip."

She frowned. "Fentus won't like a drop in my sample deliveries." She hummed. "The mission did sound serious, though. Children in danger doesn't sit well with me. Did you ask for more detail?"

"Kind of, said it was a big black monster with red catlike eyes. Still, no actual imagery."

"Maybe it moves too fast. Sounds like fun." It did, as bored as she was.

And with NOX not stopping at every habitable planet, that meant she was left to her own devices. If it wasn't for the sizable tokens offered for the capture of this red-eyed beast, she'd be too busy to worry about what awaited her in Libra with her mother.

She hitched a thumb in the direction of the mess. "Gonna grab a coffee, then...sort out Dad's cabin."

NOX blinked at her. "Think you're ready?"

"As I'll ever be." She strode off, keeping her true motives to herself. Secrets, history, nostalgia, and sadness she could expect to find in Dad's things, but facing her mother without knowing much was a nope.

She tapped her booted toes, arms folded across her chest, to the discordant gurgle of the coffee percolator. "It makes no sense," she muttered.

Mom faking her death? Why? And why had Dad agreed to that? Despite the state of their current 'relationship,' before Mom 'died,' Mick's memories were of happier times. Not once had her parents argued...in front of her, that is. Though many a night, their garbled yelling had penetrated the bulkheads and kept her awake. Divorces, these days, were easier, by far. Submit two signatures, a copy of the marriage e-certificate, and boom, divorce issued.

With coffee in hand, she trudged to Dad's cabin, pressed her palm to the cracked access panel, then grimaced when the door slid open. The air was cold, like it was devoid of emotion. In her imagination, but still. She ventured in, drawing a deep breath of his cologne, old paper, dirt, and something chemical. Tier had taken the entire stack of journals instead of coming and going and disturbing Dad's things.

Time did heal, or perhaps, help her forget. Eleven years had passed since he died. Though, with just her and NOX on the *Jinsei*, it had been easier to seal this cabin when she hadn't needed it. When the Soldiers of Solomon mercenary group or S.o.S was on board, their presence hadn't driven her to clear Dad's things either. The *Jinsei* was a retired research vessel with tons of space and detachable compartments for the deployment of instant labs in situ. Those parts of the ship had never been utilized or occupied, even before Mom 'died.'

Dad's cabin was a replica of hers. Where he had shelves, a desk, a holographic-glass cabinet, hers had none of that. Her personal touches were dirty laundry or an empty grit glass. With Tier moving in, his clothes filled half the closet and a few weapons were mounted to the bulkheads. She loved his scent though, permeating her body and space. No longer did loneliness plague her, and with the mutations at peak performance, having him with her gave her comfort.

She ran a finger over the spine of Dad's collection of real scientific books—hence the smell of old paper. "NOX, put these books on the market. Might as well make some tokens."

"Sure thing, sweetie pie," NOX said, using some hidden speaker.

He was in the *Jinsei's* system and ran everything, including her life, despite having a new suit. Now she had double the back-up with NOX and Tier heading planetside with her when she tagged alien creatures and bagged biological samples. If the poor thing died, she sent its body. When she'd agreed to work for Fentus, they'd fully stocked her drones, fuel, sol, water, and pantry.

"Do you want me to catalog each of his books?" She raised her chin to the ceiling like an idiot—a habit she hadn't been able to break. NOX was everywhere, and technically, his memory banks were levels below her.

"I have them documented, already posted. We might need to drop them off wherever we travel. I'm telling you now, babe, zigzagging across the universe to deliver books makes my ass twitch."

She chuckled. "Let's not get excited. We could dump them on a way station and have the buyers fetch them their damn selves."

"True." He whistled. "No offense, honey buns, but had we done this sooner, we wouldn't have been so desperate for tokens. These babies are worth a fortune."

She smiled, tears stinging the backs of her eyes. "So, Dad left me more than the *Jinsei*."

Energized by this discovery, she swung open his closet with all his clothes. With each jacket, pants, and shirt she pulled out, she pressed them to her face to inhale his scent for the last time. "NOX, bring me a crate, would ya?"

"Coming right up," he said.

She started to fold each item, stacking them according to their kinds. "Make that two."

"Damnit, woman." NOX glared at her from the door.

"Oops," she said. "We'll store the books too."

"Oh, by the way, just a random thing to know," his tone conversational, almost too casual. "We should be hitting Aibra by lunchtime tomorrow."

She froze. "I thought we were days out."

"We calculated our ETA using fuel-saving, but we've been firing all engines." He arched a rubber brow.

She scowled at wasting tokens. "Why the frig would we—"

"I want all systems focused on getting there. Not a single child will be lost because we were cautious with our fuel. Frig it." Her recorded voice played through the room.

"Y'know, I'm getting tired of losing arguments," she said, wagging a finger at an unrepentant NOX.

"They also paid upfront."

"Shit. The situation must be dire." A miner and their tokens weren't easily parted. "Get me more crates..." She hesitated then added, "Please."

He dipped to peer through the portholes. "Is it raining?"

She chuckled. "Very funny."

"Be right back, babe," he said and left.

She too glanced at the space outside. After Aibra, she had no more adventures lined up, which meant she had no excuses to avoid heading to Libra. To face Mom.

Dad hadn't mentioned faking her death in any of his journals, or so Tier had said. And he'd yet to find a single mention about the mating amulet she now wore. The mystery continued. How had Dad stumbled on a yet-to-be-charted planet's jewelry without violating the Primary? She winced. She was just damn lucky the powers-that-be hadn't come down on her ass. Yet.

Perhaps they didn't know about her revealing herself to a primitive species. Or they did but because she was all over space, they couldn't catch her. Would there be a fine, jail time, worse, grounding the *Jinsei* so she could never travel again? *Frig*. Not good. She studied her palms. These hands weren't made for serving beer. She curled her fingers into fists. They were made for killing.

A throb formed behind her furrowed brow. She needed grit, stat.

Leaping to her feet, she hurried down to the hydroponics lab for a refill. Sure, distilled spinach couldn't compare to Dad's stash of expensive brandies and what not. But those were for special occasions. Her mutations acting up didn't classify.

In truth, what she feared was one swig of his Ganymede wine and she'd never be able to stomach grit again. As it was, Tier's wine had been delicious. "NOX, why the hell didn't we bring a wineskin or two of Jaketta?"

"Oops," was all he said.

"Might have to swing by, fetch a few, visit Nona, see how Wyatt's doing." She beamed at having a grandmother-in-law. It still boggled her mind.

He scoffed. "Swing by? Like it ain't light years off our current trajectory." A long puff of air mimicked a sigh. "I suppose, when we're in that neck of the woods, sure. Adding it to the itinerary."

The smell of the lab hit her first: rich soil, organic plants, and the alcoholic sharpness of fermenting grit. Spinach spilled from the bulkheads and pots dangling from the ceiling. In tanks to the side, green goop gurgled. She took a glass and used the tap to 'sample' each tank. Like always, it was vile, like munching on soil and grass. Within moments though, her headache faded and her enhanced hearing, despite the earbuds, dulled. While she sipped, she read the holographic statuses. She didn't have to when NOX was the best moonshiner she knew.

"I have thee crates but am missing me missus," NOX sang through the speakers. "Finish that grit and get yer ass here. I ain't got all day, honeybuns."

"Hold your horses, I'm coming." She huffed, swigged back the grit, then left. "No need to get testy."

NOX had packed most of the books by the time she reached him. So she went to work on Dad's clothes—none of which would fit or suit Tier. Though he preferred to waltz around in a pair of harem pants he called *dowo*. Not that she was complaining. That man had some fine calves. And if he went shirtless, the better the eye-candy for her.

"Were we not meeting for a sparring session?" Tier asked, peering through the open doorway and into Dad's cabin.

"In a bit. I thought I'd tackle this space." She swept out a hand as if to say, 'look, see how well I did.'

He scanned the chaos and settled on the brandy, whisky, and Ganymede wine tucked behind a holographic glass door. A quick cross to it brought his unique cologne with him. She hummed, ogling him while folding and packing a shirt.

He opened each bottle for a sniff and a sip. "Bitter, yet there are hidden flavors that layer my tongue at different intervals. I like the burn too when it travels down my throat." He turned his back on the cabinet. "Need help?"

"All good," she said, kneeling to better stuff a crate. "Have you eaten?"

"On my way when I heard the commotion." He bent to give her a kiss. "I will bring you a coffee."

She stared after him, her heart swelling to overflowing. Just like that, she'd gone from being single and alone with an A.I. for company, to having a 'soulmate.' Not that NOX wasn't entertaining with his stage musical addiction or that his latest upgrade had taken him from formal to...whatever this was.

"NOX, what do you think of this fake-death nonsense?" If anyone would know, it was the A.I. who'd been on the *Jinsei* longer than Mick had been alive.

"With Elizabeth?" He furrowed his brow, ran his forefinger over it, then nodded in a mission-accomplish sort-of way.

A lance of pain skewered Mick's heart. Yes, that was...is...was her mother's name. *Frig*.

"Perhaps she should tell—"

"So it's true." Tears slipped past Mick's defenses.

"It started as a hobby, listening in on channels or when we passed planets and the snippets the recons picked up. She loved a good story, their folklores as entertaining...Just for the fun of it she documented them all, probably for something to read and re-read. But your mother's a smart woman, something Thomas never realized. She figured out his gambling—"

"His what?" Mick whispered, her eyes wide. Her mouth fell open. "Is that why we never had tokens for...things?"

"Yup. In desperation, Elizabeth sold a few of those secrets she'd picked up. On Goliath, a merc found her—"

"Goliath." Mick slumped, wiping her cheeks so she could catch any expressions NOX chose to use. "I remember. She was acting weird at the shop. I thought it was because I bought too many things."

"Never, sweetheart. She really did have the tokens to splurge on you. But an inch to the right and that knife wound would've done her in." NOX hoisted the crate and stood. "The exploding shuttle was her idea. Worked though, convincing Holcomb that he'd been successful. Elizabeth Danvers died, and Selira Myers was born."

"Holcomb?" Mick jerked back. "Why does that sound familiar?"

"One of S.o.S. Or used to be." NOX's voice trailed off. "Wonder if he's still being digested?"

"Frig. Well, live by the sword and all that." At least she didn't have to worry about some revenge assassination attempt. "But all these years? Why now?" She glared at NOX. "And why the hell didn't you mention it when we got the data crystal from that peacock?"

"I didn't know Elizabeth became Selira. Extensive digging after Rebirth revealed little. Info brokers cover their tracks well, and she'd done a bang-up job with everything I taught her. So, I figured she'd spill the tea when you finally meet."

"Info brokers?" That headache was back. She massaged her temple.

"Are you planning on repeating everything I say?" He harrumphed and left, carrying the crate of books.

Mom mentioned a new job that paid well. That alone had convinced Mick she could finally get a few things she needed. But Dad gambling? Part of it rang true with the meager tokens they had to survive on, but why would he throw away what little they did have? That didn't seem like something her brilliant father would do.

She sat on the crate to clip it shut, then slid it to the side to tackle the next one. With Tier trawling Dad's journals, he might stumble on Dad mentioning this. Somehow she doubted it, since Tier had yet to find a single sentence pertaining to the amulet. She cupped it through her T-shirt and stroked her thumb over the carved griffin's nose so reminiscent of Tier's.

"NOX, are you a thousand percent sure Dad gambled?" She held her breath while she waited.

"Yup."

That one word hit her like a sledgehammer to the chest.

Frig.

She didn't like how these revelations painted Dad in a negative light, nor did she like not having ammunition to thwart whatever her mother planned to talk to her about. She'd died. Mick had mourned her, sobbed at the funeral while trying to act like a boy. It had seemed as if Dad missed Mom too, though now, in hindsight, she couldn't be sure. He'd thrown himself into his work, busier than ever, but that was nothing new.

And when she'd mentioned Mom, like how much she would've liked to see an exploding star or made Mick the best cup of tea, Dad had fallen silent and abandoned Mick for his labs. She'd thought it was because it was too painful for him.

Every damn time? To act like a grieving husband when he was far from it?

And she should've been able to spot any odd behavior. Right? As the daughter? But she hadn't, not when she'd been devastated, mired in her own sorrow. It had taken her years to put aside the clothes Mom had bought her, wearing them until they threatened to split in two. She had them still, tucked in the back of her closet.

Perhaps listening to what Mom had to say would at least fill in the details missing from her memories, or answer all those whys she'd screamed into the void. Hell, during a teenage tantrum, she'd blamed Dad for killing Mom with their constant bickering.

He'd been furious with Mick, not sad, accepting, or compassionate. "Your mother brought this upon herself, dragging us into it. She shouldn't have started her silly hobby. Everything was perfect the way it was." He'd disappeared into his lab and ignore Mick for days.

She hadn't understood him at the time, but with the tidbits she was learning, it was all beginning to make sense. Now all she had to do was get over this anger simmering inside her, fueled by a hurt so deep, she didn't know how to heal it.

For now, she'd take each day as it came. When she saw Mom, maybe by then, her chest wouldn't feel like it had been crushed by an anvil.

Chapter Six

"Boss, it's bad." Iane's voice filled Selira's bedroom. "He's escaped."

Ice drenched her spine. "Frig." She leapt out of bed to yank on a pair of jeans and a T-shirt. Clipping her boots on, she eyed Five watching her. "Well?" she snapped, stuffing a pistol into the back of her waistband.

"Calm your tits, babe." Five shrugged. "He hasn't gone far. I sent his current co-ords to you."

She jerked to a halt. "What? Not coming with me?"

"Nope. You're armed, and he showed no intention of killing you. I figured you could do with some action anyway. Can't be lazing about making me do all the work. You gotta meet me halfway here, babe." Five returned to the office, leaving her to gape after him.

She grabbed her cape and left, sprinting down the passage to the elevator. It chugged, slow and lethargic. She cursed it while chewing on a thumb nail she must have ripped at some point. None of that mattered. Diaz was gone, and maybe if she caught up to him, she could convince him...somehow, to stay. Not that she blamed him either. She'd asked him to play his role even though he could leave at any moment. With his strength, keeping him in a rusted cage was stupid, but she'd needed his trust and hadn't wanted him to feel threatened. She doubted a pissed-off Gy'Ruxian man would be easy to placate. She almost giggled at the idea of throwing grapes at him and hazarding a guess at his reaction.

Despite the fleeting time they'd spent together, she did like him. Five hadn't been wrong about that. She could claim her interest was purely business, but Five wouldn't believe her, despite a justisaar traveling the universe being an excellent source of information.

When she left the Hidden Depths, the sun was on the cusp of rising. She glanced at the band on her wrist and followed the blip. Five was right, Diaz hadn't gone far. In fact, he wasn't moving at all.

"Frig, frig," she muttered, stomping up dust when she rounded the cave to the south. "He's dead or eaten; neither is good."

But when she stepped onto a flat ledge, she froze.

Before her stood a warrior as old as time. Barefoot, in nothing but his military pants, he gripped his greatsword and swung it with precise movements, all while facing the sun.

Her breath hitched, and her eyes stung with her refusal to blink and miss a moment of this beautiful man. In the sunlight, his tattoo shimmered, though that could be her imagination or the sweat glistening on every inch of his bare chest.

She swallowed hard.

"Thought I had run?" he asked but didn't glance at her. For that, she was grateful.

"Yes," she said, then hurried to clear her throat when she croaked the word.

He chuckled.

She shivered and pulled her cloak closed, more to hide her taut nipples than for warmth.

"My apologies for waking you." He pressed the flat of the blade to his temple and raised his gaze to the sky. Then with one smooth swing, he brought the tip of the greatsword to the ground.

He strode toward her, his sword arm lax. In the shadows, his red eyes glowed, but when he stopped in front of her, his irises were normal. He didn't say a word, just studied her upturned face.

"I'm sorry for thinking the worst." She released a shuddering breath. "I've been searching for Micky for so long. This is the closest I've come..." She bit her lip, hoping to silence her loose tongue. As an info broker, it paid to be observant and less talkative.

"I will wait for this Shikari, more out of curiosity. I too have heard of her achievements and wish to document them for my council." He flipped her hood back, startling a gasp from her. "Better."

The urge to touch him inches from her had her stuffing her hands into her pockets. Some things were better to ogle, though she imagined he'd feel incredible.

He swept his gaze down to her boots and up, lingering on her breasts straining her T-shirt. Only then did she remember what she'd been hiding behind her cape. She didn't rush to cover herself when doing so would embarrass her further. No, it was best to pretend she found the morning cold, rather than admit the man before her was the sexiest she'd ever met.

He closed the distance between them, forcing her to step away. A smirk toyed with his upper lip when he inched her back until her ass hit the rock. Her heart pounded in her chest, sending flutters to her core. She held her breath too, though how that would help her, she couldn't say. With this man, she was out of her depth and knew it.

He delved his fingers into her unbound hair, his touch firing a frisson heat outward. "Selira."

She didn't dare move, even when he cupped the back of her head and tilted her gaze to meet his.

"We should not start our...relationship based on apologies," he said.

"Relationship?" she whispered, raising her fingers with the intention of tracing the dragon's snout on his tattoo. Caution caught her just in time, and she tucked her hand between her back and the rock.

"Why do you fascinate me so?"

She blinked at him, not sure she'd heard him correctly. What could she say to that? That his admission sent a thrill to her toes? A rumbling that vibrated— She gasped, splayed her fingers across his chest and shoved him. He didn't budge, so she squeezed under his arm to peer around the edge of the cave wall.

"Frig," she snapped at the sight of Titan Exploration's underground transport trucks drawing to a halt. "What now?"

This she hadn't anticipated. Not with all those miners crowding the bin. Good business for Gladys, but with Micky arriving and Diaz out of his cell...

"A complication?" Diaz layered his body to hers and peered around her.

Heat seeped through her cape, drenching her with glorious warmth. She shivered and pulled her cape closed again to hide her reaction from him. As smug as he was, she had no intention of giving him an insight into what he invoked in her.

"The mining corporation with the rights to Aibra is Titan Exploration or T.E. I was hoping to not have to deal with them." She peered over her shoulder at him and stilled, lost in the iridescent beauty of his red irises.

A man jumped off of the vehicle and strode toward Gladys, who left her brothel while drying her hands on her apron.

"Gladdy," he said, throwing his arms wide.

"What brings you to our side, Javier?" She gestured to the trucks. "Let's get your men inside for breakfast."

"Indeed." He spun, his gaze sweeping over the sleeping town. "Heard we're expecting a visitor."

"Oh?' Gladys asked, as if this bit of news surprised her.

"If they're here for you, we're in deep shit." Selira didn't peek at Diaz, just leaned back to touch him. "And even if they're not, they can't find out about you."

"Why not?" he growled. "I have dealt with their kind many a time."

"Because killing any of them will bring down the full might of T.E.'s security forces. They take their miners's safety to the extreme." She twisted to press her back to the rock and her shoulder to his chest. "We're going to have to hide you."

"Are you saying there's law and order on Aibra?"

She nodded. "In a way. They handle most crimes and sentencing." She met his gaze. "Which was why I thought it odd a justisaar would choose this planet. No one at Cooksey told you or you wouldn't have headed to Richwood."

"We have a little...monster problem in the Sosrak mine," Javier was saying.

Diaz opened his mouth to speak, but she held her forefinger across his lips.

"Is that why the ground's arumbling?" Gladys flounced aside to let the miners file into the Hidden Depths.

"Sure is. We've been trying to blow up the thing, but it keeps coming, slashing and killing any in its path. The mine's come to a standstill, and you know how the execs at T.E. hate an unproductive day."

"But I haven't heard anything of the sort." Gladys frowned.

"N.D.A. prohibits any miner from discussing mining business."

She laughed and patted his chest. "Come in, eat, and you can tell me why a monster is any of Richwood's concern."

Selira did a quick scan of the main street to confirm no one lingered. "This isn't good. They're looking for Micky." She hurried around Diaz, planning on leading him farther away from the cave entrance. When she was certain they wouldn't be spotted, she fell into a pace while wringing her hands. "You'll have to hide with me. Do you have your things?"

He twisted his lips and studied her before saying, "I do."

"Oh, good." She smiled in relief. "Come, we need to hike to get to the exit tunnel. And if we hurry, we can listen in on what these men have to say."

She spun on a heel, ready to speed-hike a mile north-east to a hidden entrance.

"Wait, female." He slipped into his V-necked shirt, strapped on his holsters and belt, then pulled on his coat with its built-in sword holster down his back where he sheathed his greatsword. He looped his satchel over his shoulder and flicked his fingers in the direction she'd pointed.

With the mountain of a man at her back, she followed the blips on her wristband to her secret door. She snuck glances over her shoulder, to check if they were being tracked, or so she told herself. The truth was, she couldn't believe he'd come with her so readily.

His assessing gaze had implied he'd been about to leave and have done with her. Instead, he'd agreed. Too delighted, she didn't want to question her luck. He'd been the lure, but with a real monster terrorizing miners, she didn't need him anymore. She knew the daughter she'd raised, and Micky wouldn't turn her back on a chance to save lives.

So why keep Diaz around?

Over the rocky terrain and into a shallow ravine Selira led him; their footsteps cast up mini dust clouds. She wanted to call him a fool for trailing her without question. Instead, she savored the crisp morning air, the scent of water tickling her nose, and the cool breeze tossing her hair. Having practiced this path before, she didn't have to give it her full attention. She peered at the horizon, the variances of browns and beiges mesmerizing. It had been decades since she'd been on Prime Earth, and for some reason, Aibra felt like Earth 2.0.

She veered east, dipped behind an outcrop of boulders, then slid between a narrow gap forming a vertical scar on the rock face. In the dark cavern, she released a slow breath while she waited for Diaz to squeeze himself through. He tossed in his bag, sword, and other weapons, until a pile sat at her feet. With a slow exhale, he sidled through with an inch to spare between his chest and the crevice.

She snatched up his bag then grimaced at its unexpected weight. What did he have in there? Rocks? One by one, he sheathed his weapons, before taking the bag from her.

Dipping her gaze, she hurried ahead. What would he say if he caught her ogling him? She gritted her teeth but her imagination ran with it. What she should be worried about is where he'd be sleeping. Her satellite homes were designed for her and Five. She'd never had anyone visit or sleep over. She snuck a glance as she led him down a tunnel. Would he even fit in her shower?

She shuddered at the imagery of water trickling over his bulging muscles. *Get a grip, Selira.* A smile formed, despite her internal reprimand. He was in her home; he might as well be in her bed too. At the white door, she pressed her hand to the center until it thunked open. Five stood to the side, one arched brow conveying his surprise which didn't ring true when he always eavesdropped. It had to be her judgment or motivation he questioned.

"Welcome, Justisaar Diaz," Five said.

"Just Diaz will do, machine," he said, dropping his bag beside the now-locked door.

"Want a shower?" she asked, then pinched her lips together. She headed to her office instead of acknowledging this attraction between them. "I'll get Gladys to order more fruit. We'll stock up for the next few days."

She sank into her chair and tapped keys to fill the surrounding screens with security videos of the Hidden Depths. Not the rooms, though. She didn't need to see what happened behind those closed doors.

Any tidbit of information Gladys deemed juicy, she shared with Selira anyway.

Diaz entered the office and stood behind her, dominating the confined space with his presence. So aware of him, the hairs on the nape of her neck rose. She quelled a shiver and added volume, covering her ragged breathing with conversation and the clink of utensils on metal plates.

"Do you think the Shikari will help us?" someone asked.

"With the tokens T.E. is throwing at this...problem, for sure," Javier said, raising his white-frothed Miner's Hopper as if to say Micky helping was a fait accompli.

"How long we waiting?" a man called.

"Time for a little fun?" Another man's flashed a big toothless grin. "Might be the last time I get to dive between a woman's—"

She muted the audio, gathered her courage, and swiveled in her chair to face Diaz. "Seems like I don't need you anymore. You're free to go." With him looming, her impulsive decision to hide him here had come home to roost. "As promised."

"Is that so?" He gripped the armrests and leaned in, his nose almost touching hers. "I wish to meet this Shikari. Like I said, my council should hear of her deeds."

"Is that why you wish to stay?" She folded her arms across her chest, trying to show she wasn't in the slightest bit intimidated...or aroused.

"Among other reasons," he said, his focus unwavering.

This close, yellow flecks were visible in his eyes. And the smell of him should've been offensive. Instead, dust, sweat, and sunshine poured off him. Desire slammed into her, snatching her breath and stealing her thoughts. She could do nothing but stare at him.

"You brought me here to protect me." He smirked. "A noble gesture but pointless. I do not kill indiscriminately, but I do not hesitate when it is necessary." He straightened and glanced at Five. "Machine, I will take that shower now."

"This way, Diaz. Name's Five. Try to remember it."

She widened her eyes at Five's sass and whether he was risking a disembowelment.

Diaz pursed his luscious lips then gave Five a curt nod. "Fair enough."

The moment they both disappeared into her bedroom, she released her breath in a whoosh. This was madness, like stacking gold nuggets in front of a gambler. And yet, Diaz had been right. She had needed to protect him. She'd gotten him into this situation and had promised he wouldn't be harmed. Leaving him in that cell might have tempted the miners. One man, maybe two, that she could control, but a mob?

She stilled. A monster in the Sosrak mine? And she hadn't heard of it? She summoned security videos of the mines, any reports submitted, the list of dead...

A gasp escaped her. Only glimpses revealed the creature, but still, Micky could face that thing and live? The mother in her prayed it wouldn't come to that. But the info broker she was, knew her daughter had dealt with worse.

Even as her mind reeled, her thoughts kept circling back to the fact she had her very own red-eyed monster in her bathroom. This was a turn-about-face, with Diaz not leaving when he could, and her wanting him to leave but he wouldn't. She wasn't sure about his intentions with Micky. Reaching behind her, she took out the blaster and set it on the desk. Could she shoot him if she had to?

The only person she'd ever dreamed of killing was Thomas. Harming another soul went against everything she stood for. No. She shoved the blaster to the side. If Micky could handle such a creature, she was more than capable of taking care of one six-foot-six justisaar.

Selira only had to have faith.

And a back-up plan.

Chapter Seven

DIAZ RELISHED THE COLD water sliding over his body. Tension had hardened every muscle since Selira had ogled him at first light. And her scent was everywhere in her sleeping quarters. After sniffing every bottle in an alcove, he found her soap. No wonder she appealed to him when she washed with strawberries—whatever that fruit was.

Oh, Remyi, how I ache for her.

For a female of her maturity, she shouldn't think this heat between them alarming. She should be the one to approach him, to demand he...dive between her thighs. And that soft peach blossoming on her cheeks... He wanted to be the one to summon those flushes, gasps, and her lingering gazes she tried to hide from him.

He'd known he could leave when the mining vehicles arrived. But one glance at the concern in her eyes, her unbound hair, and her nipples tenting her garment had convinced him otherwise. Companionship wasn't denied to an exile, and it had been so long since he'd been this tempted.

He pinned his elbows to the wall and raised his face to the spray. A chemical tang saturated the water, no doubt purified to the extreme. In this small space, where she expected him to sleep was a mystery. Her bed looked too soft to interest him. And the warmth rising off the floor said that was a no-go too. Perhaps the tunnel they'd traveled through?

He hummed. The cavern had been a pleasing temperature; the way his kind liked it. Here, in her home, he couldn't spread his wings. He needed shadows, chilled ground beneath his feet, and solid rock at his back.

And yet, here he stood. He offered his back to the water to stare at her bed through the door. To lay with her, he'd endure its unstable surface. A grimace twitched his nose at his willingness to suffer the discomfort. He should've left. It might be better for him not to know her intimately.

But something compelled him to stay. Instinct, magic, he knew not what. One of the reasons he'd chosen to follow her. If he documented everything, the H.G.C. wouldn't find fault.

A monster? He was intrigued, planning to go with Micky to the depths of Sosrak to discover what lay below. How did the daughter differ from her mammo? Yesterday, Selira's strength had fired his blood. This morning, her sweet concern for him had summoned his protective instincts. Her determination was there but rattled by how he flustered her.

He grinned, liking that she was as aware of him as he was of her. The hard part of him wanted her beneath him this very minute. The rest of him wanted to drag this out, to savor every glance and touch. He shuddered, just remembering the press of her finger across his lips. It had taken everything in him to not taste her mouth as these humans were wont to do. He'd never understood the appeal until now.

Five held out a rectangular cloth.

Diaz took it but stared at it. "What am I supposed to—"

"To dry yourself. My apologies, but we don't keep garments for someone of your size." Five gathered up Diaz's pants, tunic, and coat. "I'll just pop these into the laundry closet. Shouldn't take too long to dry clean."

"Wait—" Diaz grimaced when the machine hurried off, leaving him with the soft fabric.

He patted his face with it, rubbed his head, then dabbed at his body. Aerating was so much easier than this laborious task. He considered doing just that, striding out naked in the hopes of triggering Selira's blush. Instead, he wrapped the cloth around his torso like some sort of skirt. While gripping it closed on the side, he went in search of her.

Data scrolled on a few screens, one showed the miners though it remained muted, another had... He narrowed his vision. Financial stats he couldn't care less about. She tapped the glass surface of her desk, flicking her hands to send items into folders, and all while humming a jaunty melody.

With her yet to notice him, he took the time to study her.

Her temple reached his collarbone, and she was thinner than he liked. She had a good set of hips he could grab onto, and her breasts were plump enough. Still, there was just something about her that appealed to him. If he could figure out what that was, he could assuage his curiosity and leave this hell hole for the next planet on the map. With T.E. in power, the H.G.C. would accept his relocation to another world.

She gasped, snatching his despondent thoughts from his cyclical existence.

He met her gaze in time to watch an enticing peach blush travel up her throat to bloom across her cheeks. She ogled him, every inch on display. And when she licked her top lip, he had to root his feet to the floor to stop himself from kissing her.

"Oh, let me," she said, pushing out of her chair to whir-hum across to him.

She tugged the cloth from his fingers then tucked the ends in, making sure it was snug enough to stay in place. Her hair brushed his bare arm, the sway of her curls stirring up the scent of strawberries. When she stepped back to admire her handywork, he stared at her tiny teeth dimpling that supple bottom lip.

"Sorry. I didn't think this through." Her fleeting wince had him doubting he saw it. "Five's ordering some clothes for you too."

"I do have a spaceship equipped with all I need."

She nodded. "But it's west, past Cooksey." She raised wide eyes—the brown of her irises were like pools of endless knowledge. "Would you let me...see it?"

A heart stilled. Did she mean his...? What did these humans call his sex organ? Cock? Yes. It twitched in anticipation at the mere thought of her soft fingers running along his length. But since they were talking about his camis, he erred on the side of caution.

"Why would it interest you?" He chose to be as ambiguous in his response, in case she did mean his cock.

"It's a part of the Gy'Ruxian culture, which, you know, is a closely guarded secret."

He snorted at that nonsense. How safe was his civilization if an info broker knew more than she should? That would be something he needed to document. The H.G.C. had to up their security.

"I need my garments if we are to travel. Tell your machine not to bother ordering." He swept a hand down his body as if he needed to show what he meant.

Her focus trailed his gesture and settled on his badge. He'd suffered with fevers and visions for three days after the initiation ceremony. There was no way to remove it, even for an exile. The law pounded through his veins after years of studying its nuances. Yet despite his diligence, his understanding of it had failed when it shouldn't have.

"Do you have clean clothes on your ship? Or you could wait an hour."

He smirked. "Can you?"

She stiffened, her eyes flashing fire. "I have work. You're welcome to rest in the lounge or ask Five to find you something to drink or eat."

When she swiveled to return to her chair, he caught her wrist. His world tilted at the sweet silkiness of her skin. Something he hadn't needed to know. Just touching her decided her fate.

"Thank you, Selira," he drawled.

She pinched her lip, gave him the curtest of nods, then slipped free but only because he let her. While she attended to her tasks, he faced the rest of her home.

Five pointed to the padded bench. "Squat there. I took the liberty of chilling that area. Let me know if you want it icier?"

Intrigued, Diaz strolled to the corner and sat on the too-soft bench. The cooler air made him sigh in satisfaction. And the floor beneath his feet no longer radiated heat. If he could, he would toss off the too-soft cloth and sprawl naked for a nap. Selira hadn't been wrong about his exhaustion. It hovered on the edges of his mind, like his thoughts traveled through a sieve. He'd managed a few hours last night, but being imprisoned meant sleeping with one eye open.

Not that he could lower his guard here either. What if her concern was a ruse? He peered at the machine, wondering if he could take the thing apart if she instructed it to attack him? A glance confirmed his weapons and satchel untouched. They were close enough should he need them. Without further debate, he whipped off the cloth and lay down, curling onto his side with his back to the bench.

He jerked awake what felt like minutes later. Without a window to show him the passing of the day, he knew not for how long he'd slept. Lethargy saturated his limbs to the bone. He rolled onto his back and stretched, blinking at Selira leaning her ass against the counter with a cup in hand.

Remyi.

He stilled but didn't hurry to cover his nudity when it was too late. She'd seen every-thing. Not that he was ashamed of his body, but he wanted to savor her blushes each and every damn time they appeared.

"Five has prepared a platter of fruit for you. It's what we could find in Gladys's freezers." She waved her cup at the nearby table. "Help yourself. Micky will be breaching the exosphere within two hours."

Despite her glowing cheeks, her voice was calm, as if she was unphased.

He frowned, wanting more of a reaction from her. "Indeed." He leapt to his feet and faced her. When her gaze didn't dip to his...cock, he huffed, almost impressed at her strength of will. So, he sat and pulled the fruit closer.

"We have time to head to your ship."

"Why would I need to if my garments are clean?" He arched a brow, while popping a handful of purple-blue berries into his mouth.

"Because I want to see it." She placed her cup behind her and folded her arms across her chest, thrusting up her breasts. Succulent mounds formed in the 'V' of her tunic.

"It is just a camis reserved for couriers. Nothing interesting."

Her eyes narrowed, and damn, if her flaring nostrils didn't shoot heat to his groin. "It has the look of a sperm whale from Prime Earth, yet the markings are what fascinate me. A hint of its mystery is in your tattoo." She straightened and pushed off the counter. "What do the colors mean? Especially the silver."

"So you do not know everything." He smirked.

"You must know that every way station records what ships pass it. Yours is well documented. And since similar ships and their Gy'Ruxian have also been recorded, it was easy to extrapolate who and what you are."

"And what am I?" He rose when Five carried in his garments and offered them to him.

While under her vigilant gaze, he donned his pants and tunic. He'd left his boots in her quarters.

She said nothing until he was fully covered and sitting. "Not much is known about Gy'Rux."

"And you mean to change that." He popped into his mouth what looked like the image on her soap bottle. It's sweetness hit him first, but it tartness lingered on his tongue. Would she taste the same?

"I ask out of curiosity. I'll take no recording devices." She threw her hands in the air. "You'd swear I was asking for a blood vow."

He stiffened. How did she know about that but claim to be ignorant of everything else? Something was out of alignment with her words and justifications. "I do not trust you yet."

She bit her lip, dipped her head, then walked into her office. Moments later, she returned with a ceremonial dagger embossed with magnificent gems in an ivory handle. The blade glinted in the bright lighting a second before she sliced her thumb.

Blessed Remyi, she cannot be serious.

When offered, honor bound as a justisaar and a Gy'Ruxian, he couldn't decline. His last blood vow had been when he was a ruxling. Ober joined the military when the justisaar program rejected his application. It had been their big dream, to serve side by side. Within his fifth year on the frontlines, he'd gone missing. No one had heard from him since. His weyr and Diaz had to assume the worst.

He crossed to her, taking the dagger when she passed it to him hilt first. "This cannot be undone."

"I know." She held up her palm, red droplets trickling to her wrist.

After thrumming the edge, testing the sharpness, he curled his thumb across it, cutting a deep enough wound. Dark purple blood seeped out. He smeared it across her palm and raised his for her to mark him. When done, he pressed his hand to hers.

"From darkest night to brightest hour, from every plight, none shall cower." He peered into her eyes, willing her to comprehend the significance of a blood vow.

She didn't flinch but met his gaze with a boldness he found breathtaking. "No task to small, no deed too great, vengeance for all, no matter one's fate."

The urge to jerk back gripped him, his shock that she knew the words unparallel. But he dared not break contact. Delicate slivers of silver, older than Gy'Ruxian ancestry, poured out of him and into her.

"Call, and I will find you," he whispered.

"Same." A slow smile thinned her lips before her teeth peeked out. "Now do you trust me?"

He snorted. "A blood vow is not to be taken lightly."

"Nor do I." She withdrew her bleeding hand, uncaring that she dripped onto the floor.

"All this to see my ship?" He tutted. "Time would have had me trust you, if you had waited."

"When we don't know what tomorrow will bring?" She turned her smile to Five when it clasped her hand to bandage it.

"Madness," it muttered. "And for what?" It tied a tiny bow at the base of her thumb before facing Diaz to do the same. "Welcome to our family, Diaz."

"He's serious. You're part of us now." She hitched her blood-stained thumb at the plate. "Come, bring your meal. Let me check in on Gladys about Javier and his men, and confirm Micky's location."

"We will head to my camis afterward." He trailed her while picking at his fruit.

Wait until the H.G.C. heard about this. Though, he doubted they'd believe him. For no female had ever offered a blood vow, not in all the ancestral archives was such a thing documented. Well, that he knew of.

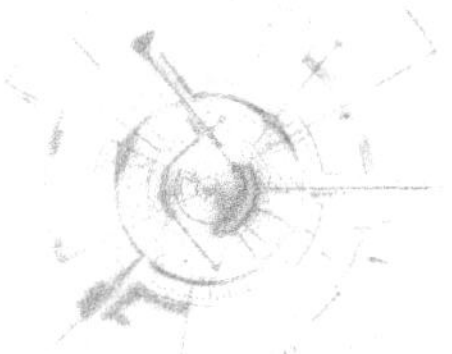

Selira sank into her chair, her body trembling. What had come over her? She almost harrumphed at that silly question. The man had slept naked, curled in the fetal position, and looking like a work of art carved from a solid block of obsidian-colored marble. She'd been nursing a cup of tea while studying every ripple of muscle across his back to the finest ass imaginable. Even his four-toed feet were beautiful.

But faced with his nudity so on display, the power pouring off him, the sheer breadth of his shoulders, to the silver flash of his tattoo... Her wits must've abandoned her. It had taken every ounce of control not to glance at his sex. The peek she'd caught was enough to send her core into an orgasmic spasm. The image of his cock replayed across her mind as she tried to focus on everything else around him. The girth was the shocker; she doubted she'd get her forefinger to touch her thumb when she grasped it. And with rings narrowing to the head of his cock, she hoped they rubbed her in all the right spots.

Heat burned her cheeks, but she dared not fan herself while he watched.

Hence her stupid blood vow. It had sounded beautiful when she'd learned of it. That she remembered the required words to speak was a miracle in itself when she'd journaled it so many years ago. Proving he could trust her was what mattered. She'd forced him to bond with her, demanded he trust her unearned, all for a detailed glimpse of his culture *and* because he flustered her? Five had been right. It was madness. But having a Gy'Ruxian on call wasn't a bad idea. Although, it also meant she was on call for him too.

Security cameras showed Gladys's clientele elbows deep into lunch.

The *Jinsei* orbited Aibra, about seven-hundred kilometers above the planet's surface. Excitement exploded outward and hitched her breath. Her daughter was here. So close, and soon, she'd be shuttling down to Richwood to battle the child-killing monster beside Selira.

All that blood vow nonsense for nothing. There wasn't time for a quick jaunt to his ship. It would have to be delayed with Micky's arrival imminent.

"Boss, she's on her way," Iane said, his voice filling her office. "Without the giant, I dunno what we're gonna do."

She smiled at Diaz leaning his shoulder against the wall. "Thanks. I'll be out in a bit."

"Giant?" he asked, his dark red eyebrow arching.

Having seen his...appendage, she had to agree with Iane, not that she'd reveal her thoughts to Diaz. "Ready?"

"Of course, though I'm wondering how your daughter will react to being lied to."

She winced. "Same. With this creature terrorizing Sosrak, she shouldn't be *that* pissed. Besides, I paid her already, so no cost to her except time."

His gaze hardened. "Luck does not mean it is right to lie." He caught her hand and guided her to her feet. "Do not deceive me, *purmoro*."

She glared at him. "Come see your mother who abandoned you when you were a child? Sure, she'll burn her engines to meet me."

He studied her upturned face. His body inches from her meant she had to crane her neck to meet his gaze. "Do not make it a habit."

"Family for ten minutes and already you're chastising me." She veered around him and marched to her room to grab his boots. "Five, get his coat."

Chapter Eight

A reckoning.

IN A BAY THAT used to house a mercenary ship, Mick sprinted across the floor, swerving and skimming obstacles NOX had laid out. Tier swooped down, his griffin wings extended, and missed her shoulder by a feather. She laughed while zigzagging, touching pads to register her passing and accuracy.

"Can't catch little old me?" she called, using a stack of crates to vault into the air.

He caught and crushed her against his chest, his wings keeping them both afloat. "I have you already." His smile teased lips she adored far too much.

"True." She dipped her head and captured a kiss. His mouth was heaven-sent. All of him was.

"I swear, I need a new set of eyes. I will never recover from the amount of salacious activity you two get up to. Thank the Lord, there's no kids just yet. They'll be traumatized for life." NOX huffed as he flipped crates over, shoved some to the side, and tossed others on top of each other. "Now quit fooling around. And don't think about taking a sex break."

"Not even five minutes?" she asked, her gaze locked with Tier's.

"I'm not being paid enough for this," NOX muttered.

She snorted when Tier lowered them to the floor. "Quit your whining, NOX. You have a new super suit, a premium software upgrade, and all the soap operas and musicals you can get your digital fingers on."

He paused. "True." He patted a crate. "One more run, then we need to head planetside."

"We're here?" Adrenaline pulsed along her veins, bouncing her on her feet. "Let's go." She swiveled to head to the ladder but slammed into NOX's titanium chest.

"Nope. Run first." He stepped to the side to stop her from passing him.

"Don't I need all my energ—" A lunge to the left was also blocked. She folded her arms across her chest and glared at him.

"No more delaying, honeybuns." NOX tutted. "I need to make sure you're at your peak. We don't know what these mutations are planning on doing to you, and I, for one, would like to know you're weakening before we find out mid-creature attack."

She gritted her teeth at his logic.

"Make that two," Tier said.

"You're agreeing with him?" She rested her fists on her hips, trying not to be pissed off by them ganging up on her.

"Of course. If you lose your speed without warning, you might be injured. That is not going to happen ever." Tier grabbed her shoulders and positioned her at the starting point.

"Remember there are children who need rescuing. You can argue all day, or just run the damn course." NOX scaled the ladder to stand on the platform to watch.

Tier lifted himself off the floor with a few flaps of his great wings.

"Fine." She bolted, aiming for the flickering red lights NOX had stuck on the crates. Everything around her blurred when she ducked, dived, weaved, and skidded to a halt by the ladder. "See? Just as fast as always."

"See?" NOX grumbled. "Then what's with all the bitching over *seconds* of your time?" He narrowed his eyes on her like Dad used to do. "We launch in five."

"Like we have to wait." She swept her arms out wide. "The shuttle's packed and prepped. What else do we need?"

"The contact," he called, sauntering through the door connecting the two bays.

She groaned and climbed up, joining Tier, who landed with a gust of air.

With pops and moans, he withdrew his wings until only his smooth back remained. "Come, *kekaseea*, we can have our five minutes when the children are safe."

"True." She snatched a kiss, before trailing NOX, who now tapped his foot on the shuttle's floor.

In her military pants and boots, paired with a simple tank top, she was more than ready. Her small armory held Locke and Flint, her cryo and sniper rifles. Beside them was Tier's greatsword clipped in place with many of his daggers pinned around it. Bottles of grit were tucked into a shelf, and on the console were her earbuds.

"What did the contact say?" She sank onto Tier's lap, who sat in the second chair while NOX took the pilot's seat.

"To come on down," NOX drawled in some thick accent she didn't recognize. "Did you see what I did there?" He laughed, sounding like the clanking of bolts in a metal container.

He powered up the engines, shot them through the bay doors, then spun to watch them seal—an idiosyncrasy of hers. When he headed for the beige planet, she had to admit it didn't look remarkable.

"What an ideal holiday destination," she crooned.

"Aibra, a dry planet with the mining rights belonging to Titan Exploration, recently renewed for another ninety years," NOX said.

"T.E.?" She frowned. "Why haven't they dealt with this monster? They've never asked us to help out before, NOX."

She didn't agree with their martial law, even though, for the most part, their employees were some of the happiest miners she'd met. Still, in the far reaches of space, when lawlessness was rife, she supposed T.E. had to do something to somehow bring order.

"What concerns you, *ateeko*?" Tier tightened his arms around her when NOX pierced the outer atmosphere. The shuttle shuddered with sparks and flames coating the shield.

"Just finding it odd, is all," she said and snuggled against him.

Beige tundra grew on tan rocky land with a pastel blue sky, as non-descript as the view from the *Jinsei*. Not the most colorful planets she'd visited. What manner of monster survived here? Well, besides humans.

The town had the feel of the space soap opera *Galactic Gunslingers*, the kind NOX liked to binge watch. He must have thought the same because he hummed the theme song while landing the shuttle beside a few mining dump trucks. Rusted housing pods lined a dirt road on either side with signs swinging in a strong breeze. Only one was double-leveled—a brothel. Men loitered on its metallic porch, and its lit sign said: *Hidden Depths*. She smiled at the play on words when there was nothing secretive about the services offered.

Sliding a blaster into her belt and Flint over a shoulder, she jumped down; the distance negligible. The observers straightened and pushed off whatever they leaned against. One ducked into the brothel and hollered "the freak's here," then came out again, along with about four dozen of his friends.

A man shoved his way through the crowd and faced her, his hands deep in his pockets. "Name's Javier." He beamed. "Glad you could make it."

Her instincts rippled the hairs down the nape of her neck. Tier launched into the air and took flight, the sunlight glinting off his great sword's blade. Those gathered stepped back and oohed, not in the slightest bit frightened. She did think him impressive too. Only when NOX stood behind her, Locke in hand, did Javier's smile waver.

"Where's this monster you want handled?" she demanded.

"He's not our guy," NOX whispered. "We're looking for—"

"That would be me," a man boomed, towering six-foot-something and splitting the crowd when he leapt off the brothel's porch.

Big, obsidian-skinned like Tier, with red eyes? And a man? This was going to be easy.

"Oh, thank Gawen," Tier said, stirring up a cloud of dust when he flapped down beside her.

This red-eyed man didn't snag Mick's attention as much as the woman who slipped around him did. Mick knew that face, so similar to her own.

"Mom?" she gasped, too stunned to think.

"Hey, Micky," Mom said, pausing alongside the 'monster.'

Sorrow hit Mick so hard, she struggled to breathe, but along with it, came a fiery fury she couldn't control. "So this was a friggin set up?"

Mom offered a shrug and a sheepish smile. "Well, you were taking your sweet time to reach me."

"Listen, this reunion is touching, I'm sure, but we have a real monster terrorizing our mines." Javier bent between Mom and Mick to wave. "Could we get to the killing then you two ol' gals can catch up some other time."

Mick spun on Javier, her skin itching with the need to battle something. "What manner of creature is it? What footage do you have on it?"

"And how much is T.E. willing to pay?" NOX asked.

"That too." Mick raised her chin but didn't let her gaze rest on her mother, not once.

Javier rocked on his toes, his hands once again deep in his pockets. "Whatever your standard fare. We're losing days of production thanks to this thing."

"I came to capture, kill, or tag a monster. Show the way." She hitched her thumb at the shuttle. "We'll trail you to the mining shaft. And send what vids you have. I don't want to go in blind."

As the crowd dispersed, most heading to the trucks, Mom strolled toward her.

Mick stiffened and curled in her lip to not spew venom. "You...should have stayed dead," she snapped, closed her eyes against what she'd said, then focused on her mother whose face had paled. Mick ignored the sting at hurting her. "You *faked* your death. I mourned... No. I'm not going through this again. I don't care what your reasons were. And even if they are or were valid, where the frig have you been?" She leapt into the shuttle, uncaring that her reactions were over the top. She'd needed the time, to think, to decide, not this, forcing her when she wasn't ready. "I half-hoped that idiot Themis lied. That this...*you* were some sort of scam. Don't reach out to me again."

"Mikaela Danvers." Mom clipped her name with a tone Mick used to wish she could hear again.

She laughed, though it lacked joy. "I'm too old for that to work. Besides, my mother's dead." She slapped the shuttle's side, telling NOX to launch. As they shot up twenty meters, Tier swooped through the door and landed inside the compartment.

"A little harsh, *ateeko*. You could have heard her out."

She spun on him, anger firing all her senses. "I last saw my mom go up in a ball of flames, only to learn she'd lied about being dead. Left me alone after Dad died, and now thinks she can waltz into my life like everything's dandy? Hell friggin no."

"At least find out why, honeybuns. Not knowing will beat you up." NOX skimmed the surface meters above the truck convoy heading west.

"She can send me an email with all her excuses. She's not mother of the decade, that's for damn sure." Mick folded her arms across her chest but splayed her legs for balance.

Tier gripped her shoulders from behind and pressed a kiss to her temple. "Whatever you decide I will support. Just remember, family is precious."

She bit the inside of her cheek, holding back tears while trying to calm the anger squeezing her stomach. Was she being unreasonable? Probably. Was she justified? Yup. And dammit, she'd hoped she'd have a few extra weeks to get her thoughts in order, to work through her resentment, feelings of neglect, and abandonment issues before having to deal with this...bullshit.

She smacked NOX's arm but not hard enough to dent it. "You know all the damn reasons anyway. But no, send me in without a word of warning? Whose side are you on?"

"Promise me you'll tell her after the funeral." Mom's voice filled the shuttle. "Thomas, I mean it. Don't wait until she's fifteen. I'm begging you. I can't go through with this if it's hurting my baby."

Tears escaped while Mick's chest tightened until breathing was a memory. "But he...didn't say a word," she finally whispered. "Did he promise, NOX?" She threw out a hand. "No, frig it. I'm about to hunt a creature. I can't deal with this while crying, you asshole."

"You asked, Mick." NOX glanced at her over his shoulder. "And yes, he promised."

Her vision spun, forcing her to suck in great gulps of air. "Why didn't he tell me?"

"That I cannot answer."

Typical. She flicked aside her tears and burrowed into Tier's embrace.

"The female she was, the one you loved, is she worth a chance to explain?" He rested his chin on the crown of Mick's head. "If not, we tag this creature and leave."

Trust her man to put things into perspective. Yes, Mom had been Mick's world. And having found out she'd been dealing with Dad's gambling and an attempt on her life while keeping Mick safe...

"Yes, she is. NOX, send her a message that I'll talk to her later." She stared at the mineshaft's pinhead-shaped headframe rising out of the surface, its shaft going kilometers deep. "Has Javier shared anything?"

Security footage played, showing a creature with eight legs scurrying like a centipede along levels and up shafts. It stabbed miners with its legs but didn't eat them—a good sign and intriguing. Then why kill?

"It is fast," Tier said.

What she wanted to say was that its pincers looked lethal and its four eyes all-seeing. Instead, she asked, "Okay, any ideas on how to take it down?"

CHAPTER NINE

To Kill a Beast.

ANGER GRITTED DIAZ'S TEETH. How dare Selira's daughter say such horrible things? As an observer, Micky's reaction was too harsh. And though Selira had hid it well, her devastation soured the air around her. This reunion was none of his business. He had no right to be furious on her behalf, nor should he care.

"What the hell is a Greeven doing with her?" he asked, trying to ignore Selira's pale cheeks and the tears glistening on her lashes. "Did she violate the Primary?"

Selira's eyes widened. She opened her mouth to speak, then snapped it shut, touching her wrist instead. "Bring the racer, Five."

"Already on my way," the machine intoned.

"You did say you wanted to see this creature? Well?" She arched a brow just as a white cone-shaped shuttle landed behind her. It's pristine exterior gleamed with not a speck of dirt on it.

He glanced at his boots already covered in the planet's beige sand. "Yes, I did."

The door slid open, barely broad enough for him to slip through. He climbed in, the cool interior bliss after the morning sunlight warmed every exposed part of him. Two seats faced the console and the windshield. Two more seats behind those faced each other. He settled into one of them while Selira gripped the back of Five's. They skimmed behind the dust cloud the convoy generated, all heading for the mining monstrosity squatting on the surface like a pimple.

"That's not how I expected it to go down," Five said.

"Yeah, though it was a possibility. If I was a necromancer, I'd revive Thomas just to kill him again." She mimicked wringing Thomas's neck with her hands.

Diaz grinned. That she knew of the dark arts no longer surprised him. Still, he might just help her.

"Unknown craft, state your business." A male voice rung loud and clear through the console.

"This is Data Reaper Atlas, envoy to Emerys Broderik. We accompany the Shikari to document her assignment as per Mr. Broderik's request."

At her words, Diaz frowned. What was a data reaper? Who was Atlas and this Broderik? Was she lying again? "Selira," he growled.

She pressed and held a button to glance at him over her shoulder. "What?"

He narrowed his eyes into a pointed glare. "Did we not discuss this tendency to distort the truth?"

She smirked. "I *am* Broderik's representative."

When she flicked her gaze away, he doubted she told him the truth. Lying was dishonorable, something that made his inner judge bristle. And perhaps a habit he needed to break her of.

"I require confirmation," the male voice said.

"Show him, Five," she said.

The machine typed buttons on the console with images flashing across the windshield: official badges, an employee number, and a letter of representation.

"And if you like, we can call Mr. Broderik himself," she said, chewing on a fingernail. "Though he doesn't take kindly to trivial interruptions."

"No... That won't be necessary. Permission granted since you'll be accompanying the Shikari and Javier. Entrance is at Gate '4B.'"

She flashed Diaz a triumphant grin. "See. All sorted."

He harrumphed. All lies were revealed in time, and their consequences soon followed. At her age, she had to have discovered this universal law applied to all.

"Oh, babe, seems Micky's had a change of heart." Five plastered a message across the windshield.

Selira squealed, jumping on the spot, her joy sweet to observe. She wrapped her arms around the machine and kissed its bald head. Diaz rubbed his, wishing he'd been the recipient.

"None of that, woman. Get your mitts and lips off me." Five swatted at her but didn't harm her.

She laughed and shimmied around the compartment, a grin splitting her glowing cheeks. Sinking into the chair opposite him, she cupped her bouncing knees. "I wanted to ask you, Diaz. What's a Greeven?"

He jerked back, her question taking him by surprise. "How can you not know when he is with your daughter?"

She shrugged. "Most planets protected by the Primary are undocumented. Without a database to mine, which is possible for a world without space tech, there is no way for me to learn."

That didn't explain how she knew about Gy'Rux. They did have archives, but they weren't available to the public. 'Mine,' she'd said. She must have some algorithm that bypasses all security—a virtual impossibility since the technology evolved too rapidly. He glanced at Five. Unless she had A.I. assisting her.

"So?" she asked, clasping her hands together and holding them to her chest. "Greeven?"

"Griffin shifters," he said.

"Oh," she gasped. "Hence the wings. And they don't mind their prince being missing?"

Prince? "It didn't seem as if he was there by force, in fact, he guarded your daughter with fierce determination." A thought struck Diaz, and he stilled, his mind running with it. What were the odds of a Greeven finding his eternal mate in a human? He would've chosen to leave with her. Whatever the reason, if Diaz didn't have to deal with the male, he didn't expect to have to battle him.

Five touched down forty meters from the gaping entrance into the pimple. Already males were striding toward it. Others gathered around Micky's shuttle.

When Selira leapt up to leave, he caught her wrist. "Where is your weapon?"

She patted her back. "I have a blaster." A smile warmed her eyes. "And I have you. If the shit hits the fan, I can hide behind Five." She tapped Diaz's chest and stepped off her racer.

His pec twitched at the softness of her fingers brushing across his badge. The silver tingled, when it shouldn't have. He glowered at the machine then trailed her.

"I have a job to do, and if you get in my way, I won't hesitate to cryo your ass," Micky was saying to the few blocking her.

The crowd scattered, summoning a bark of laughter from Diaz. He liked her no-nonsense attitude.

"Ready?" she asked the Greeven and her machine.

"We'll be joining you, Micky," Selira said. "Diaz, here, wants to see this creature up close."

"Any good with that weapon?" Micky touched the back of her neck, implying the great sword. "And a good shot with your blaster?"

Diaz didn't take offense. Only a fool ventured into battle with unknown skill at her back. "It is a bioblade and yes."

"Then come along, but you, Mom, stay back. I'll have my NOX control your NOX if need be."

Selira laughed. "NOX can try. Five's his own man."

"You can do that?" Micky paused then faced her machine. "NOX, baby, how does that sound?"

"Not now, sweet cheeks. Let's discuss this during the post-hunt celebrations." It strode past her, a rifle across its back. "I have a hankering for a little bloodletting."

"Sweet cheeks," Selira mouthed.

"Oh, you have no idea," Micky muttered to her then stomped after the machine.

The Greeven strode past Diaz, his yellow eyes narrowed.

"Greeven," Diaz said.

"Drueen," the male growled.

Well, technically, there was truth in that. But even though Drueens were Gy'Ruxians's ancestors, they had no connection with that species other than genetics.

"What's with you two?" Selira whispered, her hair touching Diaz's upper arm.

He drew in a deep inhale, hoping to capture a hint of her scent. Already the earthy dust saturated his nose, and he hated it, needing her strawberries to fill his senses. "The Greevens have been our enemy for as long as Gy'Ruxians have been in existence."

She met his gaze. Her mouth opened and closed, giving him glimpses of its pink depths. His nostrils flared when his thoughts returned to the vision of her bed, its coverings disturbed, no doubt, by his 'escape.'

She frowned. "Your people violated the Primary to take Drueens off-world?"

"Before the directive came into being, so no." He barreled her forward since they'd fallen behind.

She hurried to keep up with his long strides, a now-familiar whir and hum accompanying her steps. Her foot, leg, or hip? His fingers twitched with the urge to stroke the length of her from waist to toes. To locate the source, of course. Nothing more. Although, he did suspect the rest of her would be as soft as the skin on her arm.

They breached the entrance, the sunlight no longer blinding. Though it was cooler inside, it was also wetter, the humidity noticeable, especially when his sweat didn't evaporate but lingered.

A uniformed male scurried up to Micky, bowing while he approached. "The Shikari, what an honor." Then he dipped in front of Selira. "Data Reaper Atlas, welcome. We have prepared the observation deck for your pleasure. Would you prefer a beverage?"

"Go with him," Micky commanded. "And take Five with you."

"But—"

"This is non-negotiable or that 'chat later' won't be happening." Micky glanced at Diaz, perhaps debating whether to send him off too.

"That's...not fair," Selira snapped.

"Well, in order for me to hear your side, we must both live through this, don't you think?" Micky gave her a pointed look. "I'm not wasting a precious second having to save your ass, so skedaddle."

Selira hesitated, cast her gaze at Diaz, but left with the male. Five trailed her.

"I hope you're better than you look." Micky glared at Diaz. "I mean it. I don't want to put my team in jeopardy if your sword's just for show."

"He is a Drueen and a justisaar." The Greeven looped his arm around Micky's shoulders, drawing her near. "His weapon mastery is exceptional."

"Drueen?" Micky asked, gaping between the Greeven and Diaz. "Like the creature Fentus wanted me to capture?"

"Yes," the Greeven said.

Whatever they were discussing, Diaz didn't have the patience to unravel. He did find their open affection revealing, confirming his suspicions. "She is your *kekaseea*?"

The Greeven nodded.

The Gy'Ruxians didn't believe in eternal mates. They lay with many until accepting the most compatible. Few found someone who stirred them to forfeit honor and justice and who calmed their inner beasts. They called those heartsmates. Many dreaded meeting such a person when it usually didn't end well.

"Enough of this. Let's get this done. Diaz, we tag first. I prefer not to kill if I don't have to. But if it's slaughtering miners, we might not have a choice. Then I want to bag its body for research." She held up a finger. "What is odd is that it's not hunting for sport or food."

"Mm, intriguing." He tied back the sides of his coat, making access to his bioblade and dagger easier. With a gesture to her to lead the way, he unsheathed his great sword. The four of them joined Javier in a wire cage.

He had a blaster. "I'll show you where its last sighting was, then I'm getting the hell out of your way." He grinned. "Wow, the Shikari here. My folks back home won't believe this."

Silence settled over the cage while it descended. The deeper they went, the hotter it got, and the more Diaz sweated and struggled to breathe. His core temperature ramped, forcing him to waste precious energy to control it.

He tightened his grip on the hilt when the patter of many approaching feet traveled up the shaft. The cage swayed when the creature scurried past them, its black carapace like the endless expanse of space. The smell of undisturbed caverns tickled his nose. No one except Javier clung to the cage's wire frame as it swung wild. It ground against the side of the shaft for a moment then straightened and carried on.

"Hard outer shell," the machine said.

"Too many legs to make a difference if we hack off a few," the Greeven added.

"And too low to the ground for me to slide under its vulnerable belly." Micky glanced at Diaz.

So he said, "Four eyes means blinding it will be difficult."

She grinned, excitement sparking the air around her. "Yup, a true challenge. Not sure the excise dart will penetrate. Tagging might be off the menu, boys."

"If we can make it bleed, we'll have a sample." The machine slipped the rifle off its shoulder.

"Which means finding its weakness." Diaz stilled.

"Kill the killers," something hissed.

"Did you hear that?" he asked, glancing between them.

Micky tilted her head to listen. "A constant trickle of water, its multiple legs vibrating the ground, miners enjoying a coffee twenty meters to your left, and...a distant echo of a drill, perhaps farther down?"

"No, actual words as if spoken from the darkness." He shook his head, trying to clear his doubts and thoughts.

One: she could hear all that? He hadn't caught the drill, but the rest was accurate. Two: with the many languages he'd had to master between worlds, perhaps that explained... No, the hiss was audible, so not in his mind. Telepathy wasn't farfetched amid the hundreds of sentient species he'd encountered. Not that he spoke all their languages, just the most utilized.

The cage touched down. Javier shoved the door aside then stepped back to let them pass. "Medical is one level up if you need it. Other than that, you're on your own." He pointed at black domes on the ceiling of the rock-hewn tunnel. "We'll be watching. Ask, and we'll get you what we can."

He slammed the gate shut and up went the cage.

"Like that doesn't sound scary as shit," the machine muttered.

"Is poor NOXie shaking in his titanium feet?" Micky chuckled. "Come, scaredy pants." She veered right, striding down the tunnel with confidence, her rifle in hand. "I hear its footsteps. Stay close."

Diaz squared his shoulders and guarded the rear while they ventured onward.

"Must keep them back," the voice said.

He spun, peering behind him. Nothing lingered with no shadowed corners to hide anything or anyone.

"What is it, Diaz?" Micky paused and waited, her focus ahead.

"My instincts are saying something is odd here." He strolled past her to say to the voice, "Why attack these people?" His words traveled along the tunnel then faded.

No response came. He looked like a fool, but he just couldn't shake the weight that had fallen upon his shoulders. Dread like an anvil sank into his belly.

"Is it speaking to you?" The Greeven listened. "I hear hisses but nothing else."

"Yes, but it is not making sense." Diaz nudged his sword at Micky. "Let us continue. Perhaps it will reveal its intentions next time."

They strode onward in silence. The thump-thump of air pumps marked their progress every twenty meters, exhaling like an ancient dragon who'd lost its ability to roar. The oppressive weight of the kilometers of rock above him made his skin itch. Sure, it protected him from the glaring and overly warm sunlight, but it was damn hot like they neared the fiery core of this cursed planet.

One moment he was striding along, randomly checking behind him, when he found himself thrown against the rocky wall. The patter of scurrying feet, the cool whip of a breeze, and the smell of wet rock told him what had traveled past them. His shoulder throbbed by the time he staggered to his feet.

"What the hell?" He rolled his arm, his grip on his great sword firm.

"Sorry. Forget my strength sometimes," Micky said from the cage-side of the tunnel.

He blinked. When had she moved? He hadn't seen a thing. *Remyi*, if she was fast *and* strong, no wonder people hired her. He'd ask Five to get him the footage, just to make sure he wasn't imagining things. Part of him wished the creature had thrown him aside, for that would imply they had a worthy opponent and that it merely wanted to move around without hindrance.

"Did anyone see where it went?" He pointed his great sword. "I do not like covering the same ground back and forth."

"All right. Since we can both hear it coming, let's run for it." She met his gaze.

"Sprint for us, jog for you, is what you mean, don't ya?" The machine chuckled.

"Whatever." She bolted after the creature.

Diaz sheathed his sword and followed, keeping close to her ass. A refreshing waft of air halted him. He skidded to a stop and backtracked to a jagged gap in the wall that was in no way machine-made. He hummed in pleasure when cool air drenched him with blessed relief. The smell was intense, calling to him. He adjusted his eyes to peer into its depths.

"Micky," he said. "In here."

He glanced down the tunnel, blinding himself in the time it took to refocus. The team were hundreds of meters away.

"What is it, Diaz?" She glanced at the machine and the Greeven then was beside Diaz seconds later. "That creature wouldn't be able to fit—"

"According to the scans, it's an air vent to a larger cavern," the machine said, jogging closer.

"Diaz, you think this is worth a look, why?" She tilted her head to listen. "A thousand heartbeats merge into a steady rumble, like a tremor. Could it be…?" She stiffened, her eyes widening. "Lead the way, Diaz."

He did without hesitation. No drop awaited them, just a smooth burrowed pipe with a muted glow at the end. His shoulders were a hair's breadth from touching the sides. Micky's footsteps were light, like the Greeven's, but the machine stomped as if the use of legs was new to it. Diaz didn't hush it when the creature already knew of their presence. Something blocked the light for a moment. Had he blinked, he would've missed the movement.

In the tight confines, he couldn't withdraw his sword. Nor did he reach for his bioblade just yet. He splayed his fingers on the rock wall, its cold seeping into his skin. The final steps took him to the edge. Below and upward spread scalloped terraces holding pale gray eggs. Blinded by long tendrils of bioluminescent algae giving off a pretty yellow glow, he hurried to adjust his vision.

"There must be thousands," she whispered, peering over his shoulder.

He shuffled back to make way for them all to peer out.

"Is T.E. aware of this?" she asked the machine.

It didn't glance at her. "Nothing's been documented. A scan would've shown the cavern, though."

"Leave," the voice rasped.

Darkness engulfed their field of view, with four eyes peering at them. Its pincers smacked together in a click-clack. It spun, thrusting the spike of its tail into the vent. The Greeven leapt back, the machine threw itself to the ground, taking Micky with it, but Diaz only managed to press himself to the side.

Not fast enough.

Fire engulfed his right upper arm across his collarbone to his left shoulder. The tang of his blood saturated the air. He grimaced but staggered after the retreating tail to meet the creature's gaze.

"They will not leave, no matter what you try," he said.

It twitched, its eyes narrowed on him.

"Millions of them will come." He pointed at Micky being yanked onto her feet by the machine. The Greeven gripped her shoulders, as if to pull her out of danger. "They want us to get rid of you."

The creature rattled its displeasure.

"You're speaking to it?" Micky whispered.

Diaz didn't dare glance at her. "We do not want to harm you, but they will with their weapons and fire. They seek..." He couldn't say gold if it was color-blind, but it should be able to see shades. "The pale rock." He tapped the wall.

"This is my home," it said, sorrow drenching its sibilant voice.

"I know. They have no right, but you cannot win against them. Protect your young ones. Find somewhere with no pale rock. Let your kind know. Once they have what they want, they will leave."

It dipped its gaze, twisting to run a glance over its eggs. "I will listen, for you speak truth. They do not care."

It scurried off, snatching eggs as it traveled from scallop to scallop, then disappeared into a tunnel on the far side of the cavern.

Diaz slumped against the wall, his knees weakening.

"What is happening?" the Greeven asked.

"I asked it to move," Diaz managed and slid down to land on his ass. The jarring motion flashed spots across his eyes. "We need to give it time to do so."

The machine tucked itself under his arm and hoisted him to his feet. Pain lanced outward. He bit his lip to silence a whimper. Justisaars were trained to endure. And he would. The vent was too narrow for him to be carried, nor would he stand for the indignity of it. He staggered forward, each step almost bending him over. The burn spreading through his body implied venom. A certainty settled over him. He didn't have long.

"Help is on the way," the machine said.

Diaz didn't acknowledge it, and once he entered the tunnel, he propped himself against the wall. "If you are going to carry me, at least knock me out first."

He didn't see the punch coming.

Chapter Ten

Claiming the Blame.

SELIRA WRUNG HER HANDS, flicking her gaze from one screen to another in search of their party. Nothing. Nowhere.

"Where did they go?" she muttered, her insides twisting and yanking as if something or someone extracted her intestines.

The sensation was horrendous, driving her to pace without removing her focus from the screens. This incredible urge to grab her blaster and head down to the tunnels was a physical need she couldn't shake.

"They were in level seven east." Five tapped the applicable screen that showed a brightly lit tunnel with no one in it.

Info brokering was a large amount of her day spent on her ass, sifting data, dealing with correspondence, blackmail, and death threats. None had affected her heartbeat like today had. Proving fieldwork wasn't her forte. When Micky had saved Diaz, her incredible speed blurred her movements. Not to mention her ability to throw a six-foot-six man against a wall. Her medical documents had implied as much, but seeing was believing.

Images of the creature flashed across Selira's mind. Gray eggs lined a cavern, each one preciously cocooned in some sort of viscous. She blinked, not wanting her overactive imagination to distract her.

Her fingers spasmed so she gripped her waist and pressed the tip of her tongue to the back of her teeth. She wanted to roar at Five to let her down there, to help her do something. Anything.

"Get medical to that level. Now," Five said, facing the closest T.E. representative.

"What is it?" she asked, through the pain trembling her body. She drew in slow, calm breaths, like she'd done during childbirth.

Five took forever to answer. "NOX let me know one of them's been injured."

Ice engulfed her body from her head to her lower spine. Like a mother sensing her child in danger? That could explain the tension squeezing every organ. "Micky—"

"Is fine. Calm your tits."

"Then who?" she snapped.

"It's Diaz."

"No," she gasped, her heart twanging. Had she led him to his death when it was her fault he was even in the midst of all this? He'd have been moving on from Richwood to the town of Tenucky if she hadn't intervened.

Diaz's head popped through a hidden opening, he vanished, then staggered out only to fall against a wall. He smirked at Micky and NOX, mumbling something Selira couldn't pick up. A deep laceration leaked purple blood, staining his coat and shirt.

Micky punched him.

He slumped to the ground before she hoisted him over her shoulder. "Heavy bastard," she said, striding toward the security cam.

"Want me to take him, babe?" NOX asked, jogging alongside her.

"In a bit." She waved him off. "Glad that's sorted. To think all it wanted was to keep its home safe."

"I find it odd that that mountain of a man spoke to it," NOX said.

"I do not. He is Drueen," Tieren said, trailing Micky.

"I didn't catch a word that thing said. You, NOX? With all your brilliance, you couldn't decode its language?" She peeked at NOX over her shoulder.

"It's hisses and clicks. Cut me some slack." NOX harrumphed. "Besides, why would I bother when we had our very own interpreter?"

"Because I was trusting a stranger on faith," Micky said. "A little help from the oh-so-mighty NOX would've been nice."

"Blaming me? So typical." NOX hurried ahead to open the cage, the medical unit peering at them through the wire.

"Prep the *Jinsei's* pod or does T.E.'s medical tech cater for alien biology?" She arched a brow at the closest man in green.

"Isn't he human?" the man asked.

"Listen here, buddy," Micky poked him in the chest, "we have a griffin shifter, a whatever-he-is with red eyes, an A.I. in his super-suit, and me. None of us are human."

"Breathe, *ateeko*." Tieren gathered her close. "I'm certain NOX has landed the shuttle by the gate, security protocol be damned."

"Oh, shit, was I supposed to do that?" NOX splayed his fingers across his chest with a mock-gasp. "Well, I have now."

With a kiss to her temple, Tieren said, "We will get Diaz into the miracle pod in time."

"You're right. We'll make it." She climbed into the cage. "NOXie, my boy, let my mom know to meet us there. Send her the co-ords to the *Jinsei*."

Selira bolted, sprinting out of the observation deck, down the passages, to the exec pod that would take her to the ground level. She tapped her metallic foot, relishing the thud-thud paling the T.E.'s representative's face. With the amount of time she planned to spend here, she hadn't bothered to learn his name. She'd have Five sift through the footage and delete anything incriminating. Which she did whenever she had to man up and be around people. Data Reaper Atlas. Selira Myers. None of those personas and many others existed unless she needed them.

She paced outside the shaft entrance, the clanging of the cage's chains nerve wracking. "Send the *Usuba* to the *Jinsei*, Five. Shut down 'Unit 618' for now."

"Done," he said from behind her.

When the cage stopped and the door opened, Selira released a slow and long exhale. A hoverbed glided out with Diaz on it. A medic, on a Sunday stroll, pushed it toward the shuttles. Frustration clenched her teeth while she fought the urge to hurry him.

NOX took control of the bed and jogged it toward the exit.

"Take him to mine." She pointed at her powered-up racer.

Micky frowned. "But—"

Selira wasn't going to debate this. "It's faster, sweetheart. State of the art." She clipped each word in a tone that didn't brook argument.

Her daughter nodded. "Do it, NOX."

Five took over, steering the bed toward the racer.

NOX veered to the left, heading to the shuttle, with Micky and Tieren following him.

"See you in a bit," Micky said with a wave as the shuttle's door closed.

Abandoning the bed, Five lifted Diaz and carried him through the racer's door. He sprawled him on the floor then leapt into the pilot's seat. They shot off before Selira could grab ahold of something. She bounced off the side then sank into the spare seat, staring at an immobile Diaz. The cold, hard floor didn't concern her when he preferred it. What worried her was the extent of his wounds. That was a lot of blood.

Despite the constant pain wrenching her insides, she removed his guns and daggers, sliding them into a nearby locker. The great sword he lay on, trapped beneath him. Regardless, she wouldn't have been able to unsheathe such a heavy weapon. Five would have to do it before they lifted him into the pod.

"Almost there," he called.

She raised her gaze and stared at the *Jinsei*. Tears prickled behind her eyes, her breath cinched in her chest, and a ball of lead weighed down her stomach. She thought she'd never get to see her old home. It looked the same, as if time had no impact. As if her upturned life meant nothing to it. And why would it? The ship had always been Thomas's baby.

Five docked beside the shuttle and was out of the seat before the bay doors had closed. He hoisted Diaz into his arms and waited, no doubt for the loading bay to pressurize. Once the racer's door open, he sprinted through it.

Selira didn't hurry this time. The pod would do what it could. There was no point in rushing to be by Diaz's side. He wouldn't even know she was there, and her presence had no impact on the pod's speed.

"Biology accepted," NOX intoned through the *Jinsei's* audio system.

Her shoulders bowed in relief. With a deep breath, she climbed the ladder to the platform before striding to the med bay.

Diaz barely fit into the pod now expanded to its maximum by the look of things. Still, his stats flickered across the sealed glass, proving it was working.

Five stood beside her. "The *Usuba* is docked."

"Thanks," she whispered, splaying her fingers across the glass. He'd live. The strange pain subsided, allowing her to, at last, draw in a deep breath. "Did you get his sword—"

"Yes, but his coat's ruined."

"A small price to pay to live," she mumbled, scanning the room. "Nothing's changed, and yet, everything has."

"The pod's neutralizing the venom. He'll be his usual grumpy self in no time," Five said, confirming her instincts were right. "So, what's next?"

"He'll want to return to his ship." That was as far as she allowed herself to think.

"No doubt." Five studied the stats. "The laceration was deep and long, proving he's hardier than he looks."

She snorted. "He *looks* like a brick shithouse."

"Language," Micky said, striding into the room. Tieren hovered at the door before entering.

"Who is he? Tier says he's a justisaar?" Micky rested her back against Tier's chest. He looped his arm around her waist and pulled her snug against him. "You and him have a thing?"

"No," Selira said, a little rushed. *Guilty conscious, perhaps?* "No. Um, we just met." Her thumb twinged. And yet she'd tied their fates together on an impulse.

"If Tier hadn't vouched for him, I wouldn't have allowed him to come with us." Micky tilted her head up and smiled at Tieren before meeting Selira's gaze. "Turns out, your man speaks 'creature.'"

"He's not my anything." Even to her, the tone of her voice was weak, lacking conviction.

"Except for the blood vow." Tieren nudged his chin at Selira's bandaged thumb. "You scent of him too."

She stiffened. "Isn't it like a blood pact?"

"More. His weyr will come to your aid. Drueens take their obligations to the extreme."

Her interest prickled. "Diaz said those were his ancestors. Isn't he a Gy'Ruxian now?"

"Their mother planet is Rianus, my homeworld."

She frowned at his unsatisfactory answer. Now wasn't the time when a good digging would answer all her questions. "And you two?"

"Mick's my mate," he said, snatching another kiss.

Selira tried not to smile like a proud mother when she had no hand in this. But to find her daughter loved and protected was the best a parent could pray for.

"Mom, do you recognize this?" Micky tugged an amulet out of her tank top.

Selira chuckled. "Oh, yes, we got it off some wandering merchant." She tapped her chin, remembering the day Thomas had allowed the man to board, refuel, and spend a few days with them. "What was his name, NOX?"

"Ober Pantok," NOX said, hip-nudging Five away from the console.

Diaz sat up, bumped his head against the glass, then punched it. "What did you say?" he boomed, glaring at NOX while the pod opened. "No. No, it cannot be. Where was this? When?"

"What's wrong, Diaz?" Selira inching closer to him.

"Ober's been missing for two decades." Diaz swung his legs over the side. "We thought him dead."

"You know...knew Ober?" She snapped her mouth shut and glanced at NOX. "Share everything you know."

Without glancing at them, NOX said, "The Traveling Trader hailed Thomas near the Apus constellation. He offered to pay for a little fuel, if we had any to spare."

"We didn't," she muttered.

"Thomas welcomed him on board, especially after he glimpsed the 'treasures' on the back wall of Ober's bridge."

"Typical," she growled.

NOX continued, ignoring her. "By the time Ober left days later, we owed him tokens."

"Why am I not surprised?" she snapped. "Thomas told me he hadn't the heart to charge the poor man. In gratitude, Ober gifted us with the amulet."

"You mean, I could have asked NOX this entire time?" Tieren glowered at Micky.

She held her hands up in surrender. "You wanted something to do, *ateek*. Besides, I didn't think to ask NOX."

He grunted. "So now we need to find this Ober."

"Agreed," Diaz said. "I too have questions."

"That's like searching for a needle in a haystack." Micky patted Tieren's chest. "And may I remind you, we need to catch a contaminated hokou."

"Why?" Selira asked. "I know Fentus wants one, but what's the real reason? I don't trust them at all. Large scientific corporations aren't out for the greater good."

"To cure me," Micky said, her eyebrows knitting. "Or don't you want that?"

"I do, but that doesn't mean we should trust the first medicine peddler. Five—"

"On it, like I wasn't listening? To summarize: one Ober, one hokou, and tawdry deets on Fentus?" He hip-nudged NOX away from the console. "Share what you have, or I'll scrape the bottom of your data barrel anyway."

"You're not getting your dirty algorithms anywhere near my memory banks." NOX zapped Five with a spark of electricity from his forefinger. "Now, move over."

"How are you feeling, Diaz?" Selira raised her hands to cup his knees but stopped herself in time, leaving her standing there with her hands in mid-air. She curled them into fists and shoved them behind her back. The solid weight of the blaster still tucked in her waistband offered a little comfort.

"Good. Where are we?" He scanned the crowded med bay.

"Welcome to the *Jinsei*." Micky's warm greeting didn't lessen his frown.

"And that is?" he asked.

"My ship orbiting Aibra."

"*Remyi*, I am off world?" He caught Selira's arm and pulled her closer. "We need to leave now."

"What's the matter?" His warmth seeped into her skin, tempting her to snuggle against him.

"The H.G.C. cannot learn that I am not planetside, not with villages still on my list."

"Oh," she said.

"I must get to my ship. A quick message should appease them." Diaz accepted his great sword from Five.

"But..." She slumped. So much for a heart-to-heart with Micky. But Diaz was right. She'd taken care of her side, made easier with Five on her team. Wait, couldn't he... "Five, can you hack—"

"Female," Diaz growled. "There will be no hacking my ship when the trip down will take minutes."

"Can't argue with that," Micky said. "Mom, it's fine. I'm not going anywhere until you and I have had a chat."

"You sure?" Tears stung Selira's eyes, and she grabbed Micky's hand for a squeeze. She'd have loved a hug, but they weren't there yet.

"Besides, your ship's in my bay and you've got to explain what happened to your leg." Micky dipped her gaze. "Two joint mechanisms whirring, not counting the toes, so knee and ankle?"

"Something like that." Selira grimaced, not liking having her prosthetic limb so openly discussed.

Diaz stared at her face, his lips pursed as if in revulsion.

"Let's get you back," she said, rushing past Micky toward the racer. "Five? Staying or coming with me?"

"Staying," he called.

She nodded despite a frisson of excitement spreading fire through her veins at being alone with Diaz. The hulking man trailed her, his footsteps light. She assumed the pilot seat, and when he settled beside her, she said nothing.

"Bay clear. Doors opening," NOX said as she powered the engines. "Good to go."

She reversed out with a clear view of the doors, hovered a minute while they shut before she swiveled the racer toward Aibra.

"I'm sorry," she said to Diaz. "I threw caution to the wind and took you to the *Jinsei* without your knowledge."

"You saved my life." He stuck a finger in his coat's gaping tear across the shoulder.

She bit the inside of her cheek. What could she say to that? 'You're welcome' sounded lame. "At least I get to see your camis."

He grinned. "Yes, you do." His gaze lingered on her face. Not peeking at him took all her willpower. "Your daughter is impressive, Selira. Pity about the Greeven."

She laughed. "What's wrong with Tieren?"

"Nothing, we just don't like each other."

She rolled her eyes. "How long have you known him? Or is this a general discrimination?"

He stared ahead when she penetrated the exosphere. "Centuries of hostility."

Which made no sense to propagate it. "But you're not from his planet, are you?"

"I am not."

She dared a glance. "Do you even know why you're supposed to hate him?"

"I do," Diaz said. "Stories passed via our matriarchs cover our origins and history."

"Ah." She smiled. "Because your mom said so."

He chuckled. "In a way."

She landed the racer beside an outcropping of boulders not unsimilar from those that hid the entrance to 'Unit 618.'

"Might as well power down." He rose, towering over her.

Flicking a switch, the racer's hum slowed then cut off. She waited for him to move back before slipping out of the seat. He ducked through the door, jumped to the ground below then turned to help her. His unexpected gallantry had her hesitating. He raised his gaze to her, so she hurried forward. When he gripped her waist to lift her down, his fingers scorched her through the T-shirt. His touch lingered for a moment longer than necessary.

His nostrils flared, his lips pursed, then he shifted back. She tried not to think about the layer of tingles lifting the hairs on her arms.

This could be goodbye, and she didn't know how she felt about that. A little sad, perhaps. She studied his back when he strolled south, seemingly heading nowhere.

"*Sillstari*," he said.

Before her eyes, his ship shimmered until solid metal appeared. She gasped, taking a step forward. "Stealth?" she whispered.

She'd known where it was parked, just not that it would be invisible. Wait until she told Five. He eavesdropped through her wristband, but without a cam, there wouldn't be video footage. Besides, she'd promised not to bring recording devices.

Diaz climbed the lowered ramp at the ass-end of the ship.

She paused, taking in all its details. It had the nose of a sperm whale but the loveliest of geometric patterns in silver and red on a dark gray metal frame. Was it red because of his eyes and eyebrows? She hurried in after him and slowed to a halt. Inside was a bed, a small galley, and the 'bridge.' Handles on the ceiling had to lead to engines or storage. Perhaps its squarish shape meant it carried massive fuel reserves for long interstellar flights?

"Satisfied?" he asked, sliding off his coat.

She ventured past him to peek into his cockpit with a seat for one person. Compact, all his needs catered for, still, she'd go insane in something this small. The console was to the left and right of the pilot seat, not in front like hers. Made sense when it would save on space.

When she turned back, he was shirtless, his soot-toned skin rippling in the low lighting. Broad shoulders into muscled biceps into corded forearms drew her gaze to the dimples in his lower back, then up to his shredded back. Seeing him so reminded her of his earlier nudity. Heat burned from her cheeks to her core. She clamped her legs together and squeaked when he unbuckled his boots and stepped out of his pants.

'Warn a girl next time,' she wanted to say.

Naked, he paused before a metallic panel that flickered to a mirror, giving her a full glimpse of his front. Thinking he couldn't see her, she allowed herself the freedom to memorize every inch of him. Green lights scanned him, and she trailed its movement with her gaze until it scrolled over his face and the smirk playing on his lips.

She gasped, ice warring with the heat of embarrassment, taking turns to lash her cheeks.

His focus was on her and had been the entire time.

Chapter Eleven

DIAZ'S EMOTIONS SWUNG OUT of control. He was furious *and* aroused, frustrated *and* grateful. As soon as he recognized what thoughts crossed his mind, his hearts interfered, or his cock. What came to the fore was her gaze caressing every inch of him in the mirror. She hadn't acknowledged his nudity earlier, but now, she absorbed him like a blood-hungry *gotry*. All that was missing were rows of teeth and a lolling tongue.

He didn't know what to make of her open admiration. The male in him struggled to calm his erection, though why he bothered, he didn't know. He wasn't ashamed he found her attractive, for she was beautiful, remarkable, with streaks of honor and deceit that had him warring with his sense of justice.

In her shoes, he would have done the same: use a stranger to lure his lost child. And he'd be more remorseless than she was. She'd been the reason he'd lingered in Richwood, traveled with her to hunt a creature, and gotten injured in the process.

"I need to message my council," he said, his voice hoarse.

"That's my cue." With a whir-hum, she swiveled on a heel and headed for the door.

He caught her wrist and, using a gentle tug, pinned her back against the mirror. Her eyes widened, but this time she kept her focus on his face despite her fingers splayed across his chest.

Those enigmatic tingles radiated outward from where her soft hands registered on his skin, affecting his breathing, and scattering his thoughts. He lost himself in her brown eyes. The dark mole just below her right eye snagged his focus. How could a blemish fascinate him, or the way her teeth dimpled her bottom lip? Whatever this was, it was madness.

"It will take a moment," he said, "unless you have *seen* everything?"

Peach bloomed across her face, and without thought, he ran his thumb over a cheek, marveling at the warmth beneath his touch. He hummed, liking it when she blushed.

"I'll wait," she whispered.

He stepped back to pull on his pants and boots, again under her vigilance. With a final glance, he left her to sink into the pilot seat. He placed a hand on the left console, cupping the dome. A spike shot into his palm, the pain bright then fading.

"Councilor Hom'Garr," he said in Gy'Ruxian.

He wasn't concerned she'd listen in when he doubted she spoke his ancient language.

"What is it, Rowfallak?" the councilor demanded.

As usual, no image formed on the windshield, for which Diaz was thankful. The councilor sighting Selira behind him would raise too many questions he wasn't ready to answer.

"I found word of Ober Pantok." His hearts thumped ahead, eager to hunt down his blood mate just to learn what the hell happened to him. His fingers itched to throttle him at his abandonment.

"Now *that* is surprising. One moment." The cockpit fell into silence while Diaz waited. His senses narrowed in on Selira and her movements, her breathing, the whir of her leg, and the scent of her strawberries filling his lungs. "Locate him, and bring him in."

Diaz grinned. Just what he wanted to hear. He wiped his smile to answer, "But my villages—"

"Can be returned to when we have him in custody. Any Gy'Ruxian forsaking his duties must be held accountable, or do you no longer believe in justice?"

"You are right, Councilor. Forgive my dedication to the earlier task you rested upon my shoulders." Little did the male know, Diaz longed for a break, a chance to do anything other than bring justice to the masses. It was why he'd allowed Selira the blood vow despite being honor-bound to accept it. It was why he went with Micky into the bowels of a gold mine. Avoiding boredom was a powerful motivator.

"Forgiveness is earned, Rowfallak. Will that be all?"

Diaz gritted his teeth. "No, I met an info broker who knew what I am, my name, my status, right down to blood vows."

"How is this possible?" Hom'Garr snapped. "Are you in contact with him?"

"Her, Councilor, and yes." Diaz glanced over his shoulder, catching a glimpse of 'her' in his peripherals.

"A female? Intriguing. Discover how she breached our security. I will convey this to our archives and have them investigate from our side. She had to have left a digital fingerprint somewhere." Hom'Garr cleared his throat with a gurgle. "Dare I ask if that is all?"

"No, there is one last thing. Her daughter is the Shikari, a mutated human who is able to move with speed and carry me without an issue."

"*Remyi*, I have heard of her. A deformation of nature, Justisaar. She cannot be allowed to exist. News of her abilities would encourage others to hunt the source. No one should be more powerful than a Gy'Ruxian. Worse, if one of ours should gain such strengths, we will not be able to control them."

Diaz stiffened, dreading the instruction he sensed would soon be forthcoming. "Should I bring her in too?"

"No, a sample of her blood is all we need. Kill her, and burn the body."

Darkness swirled in his soul. It was not an unheard-of command, but his instincts rejected it. What choice did he have though?

"Will that be an issue?" Hom'Garr demanded.

Diaz drew in a deep breath and squared his shoulders. "As you say, Councilor."

"Excellent. Keep me updated on your progress."

He stared out the windshield, yanked his hand off the dome when the needle retracted, then swiveled the chair to face Selira.

"That bad?" she asked, her eyebrows almost touching her hairline.

He frowned when a dull throb formed at the back of his skull.

"You look like someone just kicked your puppy," she said, leaning a shoulder on a bulkhead.

"I am to set aside my task on Aibra and hunt down Ober." He smothered a grimace at deceiving her. Telling her the truth would gain him nothing. He needed to be on the *Jinsei* to discover how extensive her skills, to locate Ober before the Greeven did, and to kill Micky or figure out a way to do so.

All without revealing his intentions to the two A.I.s on board.

"If anyone can lead me to him, it is an info broker." He pushed out of the seat while rubbing the blood off his palm with his thumb. "Any idea where I can get one?" He forced a smirk.

She tapped her chin. "Mm, I just might." Her smile spread across her face, warming her gaze. "The *Jinsei* has another bay you can dock your camis in. Since Tieren is also after Ober, let's kill two birds with one search." She hesitated before gesturing to his chest with a flick of a finger. "Perhaps we can stop at a way station and pick up a new coat? My treat."

"Do you not like me thus?" he asked, when he knew damn well she'd just ogled him.

Again her cheeks stained peach.

He chuckled. "Now that you've *seen* my camis, will you show me something?"

"If I can," she said, though she pronounced the words with caution.

"Your leg."

She jerked back, fear darkening her eyes and parting her lips. "I..." She cleared her throat after her voice cracked. "I'm wearing pants." A quick rub of her palms down her thighs drew his gaze.

"So remove them." He waited, but she didn't move, just stood there, stunned. "Why do you hesitate? Does your kind not wear garments under your garments? Little slips of coverings?"

"Underwear," she whispered.

"Good. You will not be naked if that is what concerns you."

She didn't budge, her glowing cheeks now pale.

He scowled. "Selira?"

"I... It's not something I show anyone," she said, squaring her shoulders in defiance.

He smiled, finding her courage adorable. "I am not anyone. I am your blood mate."

She winced, pursed her lips, but with trembling fingers, unclipped each boot. The right foot was delicate, with the tiniest of toes—five of them. Again, protectiveness flooded him, demanding he guard her fragility. Her left foot was metallic, polished to a bright silver. It had the appearance of a foot but without skin, connecting fibers mimicked muscle and tendons, with bones made of titanium. It was a work of technological art.

The zip, when she undid her pants, snapped his gaze up. She hooked her thumbs into the waistband and shimmied the fabric down over her hips, only to pause mid-thigh.

His breath hitched, his hearts stuttered, and a roar engulfed his ears when no underwear covered her sex. He longed to bury his nose there, to discover whether she smelled of strawberries all over.

"*Remyi*," he muttered.

Again, she gathered her courage—stiffening her shoulders and gripping her waistband tight. At last, she dropped the pants and stepped aside. She shuffled. The whir-hum accompanied the movement, as did the stretch and pull of her 'muscles.'

He layered a hand over her clasped fingers.

She met his gaze, her eyes widening.

"Selira, it is beautiful." He knelt and ran his palm down her warm thigh to her cold knee. Eager to study her manufactured limb, he yearned more to stroke upward, her skin so silky and her exposed sex near.

"Thank you," she rasped, making him think she didn't believe him.

He stood, staying close, and peered at her upturned face. "I do not deceive, *purlievo.*"

Not truth anymore thanks to Hom'Garr's latest commands, but for the most part, he tried to be honorable. An act of dishonor could take another innocent life; something he wanted to avoid at all costs.

"How did you lose it?" he asked, running a thumb over her thigh.

In a blink, her fear and disbelief altered to fire and fury. She raised her chin. "An explosion of my own doing."

He frowned. That made no sense. "You blew yourself up?"

"Attempted to make it look like an accident." She shrugged, collected her pants, and twisted to wiggle into them. "I can't say if the explosion was a miscalculation or deliberate on my late husband's part. I have looked into it from all angles and am always left with more questions. How had he tampered with the bomb? When did he? Was NOX in on it, and if so, why hadn't the silly A.I. warned me?" She straightened and met his gaze. "Long ago, when I still knew the whereabouts of the *Jinsei*, I had Five hack it. We learned nothing from the video footage."

Diaz knelt to slip a boot onto her foot. His fingers twitched when he cupped her right heel. Even there, her skin was smooth and the bones so tiny in his hand. "Any audio recordings?"

"Zip, zero, nada, that's why it's alarming. Just grainy images. Erased data can be recovered but not after many software upgrades and so much time has passed."

He held out her other boot. When she lifted her metallic foot, she tilted, losing her balance. He didn't expect her palm on his head. Everything within him stilled, the sensation of her touch piercing his thoughts and forming in his memories.

"Sorry," she said, snatching her hand away.

Ass shit. What was it about her that he liked? As a human, she was gentle despite a core of strength. She lied with ease and kept secrets better than Hom'Garr did. Well, he'd have time to find out if he 'accepted' her invitation to dock on the *Jinsei*. He had to; her offer was too good to pass up.

"The image I have of you was when you first became a justisaar. What happened to your red hair?"

Her words chilled the rising lust burning along his veins. He grabbed her shoulders, digging his fingertips in for a firm hold without bruising her. "How have you seen those images when they were taken during the *Qaf Dahn* initiation ceremony?"

"An info broker never reveals their sources." Her tone was playful when he was far from it.

He wanted to shake her, to let loose all her secrets. Telling the H.G.C. that he couldn't succeed in something this simple would have the camis or the endless tokens confiscated. Fulfilling his exiled tasks would be a thousand times more difficult without either. But not performing any of it would bring shame upon his weyr, or worse, place his pappo in danger.

He was beginning to see why Ober disappeared. Though how he managed it from the frontlines was the first thing Diaz would ask. No, the second. The first would be why. Not once had he felt the sharp tug of a blood mate in trouble. Which made him suspect Ober had figured out how to suppress it.

He cupped Selira's face, running his thumb over her chin. "Did you feel anything when I was injured?"

Her brows knitted. "Yes, like my insides had turned into taffy and were being put through the wringer." Her eyes widened, and she gasped, parting her lips. "You know what it was."

"How can you know who I am, what I am, and what a blood vow is but not know what it does to your physiology?"

She squeaked. "Shit. That could be the fine print I didn't get to read. No wonder Five said it was madness." She inched closer to Diaz to splay her fingers across his chest. "What does it do? I mean, I can wait until I'm on board the *Usuba* to find out, or you could just tell me."

"I warned you that it cannot be taken lightly." He glared at her. "Our souls are united and to any other blood mates either of us share a blood vow with."

"Explain that in impact terms. How does that change my life?" She flicked a finger then rested it on his chest again. "I already know about the 'come to my rescue' bit."

He struggled to think, losing himself in her touch. The heat pouring off her was reason for concern, especially if his body's reaction to her kept increasing his core temperament.

"And how many have you sworn a vow with?" She narrowed her eyes. "I'm helping *you*, but no one else."

"You do not have a choice. The pain will compel you. Should I experience intense emotions or an attack on my senses, specifically pain, it will yank on your soul, like something inside you is trying to pull your life force out of your body."

"No shit," she whispered. "What if you die?"

"Then the connection is severed, but you will be adrift, alone, as if a part of you is missing."

"Frig," she said, dipping her chin and breaking his hold. "That's not good at all."

"Indeed, all because you wanted to see my camis." He arched a pointed brow while burying his fingers in her hair. A sigh slipped past his defenses when the cool, silky strands caressed him.

"That and I get a justisaar to come to my aid. That's an incredible advantage for a lone woman in outer space." Her sweet smile belied the calculating mind behind it.

He stepped forward, pressing her against the mirror. In that one movement, he had her trapped and his body layering hers. Warmth seeped into him, bringing to life the beast within.

"You trusted me without knowing me, *purlievo*." He rested on an elbow beside each ear, placing himself an inch from her face. Strawberries rose to tease his nose. His hearts pounded. Roaring not his own bombarded his ears, and yet, he couldn't break eye contact.

He dipped, closing the distance between her mouth and his. A brush of his lips across hers zinged energy through him. Another sample introduced him to her taste—sweet, smoky, and intoxicating.

A frustrated and hungry snarl thrust him off her. He rested against the bulkhead, fighting to breathe, for calm, for sanity. A glance at her and those peach cheeks had him staggering to the galley. He snatched a water packet and drank deeply, relishing the chill sliding down his throat. Already the burn of fire coated his insides.

Never before had a female inspired such a volatile reaction. Which meant he couldn't lose control around her for fear the beast would break free.

Especially not in front of a female who sold and bought information to survive. She'd not only discover what he truly was, but he might hurt her.

Remyi, how could he resist her now that he knew how decadent her taste?

"Diaz?" His name on her sweet tongue snapped his focus.

He glanced at her.

"Are you all right?" She gestured to all of him. "You're glowing."

He raised his hand clutching the packet. A red shimmer poured off him with a rippling just under his skin. "Ass shit, I am overheating."

She blinked at him. "I take it that's not a good thing?"

"No." He needed her off the camis immediately. "Leave, Selira. I need to chill the interior. I will meet you at the *Jinsei*."

She gaped at him, then bolted, striding down the ramp toward her racer.

Watching her leave, her taste on his lips, and her scent in his nose was harder to endure than being exiled. He clutched the edge of the cargo door, his fingers a bright red. When she launched her shuttle, he punched the button to close the ramp and headed to the central panel to lower the temperature to freezing. He stripped again and sprawled on his bed, willing his beast to calm.

Losing control inside the camis would destroy it, and leaving the cooling confines for the space outside might trigger the transition. As a distraction, he sifted through the list of failed villages to focus on the next he had to now abandon. Maybe permanently once he informed the H.G.C. of T.E.'s rule.

"Tenucky, Omaak, Jomar, Zorshia, Nalval." Slow breaths between each one helped calm his hearts until their beats were minutes apart. His hands no longer glowed, his beast was once again silent, and the urge to mate, though it lingered at the edges of his mind, no longer drove him to act.

This blood vow had trapped him to a female he could never have. One kiss had almost broken his control. But he yearned for more... To have her beneath him, her metallic limb wrapped around his hip, the scent of her strawberries surrounding him, her soft hands stroking his upper arms.

If he did decide to claim one night with her, he had to do it soon before he killed her daughter. If he could control the beast, that is.

Remyi, what am I going to do?

Chapter Twelve

It took one kiss.

THE MOMENT THE RACER breached the exosphere, Selira put it on hover. Her lips tingled, and she hadn't processed what had just happened. Not yet. Her mind reeled from having to reveal her most hated part of herself followed by the sweetest, chaste kiss with the biggest impact. And without underwear. She hadn't been able to list that as a problem when he'd been naked before her twice. He wouldn't and hadn't seen it as an issue. She raised her hand to eye level to confirm the tremor had reached her fingertips. Willing her heartbeat to calm, she drew in a long, controlled breath.

Diaz had kissed her. That should've been her main thought, but it wasn't.

He'd asked to see her leg.

She swallowed the bile pooling on her tongue. And he'd called it beautiful. A shiver twitched her shoulders and sent prickles through her.

From his strange discussion with his superior where the only word she recognized was 'Shikari' to admiring her knee, to finding out her biology would change due to this stupid vow, to the kiss.

Then he'd started to glow.

Chasing her off his ship should've offended her, but she understood how much he needed cold, dark spaces. The why was yet to be discovered. She pressed four fingers to her lips. How could a simple lip caress evoke such intensity? And why did it matter? A kiss wasn't a relationship. Hell, she doubted Diaz would hang around after he found Ober. What lay ahead for them were random sessions where they met up somewhere in the universe to help each other.

She squeezed her eyes shut, trying to recall what Ober had looked like. With Diaz's dark skin? No. And his eyes had been a lovely sky blue. He'd had long blue hair hanging in braids with beads clinking when he turned his head. Diaz had the same, except molten red and gorgeous with his strong jawline. That was gone now, and he made damn sure it stayed that way too.

Her instincts warned that there was significance to that. Especially with the way he'd gone on the offensive when she'd mentioned his old hairstyle. Perhaps it meant something in his culture?

She tapped the console. "Five, get me everything we have on Gy'Rux. And have you started searching for Ober? The hokou? Have you done anything?"

"Listen here, woman, I only have the skills to focus on seven things at a time. More than that, and you're pushing your luck."

"Seven?" she fake squeaked. "I need to upgrade you at the first way station. Maybe a newer model—"

"Would fall for your bullshit?" Five hummed.

She smothered a giggle, having no doubt he'd arched a rubbery brow. "I'm heading in."

"Assumed as much. I *am* tracking you, y'know. One of my seven focuses wasted." He huffed. "Is the big man coming too?"

"He said he'd meet me at the *Jinsei*." *While he flushed like a glowstick.* She grimaced. *Maybe it's my fault he went radioactive?* She snorted. *It wasn't that good of a kiss.*

"Got ya. A bay is prepped."

She steered the racer to the ship, reaching the loading bay in minutes. Five or NOX had opened the main shuttle bay closest to the mess, med bay, and bridge. She could've docked her racer on the *Usuba* which is what she would've done.

Micky peered at her from the platform, resting her elbows on the railing. "Welcome back."

Selira smiled. This was what she'd hoped for, not that emotional lambasting she'd received. Earned, but still. "Ready for that chat?"

"Sure," Micky said, waving a hand at the doors. "Interesting company you keep."

"I used him to lure you here," Selira said, choosing to be honest. "When I heard he was planetside, I had my people send out a distress call to you. Big monster with red eyes hurting children? My daughter wouldn't sit back and not do something." She climbed the ladder to stand beside Micky on the platform overlooking the bay. "It's the only thing

I could think of. I'm sorry. Diaz says I deceive too much, and I suppose he's right. It's been my way of surviving all these years." Her shrug was pathetic, and to her, it revealed her vulnerability. "I know, it's no excuse. 'If onlys' have kept me company for too long.

"I should've known Thomas wouldn't tell you. *I* should've told you, trusted you to act devastated by my 'death,' or even better, took you with me as I begged him to let me do. But he said the *Jinsei* was your home, the only one you knew." She cast her gaze down to hide the tears slipping free. "So, I left in a ball of fire, lost my leg in the process. Not your fault, so don't think that. Just a miscalculation we haven't been able to figure out. I did send tokens when I could. After I heard Thomas died, his accounts were closed as per banking policy. Five found no Mikaela Danvers but he did locate a few thousand Mick Danvers. Since your location was a mystery, I put tokens aside for you on the chance I'd one day see you again."

"When did you hire Cason?" Micky faced her, a frown furrowing her brow, but no judgment darkened her eyes.

"About two years ago. He's the best bounty hunter tokens can buy." Selira gripped and released the railing, relishing the cold metal beneath her fingers. "Hiring him was a decision I'll never regret." She smiled. "He found you twice."

"Do you think we should get him to search for this Ober?" Micky leaned her back against the bulkhead and folded her arms across her chest.

"It's a possibility—"

"What am I? Chopped liver?" Five's voice reverberated through the hidden speakers.

Selira glared at the ceiling. "You are, because even you couldn't locate my Micky."

"True. I'll give you that. Now that NOX is with me, two A.I.s are better than one." Five hummed. "Diaz incoming. Opening up bay three."

"You offered him a berth?" Micky glared at Selira, just like Thomas used to. "The *Jinsei's* my ship. You lost all claim to it when you exploded out of my life."

Selira flinched. "I'm sorry, Micky. I forgot to ask you not out of disrespect. I can tell him not to... I mean, I'd have to leave too." She threw out a hand, not wanting Micky to think she blamed her for the situation. "Which isn't your problem. I just thought since Tieren and Diaz are looking for the same man, we could combine forces."

Micky frowned. "Your logic's sound, but having him on board will impact costs. Now we're powering up another bay, making it three draining my sol tanks. Just ask next time. NOX, warm the last bay."

Tokens meant nothing to Selira, not after all her hard work had earned her a cushy nest egg. But they did matter to Micky. "No, I mean, thanks, but he prefers it cold." She cast her gaze down. "Just pressurize it. And I'm happy to pay for both berths."

Micky stiffened. "Charge family? Nope. That's not gonna happen. Besides, I'm not exactly desperate for tokens. For a while after Dad died, it was touch and go." She cast her gaze to the side. "I don't have the knack he had with creatures. They broke my heart when they died. It was on one of my insane jaunts for a hokou mate that I was bitten. I plan to head back to that planet for an infected one." With a grimace, she rubbed her shoulder.

"For Fentus?" Selira wrinkled her nose.

"No other choice. I need the best out there, and even you have to admit, their research facilities are unparallel." Micky offered a tight smile. "I don't know what these mutations are doing to my insides."

"We can hire a renowned doctor." Selira wasn't going to stop pushing this. Her daughter's medical information in the hands of big conglomerates made her 'ass twitch' as Five would say. "Someone trustworthy."

Micky smirked. "If Fentus gives me shit, I'll go on a rampage." She gazed at the shuttle. "I don't like killing, but if it's me or them…"

Speaking about murder made Selira shuffle her feet while she searched for a change of subject. The weather was out, they had their little chat, which left romance. "So…what's with you and Tieren?"

A blushing Micky nibbled her lip. A grin formed. "Soulmates… Can you believe that?"

"I can. I've learned some strange things over the years." Not that Selira would go into detail. There were too many 'wow' moments for her to count. "Diaz said his kind and Tieren's have been at odds for centuries."

"What?" Micky stiffened, shoving off the bulkhead with her foot. "And you're telling me this now?"

"I will not be harming your mate, Micky." Diaz strode through the door connecting the bays to the main ship. "My thanks for the welcome."

Selira studied the man, his presence pressing the air out of her lungs. Her cheeks warmed under his gaze. No way could he sense how nervous he made her post-kiss. "You well?" she asked, forcing herself to speak. His skin was back to normal without the red glow.

"I am." He peered at her. "I have permission to abandon my tasks for now. Ober is a priority."

Micky uncurled her fists. "What would happen if you disobeyed your superior?"

He scowled, no doubt finding the idea of rebellion distasteful. "The H.G.C. is not known for their mercy. The nearest exiled justisaars would hunt me down. If I die in the process, justice will be served."

"Peachy." Micky angled her head at Selira. "Need me to have NOX prep quarters for you?"

She caught her daughter's hand for a quick squeeze. "I'm staying on the *Usuba*. My work's there."

"Fair enough, and you, Diaz?"

He hesitated, glancing between them. "I too will remain on my camis."

"Fine, but don't say I didn't offer." Micky huffed, flicking out a dismissive hand.

"I apologize. I meant no offense. I prefer the purified water and fruit that is on my ship." He shrugged. "I must settle for freeze-dried, but at least my water is good."

"NOX?" Micky threw her gaze to the ceiling. "How pure is our water?"

"Not gonna lie, honeybuns, but the last bit of Rianus is gone. What we have is super-refined, lacking the sweetness of mountain streams."

She chuckled. "Well, there you have it, Diaz. Unless you want us to scan the worlds we pass for fresh resources?"

He jerked back like she'd surprised him with her kindness. "That would be appreciated."

"Is this the place to have a family reunion?" NOX asked, peeking through the door to the bridge. "Five's picked up a trace. I've powered up the *Jinsei* to hie after it."

"Good," Micky said, passing Selira to follow NOX.

Alone with Diaz, Selira stared down at the man, who had yet to climb the ladder. She didn't know what to say to him, and when awkward, she reacted with action. Swiveling on her heel, she lowered herself to the bay floor, intent on returning to the *Usuba*. The repetitiveness and mindlessness of work would put her at ease. But when she neared the bottom, her foot slipped. Still gripping the ladder, she swung free then slammed into the closest rung, catching it across her temple. Fire burned, and pain radiated outward, making her eyes water.

Mortification had her dipping her head. *Why am I such an idiot around him?*

"Selira?"

She rubbed away the tears before facing him. "Yes?" She sniffed.

"Female," he growled, cupping her chin and forcing her to meet his gaze. "What did you just do?"

"Bang my head?" She arched a brow and winced when the action summoned fresh agony.

"You are bleeding," he said.

She gasped and grabbed the rung, planning on using the med bay, but he caught her waist and pulled her back until his chest warmed her. "Diaz, the pod..."

His scent engulfed her. Romance novels would describe a man's cologne as cut grass, citrus, or cinnamon, but no, Diaz smelled of sunlight, sweat, virile male, with a hint of something fruity—no doubt his last meal.

"Come." Before she could say anything, he whisked her into his arms and carried her out of the bay.

"I can walk." She clung to whatever part of him she could reach, having never been carried. "And why can't I use the pod? It will fix me in seconds."

He glanced at her then ahead, revealing a pulse ticking against his jaw. "I will heal you." His lip twitched into a smirk. "A ladder..." He chuckled.

Despite the pain, his laughter was worth it. She couldn't recall ever hearing anything sexier.

She glared at him, hoping to hide how he affected her. "Listen, my 'beautiful' leg isn't graceful, nor is it advertised as such."

He kept quiet, strolling past her *Usuba* to the next bay. His camis didn't take up much space at all. A chill raised the hairs across her skin. NOX had even dimmed the lighting. She could barely make out the ship with nothing but a pale green glow of the cooling engine nozzles to guide her. Up the ramp he strode then lowered her onto his bench-bed. The urge to leave seized her, but visions of him fetching her and carrying her back made her stay put.

He opened a hidden panel and pulled out a device the size of her hand. Of the same metal as his ship with flickering white lights, there was nothing to denote its purpose. Before she could ask him what it was, he flicked his thumb forward to power it up then scanned her with a white beam.

"Is this even human compatible?" she whispered, closing her eyes against the beam's brightness.

Tingles like a thousand fire ants swarmed her temple, shifting her ass on the bench. She bit her lip to keep from screaming. While the compulsion intensified to do so, the pain lessoned.

"See," he said, stowing the device.

"Thank you," she said, touching her temple and the smooth skin where the epicenter of the pain had been.

He grabbed her by her upper arms and hoisted her up, moving her like a doll to a spot on the floor. A green light ran over her, and where the incessant need to pee had been, that, too, was gone.

"You are now clean." He sniffed the air. "I do not like the scent of your blood."

She frowned at that...insult? "Um, neither do I."

He swept a curl behind her ear, his touch delicate. "It is rich with emotion, your pain acidic."

She gaped at him. "You can smell that?"

He drew in a deep inhale. "And more." He hummed in pleasure. "Strawberries."

She frowned but resisted the temptation to sniff herself. Instead, she pushed her ass far back to create some space between them, especially when she longed to close the distance. Where was her strength, her professionalism?

When in doubt, go to the basics.

"What was your childhood like?" she asked.

He stepped to the side, opened a drawer, and pulled out two packets of pinkish liquid. "Like many Gy'Ruxians."

She accepted one while he continued.

"Pappo was on the frontlines. Every day he came home was a miracle." He paused; his gaze far away. "Mammo would weep while setting a lavish meal before him. He always looked drained; his voice hoarse from the day's exertions." Diaz smiled and gripped the dagger sheathed to his belt. "An admirable male who cherished his weyr. Even when we were ruxlings, he had time for our foolish nonsense."

"Our?" she asked.

"My sassa and I." He took the packet from her, popped the edge, and handed it back to her.

The fragrance of guava drew her gaze. How had he managed to get his hands on human fruit juice?

She opened her mouth to ask but what came out was, "Front lines?"

He scowled. "We have been at a territorial war with the Okukuro for centuries. Stupid, in truth, for our archives have it that we are the intruders. We should have been grateful for any area they allowed us to occupy."

He sucked from his packet, his cheeks caving in as he did so. When he smacked his lips; the action sent heat lower to her core. She pinched her knees together and sipped her juice, hoping it would calm her.

"Our growth was too rapid with every mammo able to nurse four ruxlings every six months."

"Wow," she whispered. "We can have multiple at a time but only every nine months."

He met her gaze and held it. "I know."

Tension sizzled between them. She couldn't say what thoughts raced through her mind, but self-preservation kicked in, forcing her to rise.

Finding herself standing, she blurted, "Thanks for the juice and the healing."

Before he could speak, she hurried down the ramp. Some time alone would go a long way in restoring her sense of self. She also hoped Five had compiled some information on Gy'Rux. Facing Diaz always left her feeling at a loss. Info was power, ammunition, a shield. And against this much magnetism, she needed some sort of defense.

A strategy would also not go amiss.

She finished the juice, the tartness of guava pleasant. Silence greeted her when she climbed into the *Usuba*. No Five to torment her with questions or observations about her haywire hormones. And could he blame her? A man such as Diaz was rare.

If she survived her time with him, she doubted she'd fully recover. Some part of her would be permanently changed... Like her leg. Yet another scar she would bear.

She grimaced at her dark thoughts and headed to the bathroom. A shower should clear her mind and prepare her for work.

And she'd need a good cup of tea.

Chapter Thirteen

TIME FLEW WHILE SELIRA read through snippets Five's algorithms dredged from millions of servers. Her eyes began to blur under the strain, but she diligently sifted and stored what seemed valuable. Five came and went, bringing her a meal, a bottle of water, or a cup of tea. If her bladder didn't drive her to the bathroom, she wouldn't have gotten up to stretch.

A ping had her glancing at her notifications. When she clicked on the folder, Five's voice came across the speakers. "All I have so far, so expect this to be an ongoing research."

She blinked at the heading: Gy'Rux.

Five: What I have compiled has been gathered across way stations and stories told. Not much can be classified as factual.

So word of mouth? She frowned. Ober had spun a tale about a blood vow sworn between two friends. She'd loved the poetry. Little had she known they were Gy'Ruxian or that she'd recognize them when Diaz spoke them.

Nuberu, a planet close to Rianus and orbiting the same sun.

Okay, so that meant Tau Ceti? That made sense with the way he and Tieren 'feuded.' Since the majority of Five's sources were from the way stations nearest to Nuberu, she had to conclude that 'factual' was the best she was going to get. She hummed and carried on reading.

The inhabitants are predominantly two species: the Gy'Ruxians and the giant cockroaches.

Again, she paused. Okukuro resembled bugs? She shuddered at the thought of fighting an insect that huge. If they were hardy like Earth's, it was no wonder the war spanned centuries.

Families are called weyrs but are kept small, tight knit despite the Gy'Ruxians ability to bear young with such ease and frequency. Most mated females choose not to have more than seven ruxlings. There's a rumor that female criminals birth soldiers for their war against the bugs. *(Five: Rumor only. Cannot find anything to validate this.)*

Note: There's gibberish about the elements being tied to each weyr. I've reviewed the footage with Ober center stage. If I'd hazard a guess, I'd say he's water or air, based on the color of his eyes and hair. But what part the elements play or whether they even matter are unknown.

Wow. Was that why Diaz had red hair? For fire? Then why did he not like the heat? Something she'd need to ask him about. She huffed. Not that he was approachable. She was lucky to get some information out of him regarding his childhood. Although, he hadn't mentioned much, come to think of it. He had a mother and a father who 'worked' too hard. What did his mother do all day? He had spoken of his sister with fondness. Did he get up to antics as a young man? He'd said foolish nonsense, so he must have. Men given half a chance would drone on about themselves; she'd expected him to be the same.

She tossed the stylus onto the desk and pushed out of the chair, desperate for a cup of tea. Discovering his secrets would take a lot more digging and perseverance. An image peeking out snagged her attention. She tapped on it, enlarging it. With dark skin against shocking white hair, a man's white-eyed gaze peered into her soul. What element was white? Ice? Water? Lightning? Just under the 'V' of his shirt sat the corner end of a tattoo just like Diaz's. This man must be an exiled judge, as well. She hadn't seen any markings, scars, or tattoos on Ober, not when he'd dressed like a human: normal T-shirt, jeans, and a long waterproof coat.

She flicked the image aside for the next one. A familiar scene played out; one she'd seen before. A young man resembling Diaz, by his broad shoulders and sharp jawline, stood in nothing but a loin cloth with his beaded red hair tumbling down his back. What had he called the ceremony? Quaff Darn? Something like that. She typed a footnote for the image.

He'd seemed upset that she'd seen this...or him with his red hair. Picking up the stylus, she circled his head on the image hologrammed onto the glass surface. Leaning back, she studied the man's visage while rubbing her hip.

Exhaustion burned her nostrils, fuzzied the edges of her vision, and dampened her hearing. She slumped, abandoned the stylus and the idea of tea for her bed. A nap would be good for her or, if at all possible, a full night's sleep—something she hadn't experienced since she'd lost her leg. Now that she'd 'reunited' with Micky, peace would surely be hers.

But after hours of trying, it wasn't.

Not when memories of Diaz stroking her metallic leg tormented her or the brush of his lips across hers re-igniting a zing through her veins.

"What's the matter?" Five stood in her doorway. "Can't sleep?"

She thumped the pillow and smashed her face into its softness. "What gave it away?"

"The lack of snoring."

"Oh," she squealed and threw the pillow at him.

With a chuckle, he caught it, fluffed it twice, then tossed it at her. "Cup of tea?"

"Please," she mumbled, throwing her legs over the side of the bed. "I thought you were chummy with NOX?"

"I can be there and here at the same time." Five shrugged. "Turns out, a passing planet has a few tag and bags. And yes, they declined my assistance."

Ice slithered down Selira's spine and wrenched a knot in her stomach. "Micky's planetside?"

She scrambled off the bed and bolted for her office.

"Relax, mama bear," Five called from the galley. "She's wearing a cam, is armed to the teeth, and has two body guards. She's more secure than you and I on this rust bucket." He curled his lip at her when she peeked at him. "I'm surprised this thing's operational. It's an antique. Even the servers, as freshly upgraded as they are, just... Argh. I need a deep cleanse after trudging through thousands of musicals NOX has a predilection for."

She grinned, left her office, and crossed to Five to accept the cup of tea he'd made her. "It can't be that bad."

"Sure is. If Micky wasn't such an anomaly and offered Fentus a rare service, they might have scuttled this thing instead of 'salvaging' it."

"That makes my ass twitch, Fentus buying into her." She sipped her tea and hummed when the hot sweetness slid down her throat to warm her belly. "What are they after?"

"For now, they seem benign. Reason enough to be suspicious." Five gestured to her office. "I linked a screen to Micky's cam if you want to watch."

She grinned. "And that's why I love you."

"Sure, and it ain't for the foot rubs, constant tea making, or my wise counsel?" He harrumphed, sounding like the expelling of an exhaust vent. "I'm deeply offended."

She ignored him and settled into her chair, rested her elbows on the table, and cradled her cup. Micky's cam showed her shoving glass cylinders and data crystals into a drone.

"Next?" she asked, facing the shuttle's compartment.

"The last one," NOX said from the pilot's seat. "Some sort of a cave. Best thing is, once you sample this one, we can stop for... Wait for it." He wiggled his rubbery eyebrows. "A sauna."

"What?" Micky gasped and leapt across to hug NOX from behind. "You're the best, you know that, right?"

"Duh." He waved her away.

She headed for Tieren, who wiped a cloth along his great sword's blade.

"Do not even think it, *kekaseea*. You are covered in a creature's blood."

"Just a little kiss?"

Tieren scoffed. "No."

Selira chuckled, liking her son-in-law more and more. What she'd observed of his behavior so far was how he grounded her gung-ho daughter. These mutations had made her reckless. Sure, she had NOX, but he was still an A.I. in a metal suit. Selira exhaled slowly, straightened her shoulders, then sipped her tea.

A sauna did sound amazing. She couldn't remember when last she'd had an actual bath or swim. Although, her prosthetic limb might drag her down like an anchor. Despite the doctors stating she could, she'd never submerged it fully. Water was a treasured resource unless the Primary was violated. Primitive worlds were protected, so stealing their water was a hell-no. Which she suspected her daughter did often, especially when she promised to do so for Diaz. All Selira could hope for was that they went under the cover of darkness. She'd have to talk to Micky about this at some point. For now, she'd make sure no documentation leaked out.

"Babe." Five pointed at the screen.

She whipped her focus there and froze. Micky was in the jaws of what looked like a gigantic worm, its rows of serrated teeth that of a shark's. It had no eyes that she could see, just mottled skin looking thicker than an elephant's, massive nostrils, and that wide mouth with its teeth embedded in her daughter's leg.

Selira was up and sprinting to Diaz's camis. "Diaz!" She raced up the ramp and almost collided with him. "Gear up. Micky's in danger."

"Female, you cannot go like that." He gestured to her between pocketing, sheathing, and loading various weapons onto his person—some of them unrecognizable.

"Pants or no pants, I'm not going to let my daughter die while I dress." She whirled on her heel and stomped off with a tossed out, "Bring your handheld healing thingy."

"I have pants," Five called through the speakers. "Hurry up, I'm powering up the racer."

"Happy now?" she asked, glancing over her shoulder at Diaz.

He snorted. "What manner of creature is the Shikari chasing now?"

After they boarded, Five tapped a console to summon footage not from Micky's cam. "According to what I've seen so far, those sauna pools are their homes."

"Their?" Selira squeaked, settling behind Five in the pilot seat as he flew them out of the *Jinsei's* bay. The small planet was purple with white clouds swirling around it—looking more like a pretty marble.

Diaz stood beside her, his shoulder and upper arm warming her through her sleep shirt. She tried not to pay attention to his proximity and what it did to her insides when she had no control over her body's reaction to him. Instead, she forced her gaze to stay on the screen and her breathing to even out.

Sure enough, circular pools with steam rising from them said sauna, but the head popping out of each hole made her think of the antique Whack-A-Mole children's game she'd read was auctioned for over a million tokens. Already a worm had been beheaded with Tieren zipping from one side to the other, his black wings keeping him from being chomped.

When the video's viewpoint glanced down at hands holding a rifle, she realized they were watching through NOX's eyes. He fired, driving the worm back but not deterring it. Micky was still clamped in a creature's mouth, being shaken like a rag doll. Tieren swooped down and swung his great sword, catching the worm just below its jaw. It squealed and released her, tossing her into the air. Tieren caught her and lowered her to the ground, setting her against a rock wall.

"You all right?" he asked, but Selira couldn't hear Micky's response with the thump-thump from NOX's rifle and the creature's dying cries. It sank into the pool and disappeared.

"A little help would be appreciated," NOX called, dodging a head sweeping out to get him. He tumbled over the floor and rose, the rifle ready.

Tieren launched into the air, then dove into the fray, swinging his sword as if it was lightweight.

"There is still time," Diaz said, cupping Selira's chin to run his thumb over her pursed lips. "I have my handheld healing thingy." He smirked, his red eyes warming with humor. "It is called a personal medic or P.M."

She smiled and let the tension ease from between her shoulders. "And she has healing."

"I do enjoy seeing you so exposed, but suitable clothing is added protection." He stepped back to run his gaze over her, lingering on her legs. Damn, if his skin didn't start to glow again.

She tried not to squirm under his scrutiny. Like a lifeline, she grabbed the pants Five offered her and hurried to wiggle into them. They were too tight, no doubt Micky's.

Diaz tutted at her bare feet. "When we land, I want you to stay back. Do not place yourself in harm's way." He faced ahead, expecting no argument.

She almost rolled her eyes. "Fine. Man go first. Woman follow. Happy?"

"I am a *male*, not human."

She chuckled. "By that logic, you can't call me 'female.'" She deepened her voice to mimic his when she said 'female,' but it was a pathetic attempt. "I hope you're not this bossy with your sister."

He grinned. "My sassa can hold her own." He folded his arms across his chest, bulging his muscles which threatened to split his shirt down the middle.

She swallowed hard and whipped her gaze to the screen, almost releasing a sigh when Five landed the racer beside the *Jinsei's* shuttle. When he opened the door, organic-smelling, rich-oxygenated air flooded the compartment. She inhaled, expanding her lungs to the fullest, like it was the first deep breath she'd taken in a long while.

Diaz abandoned her, not waiting for the ramp to lower. He leapt out, Five on his six. Together, they sprinted into the cave. She trailed at a steady pace between running and walking, then veered right when she breached the cavern. The air was warmer, moist, and the scent similar to petrichor. She'd experienced rain hitting dry soil once—there was nothing in the known universe that could compare to that smell.

Already Five was firing a blaster at a worm while Diaz hacked at its base with his great sword. Who would've thought? Thousands of years after the medieval era, men still used blades of some sort.

They seemed to have more of an impact than the rifles or blasters, when one by one, the worms died.

"Mom?" Micky frowned, shuffling to tuck her backside into the corner where the wall met the floor. "What are you doing here?"

"What a silly question." Selira squatted beside Micky to study the shredded and blood-stained fabric of her cargo pants. "My baby's in trouble." With the gentlest of touches, she peeled back strips to expose the red mess. "Oh, my," she whispered. "I can't see what's wrong. Want me to load you into the racer and get you to the pod?"

"I'll heal," Micky said, even though white lines marred the edges of her mouth.

Selira leapt to her feet and ran toward a glowing Diaz. His gaze swept to her, a ferocious scowl formed, and he bolted, meeting her half way across the cavern.

"Female, what did I say?" he snapped.

"I need the P.M." She held out her hand.

His nostrils flared. He clenched his jaw, dug into his pants, and pulled out the device. "Last warning."

"Or what?" She laughed when he said no more. "Go do your thing, big guy."

She hurried back and kneeled again, this time flicking the switch. Like she'd seen him do, she ran the white beam over the wound. Unable to see whether it was working, she switched her focus between Micky's thigh and the nearest pool.

"Give me your shirt," she said to her daughter.

"Use yours," Micky said, her eyes squeezed shut.

"I'm naked underneath. I wasn't expecting to travel planetside any time soon." Selira clicked her fingers as if to say pronto. "I can use your pants, but they're rough. I don't want to be rubbing that over your leg."

"Fine," Micky huffed and peeled off her shirt to reveal a bra.

Selira scrunched up the fabric and approached the pool. She peered at its bubbling surface and prayed nothing sprung out to bite her. When she shoved the shirt into the water, a gasp escaped her at its perfect temperature. A dunk would've been wonderful.

Little by little, she cleaned the wound, venturing back and forth to rinse the shirt now stained pink. At last, a triangular wound became visible—at its center was dark red blood with swirls of blue and white.

"Feels like it should be bigger," Micky muttered through clenched teeth.

"Maybe it was," Selira said and ran the white beam over the wound until it began to shrink. "How are the men doing?" she asked, more to distract Micky than to actually know. Five should be recording it all for later viewing.

"We're winning." Micky chuckled. "Although, your Diaz—who is glowing, by the way—has a gash across his right bicep. Tieren's missing a few feathers, but both NOX and Five are fine."

My Diaz? A shiver rippled down Selira's spine and blasted warmth in her chest until breathing was a struggle. *If only.* "Think a sauna's worth all this?"

"Mom," Micky whined. "A sauna. Are we really debating this?"

Selira laughed. "You're right." She glanced at a pool. "How deep does it go? With this leg, I might find out the hard way."

"NOX says there's one with a wide-enough ledge where only your feet would hang over." Micky pouted. "I even brought soap."

Selira focused on the color returning to her daughter's cheeks. A good sign. "Well, if the men would quit playing around, we can see about that bath."

Chapter Fourteen

"Playing around?" Diaz asked from behind Selira. With the fight over, his beast no longer pressed on him to set it free. He hoped that his core would cool enough for him to breathe, but one look at Selira, and he doubted he'd find any relief soon. "How can one female get into this much trouble?" With the great sword's tip to the floor and his elbow on the pommel, he leveled his gaze on Micky.

"Just a tag and bag," she said with a shrug. "This box thingy yours?"

At Micky calling it a thingy like Selira had, he smiled. "Yes."

"My thanks," Micky said, pushing off the wall to stand. "Are you two done?" she asked the Greeven and her machine.

"All right, hold your horses." NOX pointed to the cave's entrance. "I'm leaving. Ain't nobody needs to see your naked ass."

Naked? Diaz jerked back. "You are still going to bathe?"

"Why not?" Micky swept out a hand. "You've cleared out the creatures."

Heads, innards, and puddles of black blood littered the rocky floor and didn't make for a peaceful setting. "There could be more—"

"Which is why I'm lowering my cam into the depths below. NOX will warn me if something's coming." She gave him a look he had to assume meant she knew what she was doing and didn't value his opinion.

Diaz glanced at Selira. "You too?"

She shook her head. "Nope. I've had enough excitement for today." She rose, caught his hand, and placed the P.M. on his palm.

Her unexpected touch fired his blood, but his beast didn't stir. He curled his fingers around the device then slipped it into a pocket, using the movement to step away from her. This near to her, he could scent strawberries.

"If you're good?" she asked Micky.

"Thanks, Mom." She drew Selira in for a hug and whispered, "And take NOX with you."

"I'll wait in the *Jinsei's* shuttle," the machine called on its way out. "Just in case."

"Well, holler if you need...Diaz." Selira smiled at him then headed out.

He had to admit, from behind, with her swaying ass and the sweep of her unbound hair, she made an enticing image.

"You cannot be offering my sword arm for every minor concern," he said when he caught up to her. A breeze cooled the sweat coating his skin but didn't reach his core. It still thrummed; a soft glow shimmering off his skin.

"Minor?" Without glancing at him, she huffed and hitched a thumb at the mess behind them. "I hate to see what 'major' means in your world."

True, those creatures had been fearsome and a worthy battle. He rolled his shoulders and winced at the throbbing of his wound. The sting had been on the peripheral and now came to the fore with a vengeance. He angled his arm to assess the damage. It was slight with him having endured worse during the *Qaf Dahn*.

How would she react if he made it seem like the pain was unbearable? No matter how tempted he was to have her 'nurse' him, luring her into such a position was deception. He tutted at his silliness. When he settled his gaze on her, he froze. She was no longer in front of him, nor had she rushed ahead to board the racer.

"It's beautiful," she whispered, cupping a delicate flower the size of her hand. She'd crossed green vegetation to reach the tree to the right, no doubt thinking all was well.

He raised his gaze to the sky, then across the surrounding foliage; half-expecting a predator to charge at her. His hearts thundered in his chest, and his beast shoved against its confines, ramping the red light pouring off him.

"Deep purple is such a vibrant color. Like your blood." She stroked the petal with her forefinger, sending another wave of heat to his core.

Would she touch him like that, her hands soft, her caress evocative?

She glanced at him and frowned. "Don't like flowers?"

"I have no opinion," he said, for in all honesty, he'd never admired the fauna or flora on Nuberu.

She strode over the green patch to reach him. "You are a strange man—"

One moment she was there, the next gone, leaving a hole at her feet and her screams as she plummeted.

"Selira!" He dropped his greatsword and lunged in after her, smacking roots out of the way and cobwebs from his face. At least the drop was narrow and perhaps she would manage to grab onto something to slow her descent. His hearts leapt into his throat when she hit what sounded like water. It would dampen her fall, but after what he'd just fought, who knew what hid in the depths?

Fear seized him when he remembered she'd said she'd sink to the bottom with the weight of her leg dragging her down. He plunged in, cold water engulfing him. With his eyes open, he spun, searching for any sign of her. A trail of bubbles sent him deeper, the growing darkness summoning his heightened vision.

There! A bright shimmer faded fast as it sank.

He dove after her until the tips of her hair stroked his outstretched fingers. Scrambling for the strands, he tightened his hold and pulled her up and closer to him. Her eyes were wide when she met his gaze. She clung to his arm, his shoulder, then slipped around to his back. *Wise female.*

Something swept across his peripherals, like a large mammal circling them. With his bleeding wound, he declared their location. Propelling himself up, he prayed safety was a short distance away. A solid shadow was to his left, so he veered toward it moments before breaching the surface. Her gasp near his ear sent sweet joy through his veins.

She was well.

They'd survive this.

An illuminated strip of land lay before him, but his instincts demanded he hurry. He complied, gliding across the water despite Selira clinging to his back. Just when a sensation brushed across his heels, he crawled onto the shore. She fell off him, landing on her back to suck in great gulps of air. He eyed the waters to make sure whatever was hunting them wasn't amphibious. When nothing emerged, he knelt beside her. A splash fixed his focus once more on the rippling surface. A fin broke through then dipped as it circled.

"I'm so sorry, Diaz. I should've listened to you." She sat up to thump her thigh with a fist. "Turns out it's not that heavy. Duh, silly me. It shouldn't be when it's titanium. I just can't swim with it. Water passes right through the fibers."

"Are you hurt?" he asked, studying her drenched pants clinging to her legs.

He swept his gaze up and froze at her unbound breasts enhanced by nothing but the clinging fabric of her sleeping attire. The way her taut nipples were so clearly defined...

And his burning was back, pulsing red along his skin.

"I don't know. Something gripped me and yanked." She angled her leg to rest her metallic foot on the other knee. There, deep into the titanium were circular holes looking like teeth marks. Green liquid leaked from one of the loose fibers. "Frig. That can't be good."

He peered into the distance, adjusting his eyes to do so. There had to be a way out of here. The hole they fell through was in the middle of the underground lake, so using it to climb up was impossible. He swung his focus to the sides. If he trusted his navigational senses, the racer was ahead, the pools to his left. Narrow ledges hugged the right rock wall, curving with it as it traveled upward. *Steps? Here?*

But to get there, they'd have to swim across.

"Wait, I can see," Selira said, snapping his attention to her.

He dismissed his sharpened senses and blinked at the bioluminescent stones scattered across the ground.

"So pretty," she said.

"Oh no you do not. The last time you admired anything, we landed here. Do not touch one."

She snatched her hand back. "Fair enough. So now what?" Tapping her wristband, she called to the machine. "Five, are you receiving me?"

A crackle, pop, and fizz solidified their dire situation.

Up the ledges they'd need to climb, and he hoped there was a doorway at the end.

"Once you catch your breath, we will head for a possible escape route," he said.

She dipped her head like doing so could hide her tears from him. Before him, she squared her shoulders, drew in a slow breath, and smiled at him. "I'm ready."

He loved it when she gathered her courage. Since meeting the confident and sassy female to this one who needed him, he had to say she still intrigued him. Except the lying, he liked all facets of her, especially when she continued to surprise him.

"Come." He offered her his back.

"Right. We have to swim. Makes sense since we're on an island of sorts." She looped her arm around his neck and one across his chest, pinning her softness to his back. Though her touch didn't stir his beast, it summoned a ripple of heat. She moaned and clung to him, nuzzling her nose into the curve of his neck.

Thinking about her being naked under her garments would drive him to madness. Action would focus him, so he stood, able to bear her weight with ease. She hooked her legs around his waist and rested her chin on his shoulder.

Gritting his teeth, he marched across the short shore and waded into the water until the ground fell away beneath his feet. Long strokes carried them across the surface, but when he reached the first ledge, there was no ground to stand on. He gripped an edge and hoisted himself up, toeing the rocky wall to climb.

She gasped, pressed her nose to his back, and held on tighter.

Inch by inch, he moved, digging his fingers into cracks, locking the tips of his boots in place by sheer force. It wasn't far to go, no more than half his length, but whatever hunted them was incentive enough to reach safety.

Once on the ledge, he let her slide down until her feet touched the stone.

"Up we go." He pointed to the clear path.

"Um, Diaz, I can't see anything else but you." She threw out her hand, whacking it against the wall. "You go first."

Remyi, I forgot she has not my gifts. He squeezed past her on the narrow ledge and strode ahead. When she shoved her fingers into the back of his waistband, her touch on his skin scattered his thoughts for a second. Despite his stride faltering, he pushed onward.

While they walked to the next rise, a strange chatter accompanied her labored breathing and the more pronounced whir-thunk of her leg. Yet, she didn't complain or beg him to slow his pace.

"How can you be so warm?" she asked, her fingers twitching.

Because I want you? No, he couldn't say that to her, besides if he was forced to reveal how she drove him crazy, he wanted to see her face when he did so. "All Gy'Ruxians have higher core temperatures, crimson more so."

"Crimson?" she stuttered.

"Weyrs are separated by elements or...colors." He paused on the landing near the ceiling of the cavern and frowned.

No sunlight lured them to the outside, only a shadowed alcove awaited them. The dire situation went a long way to cool his core. He caught Selira by the shoulders, guided her to a wall, and let her lean against it while he peered through the other doorway. More ledges weaved upward *and* downward.

"Are we taking a break?" she asked, her voice thready despite the confidence in her tone.

"Yes. I hoped this was the exit. It is not. We need to climb higher."

"Oh, good. That explains why it felt like I fell for ages." She slumped and rested her head back. "If you need to scout, I can stay here."

He smiled. *My brave, little female.* "I will not be long."

He took the ledges down, sniffing as he went. Then he headed up, expecting the air to become cleaner, warmer. It didn't. He peered into the cavern's depths, scanning the rocky outcroppings, and the stream running between them. Navigating that might be difficult for Selira, but what choice did they have? On the far side was a sliver of light so tiny, without his enhanced vision, he wouldn't have spotted it. And the ledges leading up to it showed promise.

"Is it bad news?" she asked when he returned to her.

"We go down to where the air is not so stale." He sat beside her and drew her shivering body into the curve of his. *Ah.* The chattering came from her teeth. Her skin was chilled to the touch, and yet she hadn't mentioned it.

She burrowed against him, pressing her cold nose to his throat. "So warm," she whispered then moaned when he lifted her onto his lap to wrap both arms around her. "We can leave in a minute."

Without the sunlight, he couldn't tell how long they'd been trapped here. By now, Five must've realized they were missing. Micky and the Greeven too, although, that female might bring more calamity with her should she decide to 'rescue' them.

"I need to know when you are tired, weak, or sleepy. Pain our bond will share." He caught Selira's chin to tilt her face to his. Her pupils were wide, her gaze trusting.

She scrunched her nose. "I'm cold, and moving my leg's becoming difficult. Other than that, I'd kill for a cup of tea."

He chuckled, but when he gazed at her without her realizing he did, he took the time to admire her features even though his vision painted them red. Before he could rethink the compulsion, he brushed his mouth over hers. What he yearned to do was to devour her, to reveal the beast within, to have her welcome with open arms the wilder side of him.

Her smile was rueful when she pulled away. "I won't lie. I'm scared shitless. I've never been in this situation. NOX or Five have always had my back."

"Now I have you," he said, drawing her closer to slant a kiss across her lips. This time, he delved in, crushing her against him, uncaring if he burned for her or why his beast remained silent.

She sank into him, clinging to his shoulders as if her life depended on it. When she swept her tongue across his, fire blazed through him in waves, hardening his cock to an aching point. If they weren't so vulnerable, if she wasn't freezing, he'd show her what it meant to rut with a Gy'Ruxian.

He shuddered and drew back to rest his temple on hers. She'd be so soft between her thighs; about that he had no doubt. "If we do not leave now..." He left the threat unsaid.

"Right." She broke away and clambered to her feet. "Down's going to be a bit tricky with only you to light the way." She ran her hand from his bicep to his forearm. "And you're fading too."

"Next time we see a shiny rock, grab it."

"Sure, and hope it doesn't magically turn into a flesh-eating creature?" She laughed. "Wish I could see your expressions better. I'm sure they'd be priceless." She patted his chest, stroking downward to within an inch of his throbbing cock. Then around she went until she shoved her fingers between his waistband and skin again.

Drawing in a calming breath, he inched toward the doorway and out onto the first ledge.

"I find these curious," she whispered. "Like someone has taken the time to carve them. That implies they had the right sort of tools and the determination. I thought this moon was uninhabited."

"I did not think to ask, in truth," he said, leading them down, turning at every new step to help her.

"I'll have to talk to Micky soon," she muttered.

"About?" he asked, his focus ahead.

"Violating the Primary."

He snorted. "What does that matter when you gather secrets and deceive with such ease?"

"True," she said, "but in my defense, I won't be permanently grounded, fined, or thrown into some forgotten penal colony."

"Ah, so what she does is unlawful, and what you do is not?"

"I do not harm others with my 'secrets,'" she snapped then huffed. "And you weren't supposed to go down into a mine, nor fight off giant worms. I didn't expect to see you again—"

"After I served my purpose."

"Yes," she said, her tone bold.

You have courage, purlievo, but lack remorse. She'd been honest from the start, letting him know how she planned to use him. Not once had she considered how she'd inconvenienced him. She'd offered him a cold place to rest, fresh fruit, hell, even *gi'hayna*. Using his weaknesses against him? He could imagine how well she'd serve the abyss weyrs with her calculating methods, her morals flexible.

Would she be more amiable to his teachings after they rutted? He stubbed his boot against a loose rock and grimaced at his distracted thoughts. *And* she beguiled him with her sweet smiles and addictive strawberries. Did she do it deliberately? Was she aware of how he ached for her?

Remyi, I hope not.

It was bad enough fighting the temptation of her without her actively seducing him. He shivered at the thought.

"You cold?" she asked, concern clear in her voice.

"A little." He winced at the second lie he'd ever told. But admitting to her he was aroused wouldn't be wise if that was her goal. "Any idea what time it is? Where is your Five now?"

"NOX is probably singing a musical, and Five..." She fell silent. "I'll plan accordingly, making sure that if this happens again, I'll be more prepared."

He chuckled. "You cannot think of every conceivable scenario, Selira."

She harrumphed. "I can try."

He admitted she was correct, for a partial preparation was better than none. "All right, what would you have done differently?"

"Shoes, for one thing. Pack a torch and a jacket." She tightened her grip on his waistband. "Listen to a certain *male* when he suggests I dress."

"The wisest thing you have said so far," he said with a chuckle.

A splash, blasterfire, and cries of alarm reached his ears, but from afar. He angled his head to listen, trying his best to gauge the distance.

"What is it?" she asked, leaning into him to whisper as if her voice would disturb him.

"Help is on its way." He clasped her elbow and guided her down to the next ledge. "In case it is not friendly, let us continue."

She sucked in a sharp breath. "Dear God, no. I promise to never leave my shuttle again."

He laughed. "A silly vow you will break at the first opportunity."

"Fine." She grinned. "What should I offer instead?"

"Never to lie to me," he said, dipping his head to meet her unseeing gaze.

Her eyes widened. "I can try."

"Not good enough, Selira."

She jerked back. "What you have asked me so far that I couldn't reveal to you or anyone were my sources. I swore an oath to protect their identities, Diaz."

He scowled. "Which means there will always be secrets between us."

"I—"

"No, it was not a question." Pressing his lips together in defiance, he whipped his gaze ahead and continued their descent. At last, his core temperature cooled.

Chapter Fifteen

Frig, what else can go wrong?

"WHAT DO YOU MEAN Mom's missing?" Mick demanded, resting her fists on her hips.

Sure, she was as naked as they get, but when Five charged in, hiding herself from him made no sense, especially in light of the news.

"Diaz's sword is in the path between here and the racer. And there's a hole they must have fallen through." Five gestured to her. "I suggest you put on some clothes and help search for her...them." He glanced at the cave's entrance. "Or don't you care?"

Mick scowled. "I'm not about to lose my mother for a second time. NOX!"

"Already reconning beneath us. Finding nothing but solid rock, almost like the *Jinsei's* scans can't penetrate." His voice was clear through her wristband.

"Must be why you didn't know about the worms. I can't be going in blind, NOX," she snapped.

"Yeah, yeah," he muttered.

"We must follow them," Tier said, looping an arm around her waist to pull her snug against his bare chest. "I will fall first since I can fly. Wait until I let you know when to jump down."

When he loped toward the shuttles, his tight ass on display, she called after him, "Pants."

Gathering his clothes and his boots, she threw them to him. He donned them far too quickly for her liking before he was off again, sword in hand. There was nothing sexier than a well-muscled man, naked, and holding a greatsword. She was one lucky woman.

Five coughed, sounding like bolts ground over a grate. "Quit ogling the man and get dressed. Got any clothes on that shuttle? Shoes?"

Mick opened her mouth to snap at the silly NOXV when his words sank in. "Shit. Mom's barefoot. NOX—"

"Bringing them," he said.

"See. Sorted." Mick wiggled her wet legs into her pants and peeled on the blood-stained tank top. She'd taken the time to rinse it and drape it over the warm floor. Although it was still damp, she trusted her body heat to dry it fully. While fiddling with the cam pinned between her breasts, she waved at Five. "Lead the way."

It took less than a minute to reach the hole. They peered into a solid-black, ominous void. No light penetrated its depths.

"Good thing I packed a torch." NOX handed her the satchel.

"Ready." Tier's voice echoed up to them, and without hesitation, she tossed Five in. His shock was priceless.

She giggled.

"Don't you dare," NOX warned. "I'll guard the shuttles and stay here in case I need to throw down a rope."

"Scaredy cat," she said, looping the bag over her head and nestling it between her breasts. She took the time to shift the cam around it.

With a wink at NOX, she hopped into the hole.

Dirt, roots, rocks, and a fossilized creature whizzed past her when she fell. The moment she was free of the shaft, images of a vast cavern came into focus: a lake, smallish islands, blue dots of light, and absolute silence.

"I said to wait for my call," Tier muttered, snatching her out of the plummet just as her boots touched the water.

"Wasn't sure you'd catch Five or just let him sink."

"I heard that." Five stood on a shore, glaring at her.

When his expression morphed from A.I.-fury to A.I.-horror, she acknowledged the tingle of her haywire instincts. She yanked her blaster out of its holster and spun, one hand still in Tier's grip.

Leaping out of the water like a flying fish was a giant...thing; a mix between a sperm whale and a sword fish with massive batlike wings. Its gaping jaws were wide in preparation for snatching a meal. Without hesitation, she fired, but when her blasts struck, they sank into its skin like a fireworks display against a cloudless night's sky. Five shot at it but to no avail.

"Wow," she whispered when Tier burst forward, taking them out of its range.

She tapped the cam, hoping it had captured the creature. Without her rifles, she couldn't tag or bag on behalf of Fentus.

Tier lowered her to the ground beside Five and joined her. "Let us pray it cannot come onto land."

She watched until it sank under, no doubt disappointed at having lost a meal. "Right," she said. "One crisis averted. Where to now?"

"Ledges run up all the walls. Not sure which direction they went though." Five spun, sweeping his arms out wide. "That way lies the worms. Probables state that Diaz would avoid them at all costs." He dragged his fingers over the tiny pebbles on the shore. "Especially with your mother damaged." He held up two fingers coated in green goop.

"I see no blood," Tier said. "Do not scent it either."

"A leaking cybernetic leg can be fixed. Five, head to the side ledges; we'll take the back." Mick tapped her wristband. "NOX?"

The connection crackled, squeaked, then hummed.

"Can you hear me?" Five's voice came through, vibrating up her arm. "Good. I will let you know if I pick up anything."

"Same." She smiled at Tier. "Wanna hike or fly?"

"Let us climb, lest we miss a trace of them." He scooped her into his arms and flew them to the first ledge.

They didn't reach the next ledge before spotting green droplets.

"Five, we have their trail," Mick said to her wrist.

"Already? I'll catch up. Want to make damn sure they didn't backtrack this way."

Tier's eyes glowed a brilliant amber, and with her mutations, she could easily make out their path ahead. Mom would be blind. Mick didn't know about Diaz or whether he had anything remarkable about him. She had to assume he did since he found this ledge in the dark.

"Good thing NOX sent torches," she said, adjusting the satchel. "Mom's gonna need one."

"Diaz has excellent vision," Tier said in passing, confirming her earlier assumption.

"The red eyes?" she asked.

"Yes. They only appear when he taps into his beast."

She tripped over a lose rock, sending it tumbling into the waters with a 'plunk.' "His what now?"

"A tale for another time."

She pouted, but knowing her man well, he withheld the information for a valid reason. "Come, let's hurry. I could do with a coffee."

He grinned, swiveled on his heel, and marched ahead. She stuck to his ass, even when Five squeezed by them. He disappeared through a rock-hewn archway without waiting for them.

"She's leaking more and more. Not good," he called.

Mick grimaced. At this rate, Mom might be dragging her leg. "Keep going. Find her."

"Will do."

They passed through the alcove and into another cavern as vast as the other but without a lake. A stream weaved between massive boulders, and there in the middle of them roared a fire-breathing dragon.

"Frig," Tier growled.

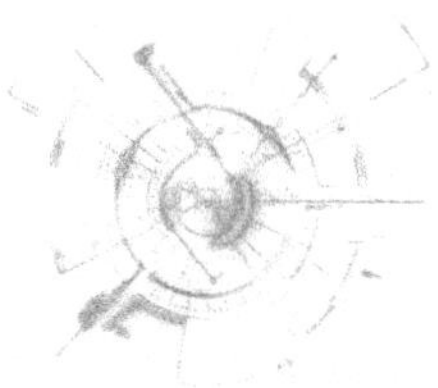

THE SECOND DIAZ SET foot on the sandy bank, his beast lashed at its confines, sending his temperature sky high. A thorough sweep with his enhanced vision showed nothing, yet they were in danger. He had no doubts there. He caught Selira's elbow and drew her closer to him. When she opened her mouth to speak, he pressed a forefinger to her lips.

"When I tell you to run, do so," he whispered.

She shook her head. "Not without you."

"Female," he hissed.

"Man," she snapped.

He threw her over his shoulder, her squeak loud enough to ricochet off the boulders. A rustle merged into a susurration then a full-blown rumble. He jumped onto the largest rock and balanced there, hoping whatever it was lost interest. Darker than the abyss, thousands of eight-legged creatures crawled out of the sand. Solid-black eyes swiveled onto them. A glimpse ahead showed how far he and Selira still had to go to reach the ledges. No way he'd make it if he bolted. She'd be of no help either, unable to see to use a bioblade. And without his great sword, his kavex would do minimal damage. If he let one slip past him...

He shuddered and carefully lowered her to her feet. Unbuckling his belt, he draped it over her hands, so grateful she didn't speak. None of his weapons would be useful now, but they were precious to him. Destroying or losing them would be foolish. He half wished he could strip, but the creatures shuffling closer told him he was running out of time.

"Do not be frightened," he whispered to her. With a deep breath, he leapt into the black, writhing mass.

Blinding light pouring off him forced him to shut his eyes, but the pain, the sheer, unbearable agony, drove him to kneel. Fabric tore, every muscle pinged and throbbed, then the crunching, bone-breaking snaps came. He gritted his teeth, fighting the beast overwhelming who he was as Diaz. For the sake of Selira, he'd stay in control if it was the last thing he did.

Up he rose, his head now meters off the ground. With a sweep of his wings, he sent the creatures flying, shaking some off, and blasting others with bolts of fire that scorched his throat and left a sulfuric aftertaste on his tongue. He couldn't take the time to find out what Selira thought of this part of him, especially not when the things rushed toward her.

He stomped over, crushing them underfoot. Then he spun, seting a few ablaze, lighting the area when he did so. The dead flopped onto their backs, their legs curling in. Some smoldered, offering meager light. Bioblade blasts hit others, and a glance at Selira had her shooting at his attackers. She broke away and aimed at the eager few nipping at her heels before targeting others around him.

From side to side, he roared, sending out streams of fire. He'd pay for that later, but for now, a dead creature couldn't harm her. When the enemy retreated and his energy dwindled, he stumbled and fell, too tired to hold himself up.

Her cool touch on his taloned hand sent a zing of fire to his core, making his beast hum. Reforming into a Gy'Ruxian happened in a blur of anguish, leaving him slumped over with his head on his forearm.

"Diaz?" she whispered, palming his temple and bringing him relief even when the cavern's chillier air summoned bumps along his skin.

He hummed but didn't dare touch her with the full force of his fire still on the surface. When she placed her hand on his without incident, he gaped at her. The heat within him had yet to diminish. *How is this possible?* It had taken long last time to wrestle control of the internal inferno. He pressed his temple to the cooling rock beneath him, trying to wrap his mind around what this all meant.

"Rest," she said, and her touch was gone.

He glanced at her, catching glimpses of her profile while she circled him, bioblade pointed outward. A smile grew and bloomed into a grin. She was guarding him, and with her poor eyesight, she had no chance of seeing something coming or shooting it with any accuracy. Still, she showed courage.

Something snapped in his chest, like the breaking of jungle vines. From tethered to free, his hearts swelled, flooding him with more warmth than he dared to bear. He clenched his jaw and sent a silent question to his beast. Only to receive reassurance that all was well.

He jerked up and clambered to his feet. As if he had the right to or that it was the most natural thing for him to do, he looped an arm around her waist and crushed her against the length of him. Her shivers calmed, but she said nothing. A few peeks over her shoulder to meet his gaze, her eyes wide, and her cheeks flushed were the only reactions she gave him.

She didn't yell at him or accuse him of hiding his beast from her, nor did she demand answers. He couldn't decide if this delighted or disappointed him.

"Mom," Micky called, dropping out of the air to stand beside them with the Greeven landing on a boulder.

"Oh, sweetheart, so glad you found us." Selira peered around, searching for something or someone. "Where's my worthless Five?"

"Coming to your rescue, babe, but I went up instead of down until I saw fire." He ran along the last ledges to skid to a halt across the sand. "Micky's got your clothes, but now that I'm here, I should've packed more." He gestured to Diaz's nudity. "Care to explain or is turning into a dragon something only I saw? Shit and corruption, maybe I have a virus?" He froze then droned in an automated tone, "Going into diagnostic mode."

"Well, that will shut him up for a bit." Selira snatched her daughter into a hug then released her to settle at Diaz's side.

He stared at her upturned face and smiled. What was it about this female that he liked so much? He'd been furious with her minutes ago, swearing there was no future for them despite the blood vow and yet... She'd come to his rescue, guarded him, *and* calmed his beast.

"I don't want to sound ungrateful," she said to Micky, "but do you two know how to get out of here? Or are you as trapped as we are?"

"The exit is up ahead." The Greeven pointed to the sliver of light Diaz had spotted.

"Excellent, Tieren. Why don't you take Micky and Five, and I'll go with Diaz." Selira waited, expectant, her authoritative tone not to be argued with. "And tell Five, when he snaps out of it, that I want a cup of tea ready."

The Greeven scooped up Micky and the machine and took off.

Diaz frowned, peering at Selira. "What are you up to?"

"I just needed a moment alone with you to say..." She splayed her fingers across his naked chest. "What the hell, Diaz? A dragon? Wow and wow. And a beautiful one at that." Her laughter wrapped around him like the first sun's ray on a crisp spring morning.

His beast preened at the compliment.

"Talk about keeping secrets," she said, "and this one's a humdinger." She patted his chest, her fingers sparking renewed fire that twitched his cock. Thankfully, she didn't notice. "What truly begs the question is whether you planned on ever telling me."

"With the calamity you and your daughter bring down upon us, it would have been soon."

She met his gaze, her expression softened, and she ran her hand up to grip his shoulder. A trail of fire followed her cool fingers. "Then I will share my sources."

His breath caught, his beast stirred, while his hearts leapt and danced.

"New ones. I can't be backtracking, Diaz; that'll take a while. But if anything I've learnt is pertinent to whatever dilemma we're tackling, then of course, since we're blood mates, I can trust you to guard my sources as I promised. After all, you did say, we now share each other's vows."

He clasped her hips and inched her closer. "Blood vows, yes. Every day promises, no."

"They are the same thing in my world," she said. "A person's word is their bond, or I hope it is. Integrity you have, therefore my secrets you will keep." She squeezed his shoulder. "Now morph, summon your dragon, do your magical thing, and fly us out of here."

He harrumphed. "It is painful."

Her eyes narrowed with an intensity that ruffled the scales along his beast's spine. His cock hardened when she blessed him with that lustful expression—the same one she wore every time he kissed her. She scooped up his belt and draped it over her shoulder, his bioblade once more holstered. "Diaz, let's leave this place and head home."

"*Remyi*," he muttered and released the metaphorical chains. His beast broke free with a roar, more eager than he'd ever known it to be. The light, the agony, the crunching bones happened in seconds, forcing her to stumble back.

She gasped and crept forward, holding out her palm. With a nudge, his beast nudged their snout into her hand then purred at her touch.

We keep her, it told him.

If Hom'Garr had his way, no. Instead, Diaz shared, *She is our blood mate. We cannot harm her.*

Harm her? His beast chuckled, rumbling its laughter through him. *Mate her, yes.*

Diaz wanted to shout his agreement. *That is for her to choose. Now grab her, let us leave this place. I am hungry.*

The beast grunted, wrapped its talons around her waist with infinite care, and launched them into the air. *Nice, cool cave. We sleep here?*

No, we have our orders.

Counselor is not to be trusted. Something smells wrong.

Diaz jerked back at the warning. The innocent bounty when all the evidence had shown her to be guilty? Had he been lured into a trap? Not once had he considered such a thing despite it not making sense. He directed the beast to glance at Selira. Perhaps she could find out more?

The beast lowered her onto the highest ledge then settled beside her, returning Diaz to Gy'Ruxian without much grumbling. He staggered to his feet but froze when she dipped under his arm, pressed her head to his chest, and steadied him.

"I've got you," she said, ushering him into the sunlight.

Chapter Sixteen

Tea wasn't forthcoming. Not when they came out on the other side of a mountain. Selira chewed on her inside lip, keeping her gaze ahead, clomp-clomping in her daughter's boots. With Micky, Tieren, and Five striding through the forest with ease, a glowing Diaz trailed Selira.

He was *naked*. Except for the belt he wore, his weapons slapping against his skin as he walked.

Not to mention *aroused*. And staring at her ass. She'd tossed him a smile and caught him ogling her. That had whipped her gaze forward, her breathing jagged. Her heart danced on the crevice of a lust-fueled volcano; each thump of her heartbeat sent waves of heat to her core.

Every hour or so, Tieren launched himself up to confirm they headed in the right direction. Why he didn't just fly them over to the shuttles had something to do with his and Diaz's mutual distrust. And moving the shuttle closer meant crushing the fauna and flora, which she refused to do.

So they hiked.

She was fine with that, needing the time to rethink her decision to see if Diaz knew what to do with that erection he sported. Hell, her mind still reeled. An honest-to-goodness dragon? In the vastness of the universe, there had to be the weird and wonderful in all forms of life. Yet, she'd always considered dragons the stuff of fairy tales.

Without anyone noticing, she pinched her arm and swallowed a yelp at the sharp self-inflicted pain. Nope, not dreaming. She'd seen a dragon. That explained the red hair, his hotter-than-normal temperature, and the glowing... Yeah. She'd ask him about it all.

Five had been spot on when he suggested that elements may play a role, perhaps influencing their colors. She'd ask Diaz about that too. What did white mean? Her brain tumbled into the downward spiral of thoughts and questions, excitement making her giddy. Oh, to learn more, to discover deeper meaning in the worlds around her, to find gems of forgotten tales and lore... Nothing compared to that.

"I can smell you, *purlievo*," Diaz whispered in her ear, his hot breath sending a shiver through her.

"Strawberries?" she asked, not daring to meet his gaze.

"Desire," he rasped.

It must have been her imagination, but the sensation of his touch along her spine resonated through her on-edge nerves.

"A natural reaction to you," she managed to say with a steady voice when she was far from unphased.

A guttural rumble raised the hairs on the back of her nape and hardened her nipples. Damn. If he made any such sound during their...sessions, she might not survive them.

A stumble snapped her out of her lust-filled daze. Her leg had locked mid-stride, refusing to bend. She had barely a second to throw out her hands when she hit the ground. A groan slipped past her lips, her wrists throbbing.

"Selira?" He knelt beside her.

Mortified as she was sprawled in an undignified heap, she couldn't bear to glance at him. Heat poured off him, his 'cologne' teased her nose, and that silky sexy voice of his—

Up she went, once more carried in his arms.

So close to him now, she could do nothing but look at him when facing ahead strained her neck. Her only choice was to accept his help. She draped her arm along his shoulder, clinging to him while relishing his glorious warmth. Where her skin touched his, the red glow pulsed. The urge to splay her fingers across his tattoo was almost too strong to resist, so she clenched them in her lap and lifted her chin in defiance.

He gazed at her, his expression intense and brooding, his eyebrows knitted. His intention was clear in the path he took while he studied her face, lingering for the longest time on her lips until she succumbed to the stupid compulsion and licked them.

He sucked in a sharp breath, flaring his nostrils. His arms tightened, pulling her snug against him.

"I could kill for a shower," she said by way of a distraction.

"Yes," he said, his voice hoarse. "After your leg is repaired."

A valid point, so she didn't argue with him. As long as there was tea sometime soon, she could bear Five fussing over her. Argh. She'd never hear the end of this.

"So what happened?" Micky called, facing them while walking backward. "Did something drag you down? Or did you just not look where you were going and tumble in?"

Selira grinned. "Fault's all mine. Wanted to admire a flower and in I went."

"Diaz leapt in to rescue you? How chivalric." Micky's knowing gaze, pursed lips, and tiny smirk said it all.

"Yup, my hero," Selira said, patting his chest.

Tieren shot ahead, drawing Micky's attention. The mini-inquisition and judgment ended when she jogged off.

"My control is dwindling," Diaz whispered, "when you keep touching me like that, *purlievo*."

"A pat?" Selira snorted. "What about..." A feathering of her fingers across his silver-tattooed, velvety skin had her sighing at the hot texture.

His arms around her stiffened into granite. His eyes hardened with the promise of retribution, even when his sexy top lip quirked.

"See you on the *Jinsei*." Micky waved from within the shuttle's compartment.

Thanks to Micky's interruption, Selira gritted her teeth at the missed opportunity. How Diaz would've reacted to her teasing or what he would've said was lost for all time.

Up the racer's ramp he carried her. The door was wide open and must've been like that the entire time. While the engines powered up, Five hurried around them to the mini galley. Before she could cancel that order for tea, Diaz drew her attention by lowering her onto the bench and stepping back. She was now eye-level with a part of him she ached to lick. Keeping her hands tucked under her ass and her focus elsewhere meant her brain misfired, unable to form a thought.

"Repair kit?" he asked Five, who handed her a steaming tea.

She yanked out her trembling fingers to grab the mug and cradle it against her chest, forcing herself to stare into the steaming liquid than to ogle a hard cock.

Five met Diaz's gaze. "You could've warned me about the dragon." He opened a cabinet and hoisted out the toolbox, placing it at her feet. With a nod at her, he headed for the pilot seat to fly them home.

Diaz knelt before her, slipped off the boot and rested her foot on his thigh. He had a multi-tool in one hand. On the floor sat a refill bottle of bio-fluid. That little bit cost a fortune, but she was more fascinated with his head bent over her. Thankfully, the tea occupied her hands.

"What happened to your voice?" She wasn't about to admit how much sexier it was all rough and guttural.

"Breathing fire damages my Gy'Ruxian biology. I will heal."

She formed an 'oh' with her mouth. *Holy cow.* She shivered, then drew in a slow breath to ask, "My ship or yours?"

"Yours but not your bed." He lifted his gaze and blessed her with a smile.

In that moment, butterflies exploded in her chest like a thousand fireworks. She jerked back, lowered her chin to take a sip of tea *and* hide her expressions. Her reaction wasn't sexual, not when his charm made her heart spasm. No, falling for him wasn't in the cards. In her peripheral was her shiny, titanium leg, her eternal cockblocker. Except he called it beautiful. She half-snorted at that nonsense. Sex was all he wanted. An experienced info broker could separate her emotions from her goals. All she had to do was get her shit together. She wasn't a teenager anymore, nor the naïve young woman who'd fallen for Thomas's 'sweet' nature.

"Five, when we dock, make yourself scarce," she said, her tone all business-like.

"Sure thing, babe." He flicked a hand up.

"This 'babe' is disrespectful," Diaz muttered.

"It gives me a sense of camaraderie, especially in the long, lonely hours in space." She cupped his cheek and ran a thumb over his lips. "And it will be there after you've left me."

She smothered a wince. Now why had she added that?

"Is that so?" Up went his red brow.

With one more tweak, he lowered the multi-tool and locked the narrow nozzle of the bottle into its slot. He met her gaze as he squeezed, forcing in the green fluid. A whir-clunk accompanied his ministrations. With a nod, he clasped her heel and behind her knee to bend the leg back and forth until the hum returned.

"All is well," he said, twisting to pack away the tools and cap the bottle.

"Thank you," she managed.

"These gouges remain from those black things." He traced with his fingertips deep scratches probably made from fangs.

She shivered, having not realized how close those spiders had come to biting her. Hell, she hadn't even known they were there until he lit a few on fire. And when they'd swarmed him, she'd reacted on instinct. From his belt, she'd unsheathed what had looked like a futuristic pistol, and fired it. The desperate urge to protect him had swept over her. Despite her fears and insecurities, she couldn't stay back and let him fight the spiders on his own.

"The fibers unclipped but didn't tear under the water creature's bite. You were lucky it only left a few indents." He stroked the holes just below her big toe.

"I have spare feet." She grinned. "I know that's an odd thing to say."

He chuckled. "Applicable under the circumstances."

"Docking," Five called, swinging the ass-end of the shuttle to reverse into the bay. When the door opened, he leapt out of his seat and raced into the *Jinsei*. "Call when you need me."

She drained her now-cool tea and set the mug beside her. Then pushing herself to her feet, she expected Diaz to shift back, but he didn't, leaving her pressed to the length of him. Frowning when he didn't move, she raised her chin to meet his gaze.

"Selira," he said, caressing her along her jaw to her ear. There, he buried his fingers in her hair. "How I want you."

She blinked, unsure she'd heard him correctly. "Say again?"

When he didn't repeat himself but stared into her eyes, she splayed her fingers over his sternum, thinking to nudge him aside. He layered his other hand over hers, trapping her.

She cleared her throat. "I thought you were eager—"

"I am, but there is plenty of time. We have long hours in space." He drew in a shuddering breath and broke away. "I shall eat, shower, as you say, and meet you on the *Usuba*."

Faced with the full length of him with just a belt on, she nodded, expecting her voice to betray her. After taking some time to calm her breathing, she headed to her ship. The tea had done nothing but highlight the emptiness of her stomach, cramping it so hard, it gurgled in protest. Her first stop was the galley on board for a quick bowl of noodles, which she shoveled in on her way to the bathroom.

It was good to be home, despite what she'd discovered on her adventure.

A dragon. She shook her head, took another mouthful, and leaned into the cubicle to activate the spray. With two more bites until her cheeks bulged, she stripped and stepped under the hot water, spinning in a circle while chewing. When she grabbed the all-purpose soap, she laughed at the word 'STRAWBERRIES' etched into the container.

No wonder he liked it. Fruity fragrances to a fruitarian would be appealing. Now how was it possible for a dragon to grow to that size with what Diaz ate? Another question she'd need to ask if she remembered to. She switched off the water after a thorough rinse and reached for the towel. Bending over, she gave her hair a good, long rub, trying to dry it before he arrived.

Why not her bed, what was wrong with it, and if not there, then where?

She flipped her head back to shimmy the towel down her back. A movement in the reflection froze her, and she squeaked at finding Diaz resting his shoulder on the doorframe.

He wore his pants and boots but left his chest bare. His glow was there but muted. Strange that, although, she did suspect it was tied to his dragon somehow. The heat had to come from somewhere.

"Sorry, I seem to have taken too long," she said, praying her burning cheeks didn't mean her face was now redder than a dying sun.

"I am not complaining." He snatched the towel from her, leaving her with nothing to hide behind. Tossing it to the floor, he caught her fingers and drew her closer.

"What's wrong with my bed?" she blurted, throwing up a hand to place on his bicep.

"Too soft," he muttered.

"Oh," she managed when he rubbed his palms up and down her arms. "I can fix that."

He jerked back, taking his heat with him. She almost pouted at the loss, even as goosebumps skittered over her skin.

"Extra-firm?" she asked, and touched a panel beside the bathroom door. "Lie down."

When he did, she paused, unable to believe he was there, in her bed, her room, her life. Not that his impressive package tenting his pants had any sway. Of course not. Hell, yes, it did. She was still a lonely woman with natural urges. Like everyone else, she had a right to some pleasure.

"Yes, this will do," he said and patted the bed beside him.

She placed a knee on the edge to crawl toward him. His eyes turned molten when she did so even though she'd swear her breasts hung like cow's udders. Not romantic nor sex-inducing to think that, nor did it seem to matter to him. He sat up, caught her by her waist, and dragged her over him as he lay down again. Skin against skin sent a tremor through her. There was something to be said about touch and how it impacted her senses. Hugging Five couldn't compare to this.

"*Purlievo,*" Diaz whispered between kisses down her neck to her collarbone.

Sparks spread outward, puckering her nipples and intensifying the growing ache in her core. Needing to feel all of him, she straddled him across his torso and arched into him. He growled but didn't cease kissing her. When he cupped her breast and rubbed a nipple, she moaned.

It had been so long since her last sexual encounter that her body thrummed in anticipation. She wanted him to hurry and needed him to go slow, leisurely so she could savor each moment.

"Diaz," she mumbled, unable to articulate what her body craved.

"Selira." He leaned back to grin.

With one hand, he traced her curves, stopping to grip, squeeze, caress, or tweak. With the other, he stroked between her legs. His hot, tentative touch shot a bolt of ecstasy through her that she writhed, rubbing herself across his fingers.

"Show me what pleases you," he said, but instead of continuing what he was doing, he caught her and sprawled her on the bed beside him.

"What—" She swallowed her question when he settled between her thighs, spreading them wide to allow for his broad shoulders.

"I knew you would be soft," he said, sliding his thumb over her sex, circled her nub, then slipped inside her channel.

She squirmed, overwhelmed with such exquisite sensations that she whimpered and let him do what he pleased. Part of her said she should be ashamed to allow him such access.

"You smell so good." He buried his nose to take a deep breath. "Strawberries and the essence of who you are, Selira." Over her mons he met her gaze, his smoldering. "Here?" he asked, swirling her nub.

She arched off the bed, her nipples so tight they tingled. An orgasm barreled toward her, the cliff so near.

"I am sorry. I cannot take the time when I long to."

She barely heard him, every muscle in her striving for that release. *I'm so close.*

"If I did not want you so much I would succumb and taste you. For now..." He thrust a finger into her channel and pinched her nub.

At the unexpected assault on her senses, she screamed and splintered, catapulting her into the void of ultimate bliss. While she drifted down from a euphoric high, he left the bed to strip, his focus on her while he freed his cock and yanked off his pants. Her mouth dried at the sheer size of him. Time to test those rings around his girth.

She spread her legs wide like a hussy, but dammit, she wanted him more than any man before.

"So beautiful," he said, settling between her thighs. "Let me know if I hurt you. You are perhaps too small for me."

"I...uh, stretch," she gasped, her ability to speak abandoning her when he rubbed the head of his cock across her sex.

"Good," he growled, inching into her.

Chapter Seventeen

Impossible.

So soft. Diaz's thoughts wouldn't form past that reality. After Selira had come apart for him, her body glowing with that beautiful peach he liked, his beast had pounded at its confines. *Mate her.*

That it echoed his greatest desire didn't bother him, but what was more potent wasn't his beast's demands, but the part of his soul that needed her more than his natural urge to breathe fire. Sliding into her slick channel was what made life worth living. Every muscle tensed. Every nerve ending leapt to life. And in a flash of fiery need, he was harder than he'd ever been.

His breath caught when he was fully seated, her lingering tremors rippling over his length. The exquisite sensations pulled him between cradling her close and withdrawing to thrust in again.

"Selira, lie still," he gritted out.

She did, except to hook her legs around his hips.

He sank deeper than he thought possible and shuddered. "Female," he rasped.

"Man," she whispered, a smile teasing her lush lips.

"You were warned," he said, withdrew, and thrust into her.

Her eyes widened, she cried out, then dug her nails into his chest. The bites of pain took the last of his control. He plunged in and out, unable to dampen the lure of ecstasy just out of reach. Her whimper cut through his lust-fogged mind, and he glanced at her, only to find her orgasming again. This time, a wet heat rushed over his cock. The sensation was so unexpected, so divine, he lost all control.

With a roar shredding his already tortured throat, he blasted his seed into her, grunting when every plunge triggered bursts of pleasure. *Remyi*. He opened his eyes to take in all of her. To absorb this female beneath him, one who hadn't complained at his rough handling, and hadn't minded the heat pouring off him. By her flushed body and her contented sighs, she'd appreciated his efforts.

He collapsed next to her, not wanting to land on her and smother her. She moaned, rolled over and draped her arm over him, pinning her length to his side. Her even breathing a moment later said she'd fallen asleep.

That wouldn't be possible for him. His mind, now clear, reeled. Desire thrummed through his veins like he hadn't just had his fill. He wanted her over and over again. She'd expected him to have her once and leave; he'd gotten that distinct impression. Now, he wasn't certain he had it in him to walk away. Whether it was the blood vow that had started this connection between them or purely Ixella, the mother of fate, mocking him, the pulse of her heart ricocheting in his chest spoke volumes. Her very life beat was now his to guard.

Idiot, his beast tutted.

How was I to know a blood vow with a female led to this?

Nothing in their archives had documented this or warned not to. Blood vowing with a female was probably rare, but still, something somewhere could've prepared him. Had he known rutting with her would feel this good, he wouldn't have taken so long to get to this point either. But now that he *did* know, he'd be doing it again. Whether it strengthened the blood vow was a chance he'd willingly take.

How long he'd remain with her was a mystery. Perhaps only after he'd performed his assignments to the H.G.C.'s satisfaction, he might be able to leave. His hearts squeezed, tightening his chest, and sending a pang of pain vibrating outward. He'd scan himself with the P.M., assess the results and what information the device carried about Micky's biology.

Track down Ober, Hom'Garr had said. The male had escaped off-world and should be brought in for questioning, but what law had he broken? If he'd abandoned his duty and stolen a camis, then yes. But how had that not been common knowledge? Unless he'd been kidnapped? For decades, they'd known of unauthorized visitors to their planet, couldn't stop the intrusion, so Ober being taken was plausible.

Until Diaz found him, he'd remain in the dark.

Discover Selira's sources pertaining to Gy'Rux. She'd trust Diaz going forward but had used the vow to ensure he couldn't reveal her secrets. And she had the right of it. He could no more go against his sense of honor than betray her as Hom'Garr commanded.

Kill her daughter. Perhaps he should have left the P.M. in the camis? Without it, she might have died and absolved him from this task. Still, not bringing it with while knowing doing so would endanger her, that smacked of deception. He had to hold himself to his moral core or chaos would reign, and all that he'd endured to become a justisaar was for naught. He only had to be patient. In time, some creature would kill her.

Or you could lie. His beast shifted like it settled its chin on its arms. *Think about it.*

He scoffed. *Hom'Garr has heard of the Shikari. News of her endeavors will continue to reach his ears. So no, lying about killing her would only bring dishonor upon me.*

The beast sighed. *Yes, and we do not deceive. You have said so before. And yet, did you not say you were cold when you were not? Mm?*

He winced. Yes, he had; his second lie, and it had flowed off his tongue with wicked ease. *I had a reason,* he snapped. *Now leave me be.*

A whimper grabbed his attention. He gazed at Selira, snuggled against him. She kicked with her leg, shoving it down as if something had yanked at it.

She moaned, shaking her head. Her cheeks flushed. She flopped onto her back, her body twitching. A cry filled the air in the room. Then she stilled. Tears flowed over her cheeks, dripping into her hair and the linen.

He caught her in his arms and cradled her, tucking her face in the curve of his neck. She didn't stir, but her breathing returned to normal.

"Five?" he whispered. "Can you hear me?"

"Yes," it hissed.

"Does she have night terrors often?" he asked.

"Every night," it said.

"Bring me what information you have on the explosion that took her leg." Perhaps he could unravel the mystery.

"Sending it to your ship."

He stroked her back, running his hand up and down in the hopes that his touch offered her some comfort. Maybe he could figure out what had happened. Not that he believed he could outthink an A.I., but he'd fixed a machine a time or two, had a few bounties who'd tried to outsmart him, kill him, or try to. Some had even set explosive devices.

Worthy opponents were those who'd injured him, sent him off in the wrong direction, or made him question the evidence. In the end, he'd always trusted the data the H.G.C. had supplied.

She'd been worthy purely because she *was* innocent. Pyia—a petite sky dragon with her abundant blue curls and bright blue eyes. So like Ober.

Now that he knew his blood mate to be alive, he tested their bond and found it weak, a faint whisper of energy where there had once been something solid. The *Jinsei* was tracking Ober, although Diaz couldn't confirm whether that was true or not. He didn't suspect foul play from Micky or the machines. And with the Greeven also wanting to find Ober, perhaps Diaz was being a little too distrusting.

Still, had he allowed the silly bird to carry him, they would have reached the shuttles sooner. Everything within him had rebelled. There was nothing to dislike about Tieren, per se, even if he was a prince of his people. Nor did Diaz care what color his plumage was. A Drueen never let a Greeven fly them anywhere, not when dragons had bigger and better wings. He smirked. He could've done that too, transformed into the beast. But trudging behind Selira with her swaying hair and ass was something he enjoyed, added to the sexual tension brewing between them, not to mention his whispers into her ear. Her reactions fueled his determination to remain on the ground.

Only when she'd fallen did he regret his selfish decision. He'd forgotten about her leg despite the broken whir-hum of the mechanisms a constant song in his ears. She hadn't complained, so he'd discarded her discomfort. 'I've got you' reverberated through his mind. Those words from her had a potent emotion curling in his chest. She'd meant them too.

He pressed a kiss to her temple. Slowly, one by one, her actions revealed who she was as a person. Stubborn, strong, courageous, impatient, persistent, and yet, she hid her suffering: her broken leg, her belief it diminished her beauty, her fear of being alone, and her inability to forgive herself for abandoning her daughter. That she'd agreed to share her sources with him said much. She took her promises seriously, would fight to protect when she said she would. But she lied, as and when she deemed it necessary. She deceived, uncaring what impact it had on other lives. He could add fraud to her crimes, especially when she claimed to be someone she wasn't, with falsified documentation to back her. A data reaper? *Remyi*. What else?

Yet, he wanted to be nowhere else but here beside her. And therein lay his dilemma.

"Five?" he whispered. "Who is Emerys Broderik?"

"A client," it said.

"Is Selira Data Reaper Atlas?" Though, why he asked when the machine could lie to him, he couldn't say. A part of him wanted to believe she was redeemable.

"Yes, in thanks for a service she provided."

Fire blasted along his veins at what kind of service Five could mean. "In person?" Diaz gritted out.

"Finding his kidnapped daughter."

Just like that, Diaz's jealousy fizzled, and instead, his chest swelled. He could save her, could bring her to the honorable side. Hope was a beautiful thing, coating his...their future in a kaleidoscope of light. And if she turned out to be who he thought she was, he had a lifetime to convert her.

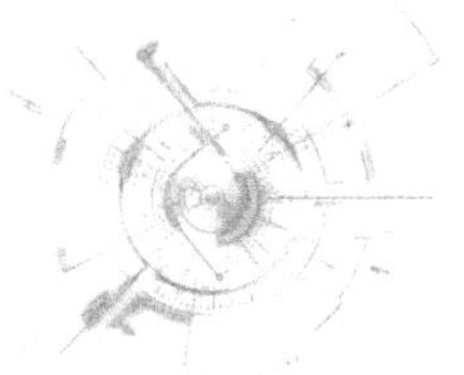

SELIRA STRETCHED, BLISSFUL LASSITUDE in every bone of her body. She couldn't remember when last she'd slept so well. No nightmares? Maybe all she'd ever needed was a sexual release?

"Note to self: research efficacy of a sex bot." She grinned. "And the cost."

"What?" Diaz asked from the shower.

"Frig," she muttered, having thought he'd left. She rolled out of bed to face the music, cursing herself for not searching for him first.

He stood under the spray, his back to the corner, his gaze on her. "Am I not enough for you?"

With the way the water dribbled over every inch of him, damn, he was more than enough man for her. She licked her lips, wishing she could lick the droplets rippling over his cock rings.

He chuckled. "I see." Off went the water, and a naked Gy'Ruxian prowled toward her.

"Diaz, I'm...dirty." She evaded his hands, just barely.

He jerked back. "My seed is in you, Selira. How does that make you dirty?"

She stilled and raised a wide-eyed gaze to him. Not wanting to offend him, she hurried to say, "If you don't mind..." She shrugged, then inched forward to splay her fingers across his chilled skin.

"I love the smell of me on you," he said.

"Oh?" she asked, trailing a pattern to his semi-hard cock. It was so pretty.

Thick at the base—needing both her hands to circle the girth, it narrowed to a decent-sized head. And those concentric rings had been amazing last night. Kneeling was out with their height discrepancies, but he could lie down and watch while she had her way with him.

"What are you thinking, Selira?" He captured her elbows and drew her closer.

"If you would let me..." She blushed and glanced away, catching her red-faced reflection above the basin. "Taste you."

He laughed, dragged her against him with one arm around her waist, and lifted her off her feet. "Where do you want me?"

She shivered against his cold body. "On your back."

This close, she could count the orange flecks in his irises. Without hesitation, she pressed her mouth to his, craving those soft lips and the sweep of his bold tongue. He placed a hand between her shoulder blades, crushing her to him. His nostrils flared. The red in his eyes swirled while he kissed her, not once breaking eye contact. Something intense lingered in their depths. She didn't know what it meant, but her body responded, thrumming and throbbing in response while her lungs gave up needing oxygen. She cupped his face and kissed him back, thrusting her tongue in to learn the crevices of his mouth.

He hummed when he broke away and lowered her to the floor. Then with a bounce, he landed on her bed. With his arms folded behind his head, he waited. His sensual and lingering gaze over her told her how much he liked the look of her, leg and all.

"Your scars," he said, "are beautiful slivers of silver."

She stroked the ridges along her side, over a hip to her thigh and stomach.

"Keep doing that, *purlievo*, and you tasting me will have to wait," he warned, his voice hoarse.

She whipped her gaze at his erection, proof he spoke the truth. Before he went through with his threat, she clambered onto the bed, nudging his legs apart like he'd done to her last night. She ran a fingertip along his length.

He hissed, thrusting his hips up.

When she wrapped her fingers around his girth, he shuddered.

His unfettered reactions emboldened her, giving her the confidence to follow her touch with her tongue. A growl was her reward. She grinned and slipped the head of his cock into her mouth. He gasped or groaned at every flick of her tongue or graze of her teeth. And the taste of him was sublime. The hot texture of his velvety skin, the sweet tang of his pre-cum, and his dramatic responses had her taking more of him, as much as she dared.

"Selira, *purlievo*," he rasped. "I cannot endure more."

She leaned back to look at him, licking her lips to catch every drop of flavor. "Are you sure?"

His body was taut like a bowstring, ready to snap. His cock twitched, more pre-cum dribbling free. She straddled him, sliding up his thighs to settle on his lower abdomen.

He gaped at her. "You cannot mean to—"

She gripped his cock, positioned the head at her channel, and sank onto him, moaning when he filled her. Arching back, she angled her hips until it felt so good, she was loathe to move. But she did, sliding up his length then down, rubbing all those gorgeous ridges of his cock along her insides.

A shiver raced over her skin, raising goosebumps and puckering her nipples. She held her breath and repeated the motion, closing her eyes to better savor the sensations.

His hands on her breasts snapped her focus to him. He watched, not blinking, while she gyrated and rode him, chasing that high only he could give her.

"Diaz," she hummed. "I need...more." She stilled, dipped and caught his lips for a kiss.

He rolled her onto her back, catching her legs to pin the backs of her thighs to his chest. The new position made her whimper it was that effective. Clasping her above her knees, he bent forward to pound into her with amazing stamina she couldn't match. He owned her; every cry, moan, sigh, were his.

An orgasm slammed into her, shaking her world. She screamed, chanting his name as pleasure flooded her in waves. Just when she thought she couldn't bear anymore, another hit her. He didn't stop, thrusting in and out until she lost count. Her muscles had melted;

she couldn't lift an arm, no matter how much she wanted to touch him. He stared at her, his intensity unparallel.

His eyes widened, then he froze, pinning his hips to her thighs. A low, drawn-out grunt escaped his parted lips then he collapsed on top of her, but somehow didn't smother her. His ragged breathing in the curve of her neck merged with her erratic heartbeat thundering in her ears.

"Can a sex bot do that?" he said, feathering kisses up her throat to her lips.

"If they can, I'll definitely buy one." She laughed when he jerked back to look at her. "Just kidding, my hero."

His lips twitched into a smirk. "Not the reply I was expecting."

He pulled out of her to run his fingers over her scars. "Mine are iron colored before the P.M. removes them. Scarring is rare for a Gy'Ruxian. Why does your pod not take away yours?"

"It will if I let it, but I haven't been in a pod since the explosion."

He frowned. "But...were you not placed in a pod then?"

"Medical tech wasn't advanced like it is today."

"Can you keep these in future?" He pressed kisses to each one. "Please. For me."

She nodded, unable to speak past the lump in her throat. He was too sweet to ask for something she could easily give him. And his admiration was a boon to her shattered ego. She no longer doubted that he found her attractive. No, not just that... Beautiful. Tears burned at the backs of her eyes, forcing her to blink rapidly to keep them at bay.

When he left her, her heart would shatter and never recover.

She was in love with him, and there was nothing she could do about it.

CHAPTER EIGHTEEN

No man's land.
Orbiting Kepler-452B or Innara
Eluzor Way Station

DAYS BLURRED FOR SELIRA, the best she'd had in a long while. Between finding pleasure in Diaz's arms and chats with her daughter, she had more happiness than she deserved. Sightings of Ober vacillated from planet to way station, until Five and NOX had narrowed it down to one corridor of planets. That morning, they were due to dock at Eluzor Station, orbiting Kepler-452B or commonly referred to as Innara, in the Cygnus constellation. Rumors had it that Ober frequented a bar named Dig It, somewhere in the mining levels.

A few nights ago, with her sprawled over Diaz, he'd said, "I cannot sense Ober anymore. Our bond is too weak."

"Your bond?" She sat up to meet his gaze.

"Yes, we shared a blood vow from when we were ruxlings."

"Oh," she said, sliding down to rest her cheek on his chest, more to hide her surprise. What were the chances of Ober sharing a tale of Diaz?

He stroked her jawline to her chin, pinched her there, and raised her gaze to his. "Perhaps my soul is overwhelmed with our bond, making his unreachable."

She stilled, her breath catching. Now he'd tell her he had to leave her. Ober was his mission, after all. Sadness drenched what happiness she'd found. She released a shuddering breath, gathering her courage to accept the news of his departure with some dignity.

"He must have learned how to dampen it." Diaz frowned. "I have been pondering this since I discovered he lived."

"It's not possible then? To cancel a blood vow?" Damn, she hoped it was. Missing him while her heart ached for him would make getting over him a thousand times harder.

"No, not that I know of. Have you found anything from your side?" He stroked her shoulder to her fingers then up again.

To be an info broker and not be able to unravel this? She winced. "Nothing of pertinence other than what Ober revealed years ago."

"I too listened to the recordings. I am glad he retained his charm."

"I can't believe I didn't know he was Gy'Ruxian," she said. "He looked nothing like you though." She ran a thumb over Diaz's crimson eyebrow.

"Oh?" His forehead furrowed, enticing her to smooth it. She did, marveling at the light playing off his skin. "What is different?"

"The blue eyes and hair, colorful beads in his braids. Paler than you and more slender than muscular." She stole a kiss. "Not as grumpy."

He scowled. "I am not grumpy."

She hummed, spreading kisses from the corner of his mouth to an ear. "What type of dragon is blue? White?"

"What? You do not know this?" he teased.

She shrugged. "I assume it's tied to elements, like your red hair for fire."

He grunted. "Yes. Blue is water. White is air, lightning."

"I bet fire are the biggest, baddest dragons." She slid her hand down to give his cock a gentle squeeze. "You have my vote."

He chuckled. "You are insatiable."

"I am," she said. "Tenacious too. I may not be successful regarding Gy'Rux, but I have learned much about Fentus."

"Fentus? You have mentioned this before. Do you not mean *fentusir*?" he asked.

She sat up, keeping one hand splayed on his lower abdomen, his muscles rippling under her touch. "Why do you ask?"

"It is Lyken for a friend who follows you with murder in mind."

She gasped and scrambled off him, running pell-mell to her office. Flicking aside files on her desk, she tapped the appropriate folder and zoomed in. "It can't be," she muttered.

"What is it?" he asked from the doorframe.

"Fentus is the Followers. They are one and the same. How could I not have put the two together?" She paced before the wall of screens, each swivel reminding her that the clues had been there the entire time.

"The religious fanatics intent on converting the universe to their doctrine?" He strode into her office then, from behind, looped his arms around her. With his chin on the crown of her head, they gazed at the information she'd gathered.

"Look how many research companies are under the Fentus umbrella. And the planets that have Followers stationed there in the guise of missionary work." She summoned a map of the universe and flicked both sets of locations onto it.

Dots speckled it from Auriga to Gemini, from Comma Berenices to Sculptor: yellow for missionaries, green for Fentus. The colors mimicked each other, paired at every spot.

"What is common between them all?" he asked. "Metals, water, fuel sources?"

She tapped the screens, summoning the data. "Nothing consistent."

"Oxygen?" He buried his nose in her hair for a deep inhale. "Life?"

She froze. "Genetics? That would explain their interest in the creatures Micky tags and bags."

"Or their offer to help her." He jerked to the side to meet Selira's gaze. "Or the Followers' interest in Drueens when they hired Micky to capture one."

"Frig," she whispered. "They're on a mission to create a genetically enhanced human race." A chill shot down her spine. "Like Micky."

"But can you prove this, and if you can, what can we do to stop them?"

Selira raised her head to the ceiling. "Five—"

"I've been trying to hack their servers for months now. Don't be asking me if I've made any progress," Five said from the doorway. "Now, listen, I know I'm just a humble slave...A.I., but could you people put some clothes on. Please. For the love of all things holy."

She rested her hand on Diaz's chest, uncaring that they were naked. "Isn't Micky a Fentus employee?"

Five froze, his hand halfway to tapping a screen. "She would have employee access, a way for me to sneak into their servers and do my thing. NOX?"

"Forwarding her initial deets, though she hasn't used their staff portal ever. It might look too obvious if you go poking around now."

"Then start using it," Five snapped. "Nothing too alarming."

"Will do. She also has some undroned samples she can deliver to the Fentus branch on Eluzor. Any way we could use that?"

Five hummed. "Intriguing idea but might be too risky. The staff portal is the way to go." He glanced at Diaz. "If the Followers want Drueen DNA, what makes you think they haven't tried before or after S.o.S's epic failure?"

"Who?" Diaz asked.

Selira gasped. "What do *they* have to do with this?"

"Micky went into a joint venture with them to capture a dragon-shifter. NOX, the sly devil, targeted the wrong side of Rianus, and sent her down to tag and bag a Greeven. But when she learned the sample chosen was a young boy, aka, Tieren's brother, she tried to return him. An epic battle ensued involving a giant centipede. Needless to say, all but one missionary died."

"Who? Be specific? Solomon?" Selira had liked the old coot and Kiros too.

"Burger had handed over the reins by then. Lemme see: Caldwell, Lyons, Woodard, Spencer, Reynolds, Holcomb, and Morton."

A sliver of fear bloomed from the back of her mind. "Holcomb?"

"Yup, Ruben Holcomb, the one and same."

"He's dead?" she squeaked. "Are you sure?"

"Yup, the bebbayaya swallowed him in one gulp," NOX said.

Selira slumped. "No wonder we couldn't find his whereabouts. I'm free." She grinned. "I don't have to watch my back anymore."

"We still don't know who hired him," NOX pointed out. "But since no one has tried to kill Selira Myers, the explosion must've convinced them he succeeded."

"True." She rose onto her toes and kissed Diaz. Tears flowed amid her laughter.

A tentative smile twitched his lips. "Care to share—"

"His attempted assassination drove me to kill Elizabeth Danvers and abandon Micky to become...me." She swept a hand down her body.

"Now back to my question: they must've sent more than one mission to snag a Drueen. Anyway we can learn if they did?" Five arched a brow at Diaz.

She smiled at Diaz's puzzlement. "Well, once we breach their defenses, we'll be able to access all their experiments, right?"

Diaz arched a brow. "Or take a sample of my DNA and see if you can find anything out there."

"Yes, both are excellent suggestions. NOX, take the pod's information and start the trawl." Five glanced at them. "Breakfast?"

"Please," she said, sliding her hand into Diaz's.

"Boom, one result already," NOX called. "Seem's like Tier has a bit of you in him."

Diaz froze. "What?"

"Yup," NOX continued. "The parts that make him dark in skin and hair, and his eyes yellow, are Drueen."

"Oh." Selira gaped.

"Find out how, why," Diaz said. "And get him down here."

"I can't be commanding a prince." NOX harrumphed. "I'll *invite* him to join you."

"Maybe this is why Drueens and Gy'Ruxians hate Greevens." Selira stroked Diaz's bicep. "Anything in your history?"

Diaz shook his head. "I am starting to believe our archives have been censured. No mention of how Ober left Nuberu, about the merging of our DNA, or why we despise each other except for vague ruxling stories." He gazed at her upturned face. "Nor how my bond with you broke all others." He cupped her cheek and caught her lips for a sweet, lingering kiss.

"Morning," Micky called from the *Usuba's* entrance. "What's this about DNA?"

"Frig," Selira cried out, ducking behind Diaz. Which was silly when he was as naked as she was. And the thought of her daughter seeing him so churned nausea in her gut.

"Wait, Micky, please. My...Selira is unclothed."

"Mom," she whined. "Fine, we'll step outside."

Diaz tilted his head to listen, then ushered Selira to her bedroom. He yanked on pants while watching her slide into the first thing she grabbed—a summer dress with spaghetti straps.

"That is a garment?" he whispered, fingering the thin fabric.

She glanced down at the floor-length skirt hiding her legs. "Yes, what's wrong with it?"

"I will show you later," he growled. "You may return, Micky," he boomed, making Selira wince.

"Coffee?" she offered, striding to the galley as her daughter and son-in-law entered.

"Please," Micky said. "So spill. NOX made no sense with the gibberish he spewed."

"Well, you were busy, distracted. I can't help it if you don't listen," NOX muttered.

Micky waved a dismissive hand. "DNA?"

"We just realized that Fentus and the Followers are the same." Selira tossed her daughter a glance. "Seems like they share a goal—one we can deduce, anyway."

"The creation of an enhanced human race." Five served mugs of coffee to Micky and Tieren. A glass of fruit juice went to Diaz.

Selira cradled her tea and faced the room. "They hired you to catch a Drueen. And since Gy'Ruxians are descendants, we had Five use Diaz's DNA to see if any data matched. This would confirm whether the Followers were successful in finally getting their hands on a Drueen."

Micky sipped her coffee, smacking her lips. "They were desperate. I can believe they'd send more than one team."

"And NOX found a match within seconds." Selira settled her gaze on Tieren.

"Impossible." He scowled.

"I thought so too," Diaz said. "But it would explain your darker coloring. Since a white Drueen with a white Greeven would not a black Greeven make, that leaves a black Drueen with a white Greeven to get you. I'd like to know how and when your DNA changed to include fire Drueen genes."

"Fire?" Tieren frowned.

"Yellow eyes." Diaz drained his juice and handed the glass to Five. "Our eye colors vary depending on the ability to breathe fire. The weaker, the more yellow. The stronger, the more red. And no one expects a Greeven to have such a skill."

Tieren sank back, his face ashen. "How this transpired, no one knows for sure. It cannot be a closely guarded secret on both our sides. That would mean Drueen and Greeven being in agreement on something."

"And that has not happened in centuries." Diaz chuckled. "Still, for there to be darker Greeven implies more than one royal rutting."

Tieren's amber eyes widened. "I always wondered why the farmers had a higher-than-usual mutation. They are on the borders between our lands."

"If this is true, *ateek*, then it's not a mutation but a blending of DNA." Micky smiled, giving his hand a squeeze. "Someone in your ancestry fell in love with a Drueen."

"It would have to be a female," Diaz said. "A Drueen would never hand over a youngling, no matter their coloring."

"Hate to intrude, but I have confirmation of Ober's whereabouts. Suggest we depart in ten." Five glanced at Selira. "I'll prep the racer."

Micky frowned. "Why not just use my shuttle?"

"NOX says you have samples to deliver." Selira smiled.

"True." Micky let Tieren lead her out, but her confusion remained.

"What is the real reason?" Diaz asked.

"Tying Micky to me will bring suspicion on Elizabeth's death."

Diaz caught Selira's hand and tugged her closer. "And endanger you both again."

"Yes." She held her hands to his chest, leaning in to inhale the hot fragrance of his skin.

While nuzzling her neck, he gathered the fabric of her dress, inching it up her legs. "Why not tell her that?"

"I will, just not now when we need to leave. I want to have the time to answer her questions should she have any." Selira arched her back when he gripped her ass and massaged her.

He hoisted her up, bringing her breasts to eye-level. "Five, is there time—"

"Argh. Yes."

Clinging to Diaz, she let him pin her to a nearby bulkhead. Using it to prop her up, he juggled her while opening his pants. She laughed, watching him fumble like a horny teenager. There wasn't time for foreplay, but since they'd started this affair, her desire for him was constant and intense with no signs of the passion fading.

"This garment is made for rutting," he said, moments before thrusting into her.

Between kisses and grunts, he had her screaming his name amid blinding eruptions of ecstasy. After he roared his release, he didn't step back to let her stand. He kept her in place, his gaze intense, his breathing ragged. The kiss he snatched was potent with unsaid emotions. She returned it, her chest swelling with everything he invoked in her that she dared not confess.

"I suggest you dress...appropriately. If we need to run, I do not want your movements hindered." He pressed his temple to hers. "Wear this garment for me alone, *purlievo*."

He lowered her then, nudging her toward her bedroom. She headed there, her knees weak, every stride accompanied by tremors of residual pleasure.

"I will await you on the racer."

She slumped against the nearest wall, drawing in deep breaths. Then with a squeak, she hurried to pull on slacks, a bra, a blouse, and boots. With quick flicks of her hands, she had her hair pinned on top of her head. It didn't take her long to join him and Five.

Diaz was armed to the max.

She grinned. "I have a private berth, so weapons are allowed. Just not this many." She stroked her fingers down his chest. "Choose one. I'll claim you're my bodyguard."

He scowled but unsheathed and de-armed himself until only his techy pistol remained.

Five exited the bay and swiveled the racer so that the screens displayed the *Jinsei's* shuttle waiting for them.

"Open comms. Meet you at Dig It on the eighth level," she said. "Try to ignore me. We look so alike, anyone seeing us together would think we're family."

"Got ya," Micky said. "Can't be scaring folks with a not-so-dead mother."

Selira chuckled. "Something like that."

"See, you could have told her the truth." Diaz rubbed his nose along the shell of Selira's ear, summoning a delicious shiver. "Try it next time." He sank onto the bench, his gaze fixed on her.

She nodded. Perhaps he was right, that lying *had* become a habit.

The shuttle shot off, dipping toward the white structure orbiting a yellow-white star. Beyond that, amid the endless space, sat a larger version of Prime Earth. Space traffic to and from it looked like the buzzing of bees around a hive. She'd been to New Eden, the tourist hub on-world. As a shopping destination for all things human, there was no other place.

"Five, track down some fruit for Diaz. Find him a few coats too."

"Done," he said, tossing her a glance. "The cryo-crates will be loaded in our absence. The garments delivered within the hour."

"That's my Five. Always so efficient." She patted his shoulder and settled on the bench beside Diaz, who wrapped his arm around her.

He blessed her with a kiss to her temple. "Nervous?"

"Nope. I have you and Five. Whatever happens, we can handle it."

He grinned. "Yes, we can."

Chapter Nineteen

WHILE MICKY HAD TO dock at the public ports, Five veered the racer upward to the individual bays for each penthouse suite. Diaz arched a brow but said nothing. A man in a white uniform stood just past the pressurized booth.

"Lady Ellison, what a pleasure." He bowed, then swept out a hand toward her apartment. "Everything is as requested. Your clearance is on the table by the exit. And I am on call should you need me." He touched his chest. "Kelvin."

"My thanks," she said, raising her nose to look down at him. "This is Diaz, my guard, and that is my personal NOXV. I expect you have organized their clearance?"

"Of course. Please enjoy your stay and the complimentary fruit basket from Governor Hyson." Kelvin left, walking backward until the front door closed over his practiced smile.

"Lady Ellison?" Diaz quirked a brow. "Another fake name." He frowned. "Like Data Reaper Atlas."

"If I was Selira Myers everywhere, I'd be easy to track down and kill." She met his gaze, unflinching. "I learned my lesson after the first attempt on my life, Diaz. Would be silly of me to let them try and try again."

"Are you saying you *are* this Lady Ellison?"

"I am. In payment for reuniting Countess Louise Ellison with her long-lost brother, she adopted me, hence the ladyship title. According to the universe, I am Elise Ellison, her daughter."

Confusion furrowed his brow, itching her finger to smooth it. "Surely the *Usuba* or your shuttle is known?"

She laughed. "Five changes their markings based on the persona I'm portraying. No one will find me if I don't want to be found." She unwrapped the fruit basket and tossed an apple to him. "And we upgrade both ships often."

He choked on a bite. "You cannot be that wealthy."

She shrugged. "Come, let us head down to the diseased side of this station." Pausing in front of the mirror by the door, she commanded it, "Strawberry blonde hair and sky-blue eyes."

Beams of light scanned her, changing her appearance. Her reflection made her double take, but she only had to endure it for a few hours before it faded.

Diaz scowled when she curtseyed for him. "I do not like you thus."

"You like me beneath you, panting your name." She winked and opened the door.

Five marched out, waiting a few steps ahead as if programmed to do so. He was her lookout and first line of defense. Diaz was supposed to be her bodyguard and should trail her, but she wasn't about to force the issue. If he stayed beside her, she'd be fine. His height, bulk, and red eyes would drive people to veer around them anyway.

Five selected the button for the primary docking level, then settled back, his hands clasped in front of him. Munching another apple, Diaz gazed at the planets and stars around them while they descended.

"Have any idea what you'll say to Ober?" she asked.

"No." He licked his thumb. "Why? How?"

"Succinct," she said, smiling. "I suppose Tieren will ask about the amulet. With what we learned this morning about his DNA, I'm hoping Ober can shed some light on it. Him having that amulet in his possession implies he had to have obtained it from somewhere. Even if he has no other information than who he got it from, that's progress."

"I assume we won't be chasing down a mutated bat-monkey for Fentus?" Five held the door open, letting her and Diaz pass before hurrying ahead.

"When we have one, maybe we can pay for an independent medical research company to create a cure." She hummed at that idea. Calling in a few favors might get it prioritized.

"Why do you need a cure?" Diaz touched the base of her spine to guide her through the growing throng of shoppers.

"Micky's mutations are evolving. They have to reach a pinnacle at some point. What they will do after that, we don't know. They could erode her ability to function like her enhanced hearing affecting her mind. They could paralyze her or kill her outright."

"You think she is dying," he said.

"We don't know, but I hope not. She's my baby girl, Diaz." Selira cast him a pleading gaze. "I'll do everything in my power to help her."

The next pod they had to take down to the mining levels wasn't so private. Despite the crush, the occupants in stained and dirty garments, smelling of stale ale and sweat, stayed clear of her and Diaz. He growled when anyone accidentally came too close.

At each stop, he dominated the doorway, stating with a boom, "Full."

A few occupants squirreled past him, probably choosing to exit and ride another pod than share one with him. She smothered a chuckle, letting him be himself. It served her well, granting her a little breathing room before they hit the busiest level on the station. Bars, gambling halls, brothels, and legalized drug dens were available for those with tokens. Hyson believed that policing one level was better than having his men scattered across the station.

It also meant the air vents and oxygen supply couldn't cater for this number of people. The smells hanging like a cloud was of burned noodles, reconstituted fish, stale ale, sweat, piss, and fresh blood. She likened it to greed and desperation.

Dig It wasn't that far, but with the weaving and dodging poor Five and Diaz had to do, it took them a while to get there. She hid behind Diaz, letting his bulk cut a swathe through. Five charged his suit so that anyone coming too close received a zap.

The mountain of a man at the door took one look at Diaz and stiffened.

"We don't let that in." He splayed his gigantic fingers across Five's chest and winced at the spark running over his skin. But he didn't lower it.

"Release it or lose that limb," Diaz said, gripping his pistol.

"They're both mine," she purred, flashing the bouncer a smile and her clearance.

His eyes widened, he coughed, and stepped aside. "Milady."

Diaz glared at her. "Tokens cannot buy everything."

"No, they can't." She met his gaze, then ran it over his face and chest. He had it right. No amount of tokens could buy her a Diaz. "Now, avoid Micky where possible."

He scanned the room, his height an advantage. "I do not see her or Ober."

"Five, get us a table with the best view." She crowded Diaz to not be jostled by the patrons.

He looped both arms around her and scowled at everyone coming too close.

"I can handle being bumped," she said, peering at him.

"No one touches what is mine," he said, meeting her gaze.

"Is that so?" Her heartbeat raced, causing butterflies to flutter again.

"Yes," he said, sweeping the room with another glance.

His angular jaw, the strength that poured off him, the danger his confidence emitted had her breath catching. This man trembled under her caresses, returned her kisses, protected her like she mattered to him.

He met and held her gaze, intensity once more in his red eyes. Time slowed, the noise faded, only her beating heart thumped in her ears, and her breathing felt like she was underwater.

"This way," Five said, bringing the world back with a slam.

She winced and pulled out of Diaz's arms as far as he'd let her. He caught her hand and tugged her behind him to where Five waited. On a dais, the half-circular booth tucked into a shadowed corner was ideal. Micky and Tieren sat on bar stools nursing Miner's Hoppers, but nowhere was a dark-skinned blue-eyed Gy'Ruxian.

Selira frowned and shuffled along the bench, flanked by Five and Diaz. "I'm going to be super angry if we've missed him."

"We've been here five minutes," Five hissed. "Patience."

An A.I. in a banged-up suit delivered two glass containers of orange juice.

"Your doing?" she asked Five.

He shrugged.

She opened a bottle and placed it in front of Diaz before tackling hers. The tart aroma of freshly squeezed oranges made her hum. A sip cramped her cheeks, but the taste was sublime, so good that she moaned. Diaz stared at her, his eyes hooded and his nostrils flaring. He sniffed the juice then took a sip, licking his lips.

"Good?" she asked, a smile forming.

"Yes," he growled and snatched a kiss. "But it tastes better on you."

Hours ticked past. Another round of orange juice arrived, after which she ordered a coffee, letting Diaz have as many flavors of fruit juice as he wanted. Still, no Ober.

"NOX says Micky's had enough," Five said without glancing at her daughter or at Selira.

"We'll be home soon. Can't leave at the same time," she said, swirling her empty cup on its saucer. "Know where he went?"

"We're tracking him on the security footage. Won't be long."

She smiled at Diaz's empty glass containers littering the table. "Had enough?"

"Delicious. I like this one." He waved the one in his hand.

"Strawberries," she whispered.

He jerked back, then sniffed the bottle. "The fruit and juice smell better than your soap."

"It does." She laughed. "But it won't clean me."

His lips twitched into a smile. "Truth."

Leaving was with more fanfare when the bouncer rushed ahead to secure her an empty pod. She appreciated the thought and tipped him well. Alone in the smelly pod, no one spoke, disappointment lying heavy between them.

"At least we know he's close," she said, splaying her fingers on the glass to peer between them at a distant moon.

"Instinct says he knew we were coming," Diaz said, taking her hand into his.

"At least he's near and not across the universe." She raised their clasped hands to kiss each of his knuckles.

They stepped off the pod on the docking level and crossed to the private pod to her suite. Up they went; the excitement of earlier was missing. Heading home empty-handed sucked. Five strode into her apartment, leaving the door open. He seemed stiff, distracted.

She didn't make it past the mirror.

Diaz caught and held her in place. "Bring back my Selira," he commanded.

She laughed. "Red hair and red eyes."

Vibrant auburn hair and deep red eyes added color to her pale face, but was a little shocking for her tastes. She much preferred the red on Diaz.

He froze, a pulse ticked at the base of his jaw, then he shook his head as if dazed. "*My Selira.*"

"Fine." She commanded all enhancements to fade, returning her brown hair and eyes.

He threw her over his shoulder and carried her into the bedroom.

"None of that," Five called. "We have Ober's location, and you're not going to like it."

Diaz spun, swinging Selira like a sack of potatoes.

"He's boarding the *Jinsei* now."

"What?" she squeaked.

Down she went until her feet were once more on the floor. With fruit basket in hand, Diaz ushered her onto the racer, not letting her get another word in. All she wanted to know was if Micky was in danger.

Neither Five nor Diaz answered her.

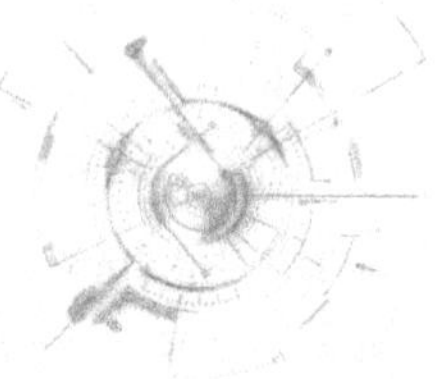

DIAZ PICKED AT THE small green balls known as grapes. Ober waited for them, for him. Selira had it right when she'd asked him what he would say to his old blood mate. Why? Why leave Nuberu? Why cast his weyr into shame? Why stay away this long? How had he quietened their bond? Why had he let Diaz believe he'd died?

Diaz leveled a silent plea at Selira when she opened her mouth again to ask a question. He couldn't answer her. Tension tightened every muscle, his gut churned, and his beast slammed against the boundaries, ready to break free. *Ober is not to be trusted*, it roared.

"He's in the mess," Five said after it had docked the racer.

Laughter met their intrusion. Selira peered around Diaz blocking the doorway. No way would he let her anywhere near Ober until he knew it was safe.

Ober pushed to his feet. His face was stuck in a friendly mask that didn't deceive Diaz, who knew him too well. "Good. Just the male I came to see. I need a moment with you...alone."

Diaz stepped to the side, trapping Selira between his back and the bulkhead. The fury in Ober's eyes had him distrusting a male he once cherished like a braddo. While Ober headed down to the bay, Diaz snatched a kiss from Selira, then shoved her into the mess with a glance at Tieren. The curt nod said the male understood to guard them both.

"What did he say about the amulet?" she asked Micky.

Diaz didn't stay to find out, racing to catch up to Ober. "My camis is through that door." He pointed ahead.

Unsaid words weighed down on him until he had to grip his bioblade for some calm. He strode into his ship, half-expecting Ober to strike.

"Greetings, blood mate," the male spat.

Diaz frowned at the hatred pouring off him. "Ober, what is going on? I thought you dead. Where have you been? How did you escape off-world?"

"None of that matters." Ober paced, his kavex in hand. Diaz didn't let that concern him when spinning the blade was Ober's nervous habit. "I've stayed hidden in the hopes I could one day free my heartsmate, or she could escape and join me."

Diaz gaped. "You found her?"

"Yes." Ober glared at him. "And no, she didn't bring trouble. Her pappo did. How I prayed to *Remyi* that Hom'Garr would die, freeing us both."

Diaz hissed at having to share his weyr with Hom'Garr. That wouldn't be pleasant.

"Instead, I'm awoken by this excruciating agony like my hearts were ripped out of me and, in their places, lumps of dead rocks formed. I raced home, despite the danger." Ober shuddered, but his blue gaze didn't waver. "Pyia's dead, killed by a justisaar I once cherished as a blood mate."

Pyia? Her face flashed in Diaz's mind. "No," he cried out, staggering back and hitting the bulkhead behind him. His hearts squeezed until he couldn't breathe, and for once, his beast was quiet. "It cannot be. All evidence proclaimed her guilt. Only after I meted out justice as decreed by our law was I told, as a judge, I should have realized the truth. I never questioned my orders. Never once considered my bounties to be free of sin."

"Excuses." Ober pressed his kavex to Diaz's throat, the sting making him wince. "It's been years since I *felt* your presence." He thumped his chest with the other hand. "Until it was silenced. Only then did I realize our blood vow had been there all along. I could've called to you. Wouldn't have had to face this alone." His upper lip twitched his mouth into a grimace. "You... *You* killed her. You doomed me to this waste of a life."

"Every day I regret not listening to her pleas." Diaz squared his shoulders and tilted his jaw, offering his throat for the killing stroke. "A life for a life, my blood mate."

Ober laughed, cold and lacking mirth. He flicked away the blade. "No, I should take *her* life."

Diaz stiffened, fear slithering like a demon into the very center of his being. "Why harm Selira?"

"Then you'll suffer alongside me. She's your heartsmate, is she not?"

Diaz knew she mattered to him. More than she should, but not once had he considered her his heartsmate. Ober had the right of it. She was the very air he breathed, the fire in his veins, the future he'd never dreamed was possible. He opened his mouth to lie, prepared to do anything to save her. To hell with his honor and his sense of justice.

"Listen, I'm sorry-not-sorry for eavesdropping..."

Diaz blinked at Five standing inside his camis. "You speak Gy'Ruxian?"

"Well, someone had to learn." It shrugged. "I was curious when Ober didn't announce his arrival, broke into a bay, and parked his ship without fanfare. No, Micky thinks NOX let him dock, and Selira's elbows-deep discussing the origins of that amulet. But after all I've discovered, and this interesting conversation slotting things into place for me, I wanted to ask why neither of you suspected Hom'Garr?"

"What do you know of him?" Ober jerked back but didn't pocket his blade.

"He seems to be at the center of your misery. I gather information, and some of it I don't share with the boss. Especially when it's not in her best interest. So no," it glared at Diaz, "you won't be killing Micky, nor will you be allowed to reveal Selira's sources. But you have Ober. Take that as a win and leave."

Diaz flicked a hand. "I have no intention of obeying any of the H.G.C.'s orders."

Five huffed. "Hom'Garr isn't the council. In fact, he is on the edges of that power circle. You, the best justisaar they had, was close to challenging him for his position."

"No." Diaz scowled. "Being a council member would be a dull life."

Five threw up a hand. "Well, he didn't know that, especially when your name was often thrown into the nominations pool. And since his daughter betrayed him for a 'worthless' soldier, he planned to use her to bring you down, especially when that soldier was Ober, your blood mate."

"How do you know this?" Ober demanded, pointing the kavex at Five. He narrowed his blue eyes, distrust in their depths.

"Five and my heartsmate gather secrets." Diaz grinned. "And never have I been more delighted. Tell me, do you have evidence of this?"

Five scoffed. "Of course: video footage, audio conversations, written communication."

"How? Our archives are impenetrable." Ober waved his blade.

"For two A.I. with decades of hacking skills?" Five arched a stiff brow.

Ober stepped back and sank onto the bench. "We can show this to the H.G.C. and bring justice to Pyia, to my weyr?"

"Whenever you are ready." Five proffered a data crystal. "Here is all you will need."

Ober took it and tossed it to Diaz. "I want to see that bastard's face when we do so. I want to plunge my blade into his chest." He twirled the kavex and mimicked an icepick stab.

Diaz tutted. "He will be exiled. You know this."

"At his age and for these crimes, perhaps not?" Ober's smile was hopeful.

"Do I veer the *Jinsei* toward Gy'Rux?" Five asked.

"Ask Micky first," Diaz called when it bounded off. "I truly am sorry for my part in this."

"Seems I should apologize. My love for Pyia was all Hom'Garr needed to take you out of the equation." Ober pocketed his dagger. "So, who is Selira?"

"Elizabeth Danvers," Five said through the camis' system.

Diaz glared at the ceiling. "Get out of my ship."

"Lizzy? Your mate is Thomas's wife?"

"Ex," Five chimed in. "And she doesn't know. Loverboy here has yet to share how he feels about her."

Loverboy? Diaz mouthed the odd word.

He is right. His beast added. *It is time.*

"Quite a pretty woman if my memory serves me well." Ober slapped his thighs and rose. "I best make my intentions known."

"Wait." Diaz halted him. "Tell me how you silenced our bond all these years? I grieved for you."

"Finding your heartsmate dampens all bonds, so does long distances beyond its reach." Ober gave him a stiff shrug. "I simply stayed on the far side of the universe."

As easy as that? "And how did you escape off-world?"

"I was sold to a passing ship." Ober winced. "By the H.G.C. or so the official documentation stated." He glanced out of the camis. "I wonder why I never suspected Hom'Garr. He'd been all smiles the last time I met him with Pyia at my side."

Diaz squeezed Ober's shoulder. "We were taught that the H.G.C. carry the highest honor. That heartsmates were to be cherished. Hom'Garr violating our trust, twisting the course of justice, and breaking apart a *Remyi*-sanctified union... Exile would be a light sentence."

Ober flashed a sad smile. "Let us pray the council shows him no mercy."

"I wish I had known Pyia. Those charges would have had me question the H.G.C.'s orders." Diaz yanked Ober into a hug and thumped him on the back. "She was beautiful, Ober."

He sniffed. "I didn't want to share the happy news just yet. Had I done so, perhaps neither of us would be here today." He glanced in the direction of the mess. "Then you wouldn't have met...Selira." He smiled when he drew back. "There's a story there."

Diaz chuckled. "For her to tell."

"Fair enough." Ober strolled down the ramp. "Claim her, blood mate, and cherish every moment you have together."

I have always liked him. His beast hummed.

Diaz scoffed at that.

Chapter Twenty

Well, that's a surprise.

THE NEXT FEW DAYS were a flurry of activity. On the *Usuba*, with Diaz's shuttle docked instead of her racer, they departed for Gy'Rux. Ober followed in his ship, and the more ponderous *Jinsei* trailed him.

Many discussions were had about revealing to the H.G.C.'s council members what they knew. Selira was all for it, thinking allies were in short supply. Her plan to destroy Fentus and the Followers was to leak the evidence to all news stations, the galactic security or G-Sec, Central Universe Forces, the Religion-For-All council, and the Galactic Science Board or G.S.B. A full-out deployment was impossible to trace and shut down. They also wouldn't see it coming.

It would take effort to set up, though. Time across the universe being the issue. She needed it to go live within seconds of each other. Which meant scheduling the releases: a mathematical nightmare. Thankfully, she had Five.

"Remind me to give you a raise," she said, sipping yet another cold tea. A sharp pain pulsed up her back from sitting too long. She rubbed where she could reach while attending to her daily tasks and mails.

In his camis, Diaz was on a comm with Ober, strategizing. Five had been invited, which she considered a definite improvement in how Diaz viewed him. Her stomach churned and gurgled, reminding her that she hadn't eaten in a while. But the thought of food made her queasy, pooling bile at the back of her throat. She rose, stretched, then grabbed her half-drunk tea, intent on making a cup of coffee instead.

"Four more galaxies to schedule," Five said. "Heads up, Diaz is done. They're going with your suggestion to garner allies. I've been tasked to compile the evidence on multiple data crystals."

"Good," she said, stretching and bending while the water boiled. "Set the press release in motion when you're ready."

She pondered their joined goal which had been to find Ober. He'd revealed that the amulet had belonged to a Greeven princess who'd fallen for a crimson Drueen. She'd given birth to the first dark Greeven. This confirmed Five's conclusions and the reason behind the DNA similarities.

And now they had two new missions: to end Fentus and the Followers, and to bring Hom'Garr to justice. Both noble, and something she was glad she was a part of. Five had hidden their digital fingerprints behind another alias, one she barely used, so losing it permanently wouldn't be too much of a pain.

The aroma of freshly ground coffee, usually the best part, made her gag. She shivered, leaned back, and stared at her empty cup. "Um, Five?" She splayed her fingers across her stomach, recognizing that feeling even after all these years. "Prep the med-pod."

"Why?" he asked, despite opening the coffin-like tube set into a bulkhead.

On trembling knees she stepped into it. The door shutting was like the hammering of a nail. The dim light flickered on, more for comfort than for any other purpose. None of that mattered when her focus was on the lettering forming in front of her.

Diagnoses: P.R.E.G.N.A.N.T.

She blinked at it, joy warring with disbelief. No, no, she was beyond her child-bearing years. She tapped it and requested another scan. Again the lettering flashed. She held her breath, torn between praying it was true and dreading that it wasn't.

What would Diaz say? Would he be happy? Should she tell him *if* it was true? Maybe she should wait until this whole Hom'Garr situation was behind him? No, she wasn't pregnant. Forty-six was too old to start fresh even though the tech these days meant women could give birth well into their fifties.

Diagnoses: P.R.E.G.N.A.N.T.

Hysterical laughter snuck out. She slapped a hand over her mouth, tears spilling free. With shaking fingers, she selected the 'more' button.

Sex: B.O.Y.

Species: U.N.K.N.O.W.N.

"No friggin' way," Five said.

"It's not saying how far along I am," she whined. "Nor is it telling me when he's due."

"Unknown species, babe." He laughed. "I don't know what you and Diaz have cooked up."

"That's not funny." She sniffed, wiping her cheeks.

"You're not happy?"

"I'm ecstatic," she wailed, sounding anything but.

"How about I make you a cup of peppermint tea and a grilled cheese sandwich." His tone was that of parent with an overly tired toddler.

"That would be lovely," she mumbled, wrapping her arms around her torso when she stepped out of the pod.

If she had any idea Diaz loved her and wouldn't be leaving her, perhaps she could share the news without concern. But she didn't want him to stay out of pity or because of his stupid sense of honor. She wanted his love, craved it, if she was honest with herself.

"Okay, spill," Five said, waiting there for her.

She hugged him, needing his solidness to ground her. "How can I tell him?"

Five patted her shoulder then froze. "Oh boy, are you thinking of *not* telling him?"

"He has this important H.G.C. thing to deal with. I don't want him worrying about me." She sniffed, smearing her snotty nose across Five's cold metallic shoulder.

He set her aside and started on the tea. "Right. Now give me the real reason."

"He doesn't love me." She slumped against a cupboard then sank to her ass, pulling her knees up.

"Cold floors aren't good for the baby," Five said, picking her up and dumping her on the couch.

"What was I thinking?" She half-chuckled half-sobbed, wiggling her ass to get comfortable. "You're going to be worse than him."

"And I should be." Five waved the tea can at her. "Your well-being is my priority. Everything I do is in your best interests. That is my core programming."

"You're going to tell him." She glared, folding her arms across her chest. "Because it's good for me," she said in sing-song voice.

"If it is, then yes." He didn't glance at her, and at that moment, she wanted to pull his plug, she was that furious.

She leaped to her feet and waved a fist at him. "I thought you were on my side."

He faced her and slipped a hot cup of tea into her hand. "Always, babe. Just give the guy a chance, would ya?"

She sat and took a few sips, sighing when the hot liquid slid down her throat and warmed her belly. The nausea calmed too. "I suppose you're right. He has a right to know. But if he leaves me, my heart will break. And if he stays because of our son, it will be out of obligation and nothing else."

Five shook his head at her as if she was being an idiot. "And if you talk to him, perhaps it will be none of those."

The sizzle of melted cheese and its aroma made her rise to watch him flip the sandwich over. The moment he offered it to her on a plate, she snatched a triangle and bit into it. A groan escaped her at the rich, gooey, saltiness filling her mouth.

"Yup, as I suspected." He sighed. "Hangry made worse by mommy hormones."

She rolled her eyes, her mouth too full to reply.

"Don't let those ruin your happiness."

She swallowed to say, "It's damn hard to put your heart out there. Crushing it friggin' hurts."

Five exhaled, puffing his cheeks. "All I'm saying is that you take a leap of faith, be the courageous woman who trapped him in the first place."

"You make it sound like I planned this, that we're living a space opera." She pouted. "It's not like that."

The moment Diaz appeared in the doorway leading from the bay, Five squeezed past him. "She's all yours."

She waved her sandwich in greeting and gestured with her tea for Diaz to sit.

He glanced at the galley. "What is that intriguing smell?"

"Grilled cheese sandwich," she said and set the remaining half and her tea to the side. "I need to talk to you." She drew in a steady breath. Worst case scenario, he spent the rest of the trip on his camis, didn't speak to her, then headed off into the sunset. She'd need the other half of her grilled cheese to survive whatever hell happened when she told him the big news. Not that she'd fully processed it yet either. But if she procrastinated about the baby, she'd never tell him.

He sank onto the couch, his brow furrowed. "About?"

"Our future." There, she'd said it. Her stomach knotted, but she refused to throw up. Her son came first above her feelings and discomforts, and if he was anything like his dad in size, she'd need every bite of food. Tears stung her eyes, the realization starting to hit her.

"It is time." He smiled. "Ober pointed out that I might have my exile revoked."

Which meant he'd have to return to Gy'Rux, leaving her to raise their son alone. She could do it. She had to, but at least she had Five. *Frig.* What would Micky say? "Yes, that's possible, and for your sake, I hope so."

He rubbed his palms down his thighs as if he was nervous. Maybe that meant something else in his culture. "It will cancel the shame upon my weyr."

She choked back the lump rising in her throat. *Don't cry. Not yet.* "Honor's important." What else could she say? *No, I refuse to set you free?* He'd go no matter what she said.

"My mammo's going to love you." His eyes filled with a strange emotion that tugged at her soul. "My sassa too."

What a sweet thing to say, and odd for it implied she'd be going down to his planet with him. "Why would they?"

"All heartsmates are revered."

Her mind spun, her thoughts in a tizz. "The what now?"

"The mate of my hearts," he said, sliding across the gap between them to draw her onto his lap.

"How many do you have?" She stared at her greasy fingers curling over his shoulders while trying to unravel this conversation.

"Two, one on each side of my chest."

"Oh," she whispered, sliding her hands down in the hopes of sensing his heartbeats. "I didn't know that."

"I suspect you will bring my pappo to tears. The news is worthy of a special trip from the frontlines if I was not exiled, but I plan to fetch him myself."

She shook her head like her thoughts were engulfed in cotton wool. "You're losing me here. What news?"

He laughed, cradling her close. "That I found my heartsmate." He snatched a kiss then blessed her with a sweet smile. "You."

Her cheeks flushed. "Are...are you saying you'll stay with me?"

"Yes, and that I will love you for an eternity, *purlievo*." He tucked a curl behind her ear, his touch so gentle. And there in his gaze was that familiar intensity, one she could now identify.

"Love?" she croaked, dipped her chin to wipe her wet cheeks, then beamed at him. "This *is* the day for good news." She swung her legs to straddle him, and inched forward, rubbing herself across his ever-present hard-on. Arousing him wasn't her intention. She wanted to pin her chest to his, to gaze into his beautiful eyes, and say, 'I love you too.' Instead, what came out was, "I'm pregnant."

He froze, and his mouth opened and closed without a word escaping. With a growl, he crushed her against him and buried his face in the curve of her neck. Kisses followed, all over her face. He cupped her cheeks and settled a lingering kiss to her lips.

"First," he rasped, "tell me how you feel."

Her heartbeat stuttered. He didn't know how risky a pregnancy at her age was.

She climbed off his lap to pace, wringing her hands as she did so. "I'm scared, Diaz. Being this old and carrying to full term isn't guaranteed. Of course, I'll take all the precautions necessary." She faced him, flicking away more silly tears. "Already Five's being a pain." She offered Diaz a watery smile.

He chuckled. "No, I meant, about me."

"Oh." She laughed. "Love you with all of my singular heart."

He leaped to his feet to gather her into his arms. "That is what I need to know. Everything else we can handle."

She smiled, burrowing into his embrace. "Yes, we can."

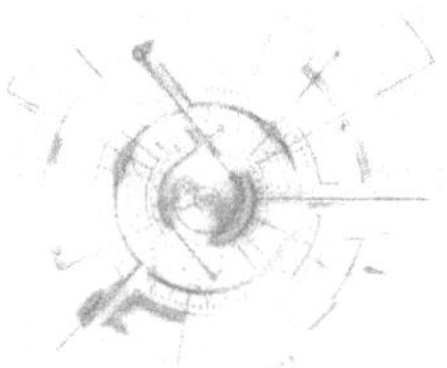

DIAZ LAY AWAKE ON Selira's extra-firm bed. One arm he tucked behind his head, the other he wrapped around her curled into his side, her soft snores adorable. What a miracle she'd become. How had she changed his perspective? When Ober had threatened her life, in that moment, he'd realized that he'd lie, kill, deceive, do everything dishonorable to save her.

And thinking of committing a crime was as bad as doing it for his thoughts today governed his tomorrow. Perhaps she'd lured him to *her* side. In her way, she was honorable: saving children, searching for distant relatives, destroying a religious-research conglomerate—fighting evil the only way she knew how. He couldn't judge her for that even if her methods weren't above board. She had her reasons, her safety being one of them. Against her opponents, her life would always be in danger. Against his bounties, he'd never been close to dying.

And now she carried his son.

Told you to claim her. His beast hummed with contentment. *Mate.*

Yes, yes, you are wise. Diaz chuckled.

Told you councilor smell funny.

He stilled, remembering that conversation. *You did. Any other councilors I need to be aware of?*

Go to Da'Ager. I like him.

That didn't sound right. *Hom'Garr's blood mate? What if he is also dishonorable?*

The beast tapped its nose. *Smell.*

What Diaz planned to do was ask his pappo. If anyone would know who to trust, it would be him. But sneaking onto the frontlines would endanger his mate and son's lives. He'd deliver Selira to his mammo then head to the camps alone, or with Ober by his side.

He grinned. Maybe he'd take Five with him just so that Selira wouldn't worry.

She loved *him*, Diaz Rowfallak, an exiled justisaar. He rubbed his hand over his head, relishing the growth of hair forming a downy layer. There'd be no more shaving it off for him. Regardless of how this mission ended, he would be free. If anyone could hide him from the H.G.C. it would be his Selira. If need be, he'd take his weyr off-world. His sassa could have more to life than bearing ruxlings.

He needed to reveal his conclusions to Selira. Many had been responsible for the loss of her leg. Had she been in the pilot's seat as expected, its back would've protected her. The grainy footage had shown her leaping up, sobbing, like she could return to the *Jinsei* after the shuttle had launched.

NOX had started to pressurize the compartment a minute too soon, filling it with more oxygen than calculated. That had added fuel to the fire.

And Thomas had knocked the device forward when carrying her luggage on board. Closest to the door would have triggered the emergency protocols and evacuated the flames while sealing her from it.

He'd shared his findings with Five, just for a second opinion. Perhaps when she knew this, her night terrors would fall away. A kiss to her temple swelled the heat in his chest. She was his, in heart and soul. He chuckled, happier than he deserved to be.

"Five," he whispered. "Get me what you can on the Gy'Ruxian councilor Da'Ager."

"On it," Five said.

"Thank you." Diaz gazed at the ceiling. "For protecting her."

"I will always."

Diaz nudged Selira onto her back. "Make yourself scarce."

From the depths of sleep, she moaned when he trailed his fingers over her flat belly and down her hips to grip her knees. With a gentle push, he spread her thighs. She blossomed, exposing her most vulnerable part of her body. He dipped in for a deep inhale, then succumbed to the temptation. He ran his tongue down then up, groaning at the explosion of her flavor across his tongue.

His temperature spiked and a muted glow painted her skin red. He was no longer afraid his beast would tear free. No, not anymore when only its peace and contentment filled him.

She gasped and twitched awake. "Diaz?" she asked, her voice husky.

"Hello, beautiful." He met her gaze before sucking her nub into his mouth.

Her breathless cries filled his ears like birdsong on a summer morning. If he could wake her like this every day, his life would be complete. And with the number of identities she assumed, the secrets she guarded, he'd never be bored. Not when she had a tendency to surprise him and often.

He laughed, flipped her onto her knees, before plunging into her slick channel. She pawed the linen with every whimper. And they'd have a son, something he'd never dreamed possible.

As desire tightened his muscles, a slow tingle building at the base of his cock, he arched his back to gaze at the ceiling.

And younger, foolish him had cursed *Remyi* for his pointless task of bringing justice to the unwelcoming.

"Thank you," he whispered in Gy'Ruxian. "I shall not doubt You again."

Chapter Twenty-One

"Um, babe," Five crooned, drawing Selira from deep sleep.

She flipped onto her back, her womanly bits tender. A groan escaped as she stumbled out of bed and into a hot shower. Fewer nightmares disturbed her sleep, but Diaz had his own way of waking her up.

"Babe what?" she mumbled.

The smell of peppermint teased her nose, and she glanced up to find Five holding out a steaming cup of tea.

"This feels like a peace offering. What happened?" She inched a little out of the spray to take a sip, letting him tip the cup for her.

"Well, all but two press releases launched. I consider that a win, statistically. The big info dumps went through fine. It's all over every way station and news channel. Also good."

She glared at him. "Quit beating around the bush."

"We've been pinged too many times to count. I have us on sleep mode, so when their dirty fingernails scratch our servers, they're getting nothing but a luxury cruise vessel out on a joyride."

"Good thinking. I'm assuming F&F's searching for us?" She wrapped the towel he offered her around her body and shuffled out of the cubicle, foregoing washing her hair that morning.

"You got it, *and* the G.S.B., G-Sec, C.U.F.—"

"Central Universe Forces?" she squeaked. "I knew we'd piss off F&F, but not the military."

"Well, it seems they've had their eye on Fentus for a while, violating not only the Primary but a dozen other laws too dull to go into. Our tidbits just blew their case wide open. They've launched an investigation into the Followers' dealings which has the Religious-For-All council up in arms and backtracking at having issued the license to practice religion."

"Frig," she muttered. This had blown up worse than she'd anticipated. Diaz had said she couldn't plan for every scenario. With two A.I. on her side, she'd damn well hoped she could. Being hunted would put a spanner in the works.

Five held out a blouse and a bra, a pair of pants tossed over his shoulder. "Tell me about it. Worst part is, C.U.F. wants your input."

"No," she gasped, clipping on her bra after buttoning her pants.

"And F&F are calling you an outright liar seeking attention. Thankfully, your image isn't yours per se, it's mine with skin." He chuckled. "NOX and I had fun playing with avatars."

"What image?" Her frown was lost on him while she wiggled into her shirt.

"I suspected they'd track the 'source' we threw out there. And now, there are 'wanted' images plastered across all way stations and media."

She chuckled. "Of your face?" She sat to pull on her boots.

"Yup." He rubbed his palms together. "It's a matter of time before they realize I ain't real."

She scoffed. "You're real to me."

He flicked a dismissive hand at her, smacking of her mannerisms. "Sweet of you to say when I'm your permanent babysitter."

"Baby," she sighed, cupping her stomach.

"I've kept Bossman in the loop. But heads up, he's not too happy 'we're' in danger... 'Hunted like gotry' were his exact words."

Whatever that creature was. She chuckled. "My grumpy man."

"I am not grumpy, female," Diaz said from the door, a scowl furrowing his brow. Fluff had grown on his head, and in the artificial lighting, it had a pink hue.

"Your 'sunny' disposition isn't something to be ashamed of," she said, splayed her fingers across his shirt-covered chest and rose on her toes to kiss him. He had to bend to meet her, and he did, looping an arm around her waist to lift her too.

She wrapped her arms around his neck, and sank into the sheer warmth of him. Strength poured off him, making her feel invincible. Together, they could conquer so much. And she had no doubt he'd be an excellent father.

"Love you, big guy," she whispered against his soft lips.

His mouth quirked, and his eyes warmed. "Adore you, my female."

Her breath caught at the sincerity in his husky voice. Tears stung her eyes, so she clung to him, tucking her face just under his jaw.

"NOX tells me you had no morning sickness with Micky. I'm hoping, for your sake, it's the same for the mini dragon." Five veered around them and strode toward the galley. "Time to feed the little one."

She chuckled but didn't move, just let Diaz hold her for as long as he wanted to. Her gurgling stomach ended the embrace too soon.

"Come, eat," he said. "I have something to share with you."

"Oh," she asked and didn't fight him when he set her down.

"I did research of my own." He went on to list his findings about the explosion that had taken her leg. "I am not certain this solves the mystery, but I hope it puts your mind at ease."

Tears flowed unhindered. "Why did you do this for me?" she asked between sniffs.

"Your night terrors disturb your sleep, *purlievo*." He cupped her cheek and wiped it with a sweep of his thumb.

She hiccupped. "I blamed Thomas for so long. Instead, it was seconds to disaster with each of us playing our role."

"Eat," Five said, placing a plate in her hands.

She stared at the bacon and eggs and gulped. "Um..."

Away went the plate and in its place was a bowl of mixed fruit. She hummed and dived in, sharing slivers with Diaz.

"Great," Five muttered. "Two fruitarians and eventually three."

"I still like cheese," she said around a mouthful of mango.

"Well, then there's hope for the tyke." He placed glasses of juice on the coffee table. "Thought of a name? I can call him 'The Spawn' or 'Mini-Fire-Breather.' Both have a lovely ring."

"Blaze?" She pressed a forefinger to her lips while she chewed, her gaze on Diaz.

"Yes," he said. "I like that."

"Unless he's not crimson?" She frowned. "Wait, you said multiple every six months. Five—"

"Only his two heartbeats," he mumbled. "If you were having a litter, I'd damn well tell you, babe."

She breathed a sigh of relief.

Diaz chuckled. "I would have mentioned it too. His hearts are strong."

Her eyes widened. "Please tell me he's coming out Gy'Ruxian and not in dragon-form?" She grimaced. "That would hurt."

Diaz laughed and stole a kiss. "No dragon until he becomes a teenager. I doubt many Gy'Ruxians would survive those first years if they were born wild."

"Why not?" She didn't like the thought of baby-anything dying.

He shook his head. "Not the ruxlings, their parents. At least, as teenagers, they have their training to distract them."

She smiled, rubbing her flat belly. "Toddlers can be a handful."

"Want me with you when you tell Micky?" Diaz covered her hand with his.

She winced. "No, I've got this. If she loses her shit, you being there might make it worse."

"Well, Five will be showing me what information he gathered about Da'Ager. Call if you need me." Diaz stole a kiss then rose.

She gazed around the empty space, a little dazed. "What do you think, Blaze?" She patted her stomach, imagining a slight bump had formed overnight. "Your sister's going to lose her mind?"

Each step to her office was like both legs had lost bio-fluid. She didn't even know how she was going to word the news. A tap of the closest screen summoned communication functions, allowing her to connect to the *Jinsei*.

"NOX, is Micky available for a chat?" she asked, folding her arms across her chest while rocking on her feet. Her heartbeat pounded, fast, slow, double-fast, until her breathing rasped. She willed herself to calm, to draw in long and slow inhales.

"Yup, having her morning coffee...again."

The screen filled with her daughter sitting in the mess, cupping a mug, her hair in a state. "Morning, Mom."

"Hey, sweetheart. How did you sleep?" Part of her wanted to mention the weather, anything but Blaze. The rest of her yearned to blurt it out, her fears and hopes.

"Better. Was worried about this whole Fentus thing. Thanks for the tokens, by the way." Micky raised her mug in salute. "It'll keep us running for quite a stretch."

"They've been yours for a while." Selira unfolded her arms, hoping to appear at ease. "Um, I kind-of have some news."

"About you and Diaz?" Micky chuckled. "Plain as day that man loves you."

Heat warmed Selira's cheeks then traveled lower. "He does."

"I'm happy for you, Mom. You and Dad stopped loving each other after a while. As a child, I didn't understand. As an adult, I get it. Relationships, marriage, both are hard work."

Any lingering doubts that Micky wouldn't forgive Selira, faded, at last. She sniffed, lowered her face to wipe away a tear, and offered her daughter a watery smile. "That's not what I called to tell you."

Micky stiffened. Her eyes widened, and she leaned back in the chair, her smile tentative. "No way."

"Yeah, took me by surprise too." Selira laughed.

Micky grinned, tilting her head as if to listen. "Twins?"

Selira jerked back at her daughter's ability to hear heartbeats across a call. "Um, no, Five assures me there's just one baby. A boy."

Micky squealed, leaping to her feet to kiss the screen. "Mom, this is the best news ever. I'm gonna have a baby brother?"

Tears flowed willy-nilly at her reaction, better than Selira had hoped. "Blaze."

"You chose his name already?" Micky darted off screen to holler, "Tier, get down here." She returned to beam at Selira. "I'm super happy for you, Mom. For you *and* Diaz."

"Aww, my baby." Selira pressed her hand to her chest. "I needed to hear this. Was so worried you'd hate me..."

"Never. What's in the past stays there. We're on a new beginning, and Tier says family is precious." She threw out her arm for her mate to join her. "I'm getting a brother."

His gaze whipped to Selira. "Truth?" A smile formed then broke across his dark face. "May the Gawen bless you, *moma*."

"Thank you, Tieren." Selira bowed her head in gratitude.

Micky flicked aside a tear and chuckled. "What did Diaz say when you told him?"

"Shocked but delighted," Selira said. "Five's been a big ol' mama bear."

"I can imagine. I got Diaz's findings on the shuttle explosion. Shit and shit, Mom. I'm so sorry." Micky drew in a shuddering breath. "I could feel your pain, your unwillingness to leave me."

"I was such an idiot, sweetheart." Selira stroked the screen, running her finger along Micky's face, like she used to. "I was thinking you two don't need to head planetside when we reach Gy'Rux. With the way Greeven and Drueen hate each other, Tier might be in danger."

"Or escalate the situation, but he won't listen to me." Micky harrumphed, tossing a glare at her man.

"My female will never be unprotected, especially before my enemy."

"Seriously?" Micky gasped. "You share DNA. That's like…fighting with your family, *ateek*."

"Extremely distant family," he muttered. "I will discuss this with Nona."

She nodded. "Good. Let her talk sense into your thick skull."

"Nona?" Selira asked.

"Oh," Micky gasped. "She's his grandmother and now mine. Isn't that awesome?"

"It is." Selira grinned. "Thank you, Tieren, for taking care of my little girl. I've been meaning to tell you that for a while now."

"It is my honor," he said.

"Well, let me leave you. We can chat some other time, right?" Selira waited with bated breath.

After all these years searching for Micky, saying goodbye on a call felt like it would end this dream and cast her once more into a life of loneliness. She had to rid herself of that fear. No matter where in the universe the *Jinsei* traveled to, she wouldn't lose contact with Micky again.

"Sure thing, Mom." Micky ended the connection from her side.

"She's behind us," Selira reminded herself. "And she has a grandmother." She sniffed. "Oh, Mom, wish you could be here."

Memories of her childhood, fleeting, blurry, reminded her of happier times spent on a farm on Ganymede. Eldest of seven kids, she'd been the one to take care of her siblings when her folks did night shift. Dad had maintained the U.V. lights, Mom had farmed the fields, as in plucking apples. It was honest work until Dad fell off a platform and died. Mom hadn't recovered from that.

Selira hadn't seen her siblings since then. She stared at the figures on the screens around her. Five could locate them with ease, but she wasn't sure she wanted to go down that route. Did they think she'd abandoned them like she had Micky? The authorities had scattered them across the galaxy and various foster homes. She'd been dragged away from their home, kicking and screaming.

"What's the matter?" Five asked, his voice filling her office.

She wiped her cheeks and faked a laugh. "All good. Just getting started on the daily tasks."

"Now can I tell you 'I told you so?'"

"Don't you always?" she asked, sliding into her chair. Her Five had to be right about everything. "Besides, no one likes a know-it-all A.I."

He scoffed. "That's my definition, the sales pitch, my middle name." He coughed like the grating of rocks across metal. "On happier news, you've been touted as a hero, a savior of all. Riots have taken to the levels, research facilities looted. Others aren't so grateful for your service."

She cast him a glance and scoffed. "Quit saying me when it's you they're edifying."

"Regardless, we're being blamed for the economic fallout about to go down. All those employees without work?"

"Frig." She grimaced. "I didn't factor that in. Which explains why Micky mentioned tokens this morning. She got fired, didn't she?"

"They're calling it furlough." He snorted. "A spade is a spade."

A lump lodged in her throat. "Just feel bad about those folks."

"They'll survive," Five said. "Most of them have been offered positions, no doubt those companies wanting them to share their research. Y'know, while pretending to be appalled at Fentus's dirty deeds."

"At least, Micky's work isn't being wasted." Selira smiled. "And now she'll have fewer reasons to break the Primary."

"Yeah, dunno how Fentus justified that." Five hissed. "Hope this doesn't come back to bite Micky in the ass."

Selira tutted, her focus on the endless emails needing her attention. "You know the drill. Find and erase."

"I do have my hands busy," he huffed.

"Pfft," she said, perusing through evidence of a high-powered judge spending his hard-earned tokens on suspect investments. "You can focus on seven things at a time, remember." For a deeper investigation later, she set aside an article on an unexpected dip in water supply. "Besides, I have eaten and am not going anywhere. Blaze's fine, and you have everything for Diaz all under control. That's three things you don't need to worry about."

"I'm flying this ship, trawling my way through databases, and monitoring this F&F saga."

"That leaves one spot open." She grinned.

"Fine. I'll pause my Galactic Gunslingers episode to handle Micky's expeditions." He sighed. "And just when I was getting to the juicy bits."

"Thanks, Five. You know I love you, right?" She raised her gaze to the ceiling.

"I'll have none of that sweet talk, you hussy."

She laughed, shifted her backside into a more comfortable position, and got to work.

Chapter Twenty-Two

To trap a councilor

The planet, Nuberu

When they strolled away from his camis, Diaz muttered, *"Sillstari."*

He scowled, not in a good mood after Selira refused to be dropped off at his mammo's. Trapped on his ship was the best he could do, other than tossing her over his shoulder and abandoning her at his weyr's front door. He'd never hear the end of his 'mistreatment' from his mammo, though.

Ober chuckled, striding through the battlefield like the soldier he was.

"Do not start," Diaz snapped.

Ober flicked up his hands in surrender but thankfully didn't say a word.

They both drew attention: Ober in his humanlike attire, and Diaz dressed as an exile. If it wasn't for his new coat—in a far superior leather that fitted his shoulders well, he was tempted to release his beast. A crimson dragon was never questioned.

"He will be in the midst of that chaos." He pointed with his chin at the fires that burned high on the south-eastern shore, no doubt the battle zone for the day.

"Expect so," Ober said.

The stench of new and old sulfur hung in the air. The wounded littered the ground with medics rushing between them, P.M.s in hand. Females darted back and forth, carrying food or water. All were in a state of dishevelment, soot coating their faces, their garments charred. A few aqua dragons lined the rear of the battleground, the shimmer of blue on their scales stated their purpose—fire extinguishers. In the distance, crimson Gy'Ruxian soared and swooped, blasting jets of fire across the swaying feelers looking like tufts of grass in a breeze. Okukuro were still at it, as gung-ho as the day the war started.

A familiar dragon dove, setting a swath of enemies ablaze. No wonder Pappo's voice was always so hoarse. Diaz cleared his throat in sympathy. He trailed the beast's flight path and veered in that direction, hoping to catch its attention. Spending hours zigzagging across the shore wasn't something he was prepared to do.

It took minutes for a headache to form, pinging behind his right eye. The constant screeching from the Okukuro was enough to make his ears bleed. *Remyi* was with him when his pappo landed meters ahead. Diaz exploded into a run, dodging scorched sand, servants, and smoldering detritus.

"Pappo," he roared, waving an arm.

The dragon's head jerked back. In a flash of white light, a Gy'Ruxian sprawled in the sand, sweat glistening off his body. Diaz crossed to him, grabbing a bucket of water from a female on the way. He offered the ladle, his gaze focused on his pappo's expressions.

"Diaz, my sanno, is it truly you?" He staggered to his feet and yanked Diaz in for a hug, knocking the ladle to the ground. "Has the council come to their senses?" He leaned aside to raise a hopeful gaze, sweat-drenched tendrils of red hair obscuring his features.

"No, it is worse." Diaz lowered the bucket and gestured to Ober. "We bear news."

"Ober?" Pappo's eyes widened. "Where have you been?" A ferocious scowl formed. "How dare you abandon your responsibilities and bring such shame upon your weyr."

"He did not. Come." Diaz threw his arm across his pappo's bare shoulders. "We have much to share and are in need of your wise counsel."

"Start with Ober," Pappo snapped, accepting the robe a female offered him. He shrugged into it, his unwavering gaze fixed on Diaz's blood mate. "Well?"

"Hom'Garr sold me into slavery."

Diaz winced. Not what he would have led with.

Pappo froze, studied Diaz's face, then cursed. "You can prove this?"

"And more." Diaz tossed a sad glance at Ober. "Hom'Garr had me kill his daughter, Ober's heartsmate, in a fake judgment."

"What—" Pappo boomed, his cheeks juddering. "That sanno of a gotry. Exile would be too kind a punishment."

"Our thoughts as well." Diaz guided his pappo across the shore to where his camis and Selira waited. "We wish to gather allies before we confront the male."

Pappo hummed. "It is risky, but he is no longer sought after for his wise counsel. I would start with Johah."

"Da'Ager?" Ober asked from the left where he flanked Diaz.

Pappo's stride faltered. "Now *that* is a risk. Rumors have been circulating that he and Hom'Garr have grown apart, but is this enough to sway him to see the truth?" He raised his gaze up the mountain to the clouds above. "It would be best to get him alone."

Diaz grunted. "What if he warns Hom'Garr?"

"That will speed things up." Pappo cleared his throat. "If the male does not ally with you, I will detain him while you speak with the council."

"We will talk with Johah first," Diaz said. "*Sillstari*," he commanded his camis.

It flickered and shimmered, forming before them. A tap to the side lowered the ramp. Excitement and nervousness twitched his fingers when he entered. Selira stood there, her hair flowing over a breast, her expressions stoic, but her cheeks were that peach he loved. She flashed him a smile, her shoulders slumping before she squared them, gathering her courage.

"*What* is this female?" Pappo asked, thankfully in Gy'Ruxian.

Diaz's chest swelled with a maelstrom of emotions. "Selira is a human and my hearts-mate."

Pappo's gaze whipped to meet Diaz's. "Truth?" he gasped, switching his attention between Selira and Diaz. "She is a little thing and so pale." He stepped closer, his nose twitching. "And fertile."

"Yes, she is with ruxling." They didn't have a word for 'pregnant.'

"I have another danno?" Pappo stumbled forward, his arm extended.

Instead of touching her, he backhanded Diaz. Pain exploded across his jaw. He stumbled back, shock tying his tongue.

Ober lunged forward, but Diaz threw out his hand, halting him. Never had his pappo hit him. This was so out of character, he wasn't sure what to expect, certainly not Selira standing between Diaz and his pappo, her body stiff. His breath caught. The urge to yank her back, to protect her, tore through him and his beast. Heat exploded outward while cold fear pooled in his core.

"*Purlievo*," he whispered.

She shrugged off his hand on her shoulder, her gaze not leaving his pappo. "You do that again, family or not, I *will* kill you." She held up the bioblade, her intention clear even if his pappo couldn't understand her.

"She will do well." Pappo laughed, nudging the bioblade aside to hug her.

Diaz exhaled, tension pouring out of him. "Ow," he said, touching his throbbing jaw.

"Please, it was a tap." Pappo cupped Selira's cheek, but her gaze shifted between them.

"It was a test, Selira," Diaz told her while poking the injury with his tongue.

"A shitty one," she mumbled. "Is he going to hug me forever?"

"You bear his first grandsanno, so yes." Diaz chuckled and closed the ramp.

"Your mammo is going to be so happy," Pappo said, releasing Selira, who shuffled back into Diaz's arms. "And perhaps you can speak to your sasso. Vasaa has gone a little wild since you left."

Diaz grunted. Calming his sasso's impulsive ways was a chore he didn't want.

Instead of snuggling against him, Selira dug into his pockets and pulled out his P.M.

Pappo sniffed, his eyes gleaming with unshed tears, as she took care of Diaz. "You have done well, my sanno. Now," he gestured to the camis, "How did you sneak through the star guard?"

"With Five." Diaz kneeled so that Selira could scan him to her heart's content. "My heartsmate has a machine. He is piloting the camis and has bypassed all security protocols." After all that machine had done, Diaz figured he deserved to be recognized for his chosen gender. No longer would he consider Five an 'it.'

"He?" Pappo peered into the cockpit. "I see."

"Take us up, Five," Diaz said, caught Selira's hand, and pressed a kiss to her palm. "Again, I ask you to please stay with my mammo."

She hesitated, then shook her head; her stubbornness clear in the tilt of her chin. "Where you go, I go. But if your father hits you again—"

"Yes, my fierce warrior will save me," he teased.

She tucked the P.M. under her arm and cupped his face. "What did he say? Is Da'Ager the right man?"

Diaz grabbed the backs of her thighs and tugged her closer. "Johah first, then we try Da'Ager. If the latter is not interested in justice, Pappo will detain him, buying us time to reach the council."

She hummed. "It's a workable plan."

Five called, "Babe, Mick's approaching Gy'Rux."

"Shit," Selira said. "Tell her to orbit. We're not ready for her."

Diaz paused, an idea forming. "Hom'Garr wanted me to take her blood and kill her."

"What?" Selira squeaked.

"We can use her to lure him to the council chambers," Ober said.

Diaz grinned. "Yes, my thoughts as well, especially if she insists on landing on Gy'Ruxian soil."

Selira gasped and gripped his arm. "No, I can't lose her, Diaz. Not after finding her. Sure, she might land without permission, *and* she can take care of herself, but please, don't put her in unnecessary danger."

His hearts cracked at the pleading in her eyes. "All right, *purlievo*." He kissed her temple.

"One minute to target," Five said, circling the peak of the mountain.

Pappo was directing him to the platform belonging to Johah, a sky dragon.

They landed, and as one, disembarked. Five trailed them, keeping back in case he needed to return to the camis. His presence alone would alarm any Gy'Ruxian with their two suns making his polished body gleam. Had Diaz come on his own, all he would've had to do was justify his unsanctioned return from exile. With Selira by his side, he expected more resistance. If Johah asked about her, that is. Diaz had no intention of divulging information if he didn't have to.

Speckled stone with markings and grooves told the story of Johah's lineage, tracing far back to their first journey from Rianus. Stained windows directed the light and painted vibrant colors across the letters. A fire burned in a hearth, adding warmth to the cool interior. Diaz wouldn't have gone that route, but when Selira shivered, he ran his hand up and down her back, understanding that his human preferred a warmer clime.

"Councilor Johah," he called, striding into the male's home as if he had the right to intrude.

"Who would dare—" Johah froze, his white eyes widening. "Justisaar Diaz, what is the meaning of this intrusion?" In his casual robe of spun silk, the male was no less impressive. White braids fell down his back and draped over his shoulders.

"I bring news of a betrayal requiring your immediate counsel," Diaz said.

Johah wasn't listening. His gaze had found and settled on Ober. "I cannot believe you survived. After all he did to you..."

"Who?" Diaz asked, more to glean what Johah knew.

"Hom'Garr returned from a luncheon with his weyr, so irate that I expected him to expire on the spot. He was most displeased with his precious danno falling for a common soldier. Worse, that they were heartsmates." A stiff smile teased Johah's mouth. "A rarity, or so they say. I suspect most do not realize the depth of their connection when they choose their mates." He splayed his fingers across his chest. "I am glad you came to see me. I have borne this burden for too long." He glanced at Diaz's pappo. "Is it at your advice that Diaz comes to me, Esha?"

"Indeed, Councilor." Pappo bowed his head.

"How may I assist?" Johah's stared at Selira, his thoughts hidden. "I assume you wish to bring Hom'Garr to justice?" He spun on a heel, the ends of his robe flicking out. "Come, we have much to discuss. Evidence is what we will need. To speak truth, the council has been searching for a reason to strip Hom'Garr of his authority. I hope you have much to reveal." He swept out an arm to the cushions scattered on a thick woven rug.

Diaz laced his fingers with Selira's and pulled her down with him. Since she didn't speak Gy'Ruxian, he didn't know whether she could follow the conversation based on expressions alone. "We have footage and recordings confirming Hom'Garr's plans... In his own voice." Diaz tossed a data crystal onto the cushion beside Johah.

Ober thumped his chest. "And an eye witness, though it would be my word against his."

"I had no idea that Pyia was Hom'Garr's danno until Ober found me." Diaz clenched his jaw against the shame of his failure. "So many things would not have occurred had we chosen different paths." He tightened his hand around Selira's, grateful that he found her. "I cannot fathom how a pappo would use his ruxling so callously. Did he not love her?"

"The inner workings of a male's hearts is known only to the male," Johah said. "But actions tell their own tales and with truth. He must not have loved her if he sent you to judge her. To pervert our sacred laws for ambition..." He tutted.

"We came to gather allies," Ober said. "Would Da'Ager side with Hom'Garr or justice?"

Johah grunted. "Your timing could be better. They went fishing just this morning, behaving like there had been no animosity shared between them these past seasons." He folded his arms across his chest. "I will reveal your intentions to the councilors I trust. You approach Da'Ager. Esha, with me. Your battle prowess alone will bring credence to the news."

"Very well, Councilor." Pappo glanced at Diaz, no longer able to detain Da'Ager if need be.

"We shall meet in the chambers before the first sunset." Johah leaped to his feet, his focus once more on Selira. "Who is she?"

"My heartsmate," Diaz said, drawing her closer after standing.

"May *Remyi* bless your union." Johah gestured for them to leave.

Diaz looped an arm around Selira's waist and ushered her out, passing Five hovering in the doorway.

Ober strolled alongside them. "That went well."

"Indeed," Diaz said, gazing at the waters below. Deep sea fishing for an aqua dragon might be enjoyable, but for crimsons, reaching the underwater homes might be difficult. "This one is on you, Ober," he said, meeting his blood mate's blue gaze.

"Expected as much." Ober grinned. "It's been a while since I swam in the Bay of Gavrev."

Diaz studied the suns' positions, measuring how much sunlight remained of the day. "Five will fly us to the shore again where we will wait for you."

"Oh, no, you're coming with me." Ober caught Diaz's arm, halting him.

Diaz frowned. "How?"

Ober shrugged, a smile forming. "Hold your breath?"

"I am not riding you into the depths of certain death." Diaz glowered and marched on.

"Then we can forget about Da'Ager. He won't believe me without you there." Ober strode into the camis as if the matter was resolved.

"Ass shit," Diaz muttered.

"What's wrong?" Selira asked.

"Ober wants Bossman to go for a dip," Five said, stomping past them to the cockpit.

"Oh," she said, sinking onto the bench. Her brow furrowed in thought, and her eyes widened. "Can you swim?"

"Aquas live at the bottom of the bay, but once I reach Da'Ager's home, I will be able to breathe." Diaz grimaced. "It is getting there that is not appealing."

She exhaled, her shoulder slumping. "I suppose Five and I stay here?" She clasped her hands in her lap, her knuckles white.

"Or we can dive down with the camis," Five said.

"A ship descending to those depths wouldn't be welcome." Ober gripped the back of the pilot's seat. "We want to sneak in, not announce our presence."

"Fair enough," Five said, landing the camis on the opposite shore to the battlegrounds.

Hating being forced to do this, Diaz snapped, "I have not agreed to this madness." He shuddered at what lay before him: frigid waters, darkness, though that wasn't an issue, but clinging to the back of Ober was definitely an embarrassment.

The ramp lowered, a gust blew sand in, and in its path stood Ober, casually stripping off his garments. He dropped them at his feet, then ventured out to morph into his beast. With a dip of its head to rest its chin onto the beach, it waited.

"*Remyi*," Diaz mumbled. If his pappo and Johah weren't expecting him to talk with Da'Ager, Diaz would have refused outright. Snatching a quick kiss from Selira, he jogged down the ramp. "*Sillstari.*"

Before he could change his mind, he climbed onto Ober's beast.

Then up they went with a great sweep of its wings, and down they plummeted, breaching the waters with enough force to snap Diaz's head back. If he hadn't been holding onto the spines, he would have been thrust off. The idiot hadn't even given him a chance to take a deep breath. The deeper they went, the darker it became. With his enhanced vision, Diaz picked up the houses shaped like coral. Large domes covered in seaweed emitted steady streams of bubbles that dissipated before they reached the surface.

His lungs began to burn and still, on they dove, aiming for a cluster of homes at the center. Other aquas came and went, none paying them attention. Spots began to circle Diaz's vision, and the need to breathe became a priority.

Calm, his beast commanded.

Peace settled over Diaz. He closed his eyes, slowed his heartrates, and focused on why he was doing this. For honor to be restored, for justice, and, he admitted, revenge. A shadow across his face snapped his eyes open to the tunnel they delved through.

He breached the surface first, sucking in air. Before him sprawled streets with many houses. In front of them were stalls selling fresh fish and fruit. Strange balls clung to the domed ceiling, glowing with enough light to bathe the area like it was dusk upside. Smaller balls hung like lanterns from arching coral, illuminating circles of paved stone.

He slid off when the beast shook his shoulders.

"Amazing," Diaz whispered, aware he stood there, gawking, drenched, with his coat clinging to every inch of him. His boots squelched when he moved.

"It is," Ober said, once more a Gy'Ruxian.

Nudity was common and would draw no notice. Diaz should have stripped before climbing onto Ober's back. But he hadn't for fear he'd change his mind. Ober took a robe hanging on a nearby hook. Along the widest street they strolled.

"The purple house ahead." Ober winced. "If my memory serves me well."

Rows of steps marked the entrance to Da'Ager's home. When they reached the top landing, the councilor waited for them. "Many have warned me of your arrival," he said by way of greeting. "Come, the news must be dire for an exile and a dead Gy'Ruxian to visit me."

Where Johah's welcome room held light, Da'Ager's had texture. Waves scoured the inside of the coral. Translucency allowed filtered light through. Tiny squares in a multitude of colors patterned the floor. No softness was offered, only carved benches in some sort of netted substance. Not wanting to offend, Diaz sank onto one when Da'Ager gestured to it. Sponge conformed to his body, offering maximum comfort. He didn't like it.

"Did you know of Hom'Garr's plans?" Ober asked. "To sell me into slavery and use Diaz to kill his danno?"

Da'Ager stiffened. His cheeks paled. "No, he would not do such a thing."

"He did." Diaz leaned forward, as best he could, to grip his knees. "We wish to bring our evidence to the council."

Da'Ager nodded. "I knew he was furious about Ober and Pyia, but I expected him to accept it. After all, heartsmates are a gift from *Remyi*." He glanced at Diaz. "And his fear of your popularity was illogical when we are not as we once were. At some point, we would need to step aside for the new councilors to rule." He sank deeper into his sponge and grimaced. "It is time. You have my support. Have you spoken to other councilors?"

"We have." Ober tapped his fingers along the chair's arm. "Johah."

Da'Ager sniffed. "Good. He is well-respected."

"As are you, Councilor." Diaz rose, considering this meeting at an end. What awaited him was yet another swim.

"Do you have a plan? Hom'Garr will know something is happening if he is invited to the chamber without reason."

Diaz hesitated. 'Escorting' Micky in would have been ideal. But he didn't have it in him to hurt his Selira. "I have Ober," he said, glancing at his blood mate. "We could use him to lure Hom'Garr. He did say to bring him in for judgment."

"Yes, and he would want to be there before the councilors arrive." Da'Ager nodded at Ober. "To silence you."

"I like this." Ober grinned. "When we return to your camis, make the call. I want done with this."

"Agreed." Diaz bowed to Da'Ager. "Thank you for seeing us. We will gather in the chambers at first sunset."

With that said, they left, marching down the street to the lake below. Diaz winced with every squelch, swish, and drip, dreading what was to come. But he would endure much for a chance to see Hom'Garr be exiled. And of course, Selira waited for him.

He squared his shoulders as she was wont to do then glanced at Ober, silently asking him to summon his beast. This time when they dove in, Diaz would be forewarned. While he climbed onto his blood mate's beast, he drew in deep breaths.

And a big one before they sank into the water.

Chapter Twenty-Three

"Five, any chance you can up the temperature? I'm freezing," Selira said, pacing to keep herself warm. With each step, her left foot thunked on the metallic floor.

"Sure, though why you're cold is beyond me. With a bun in the oven, you should be cooking." He chuckled. "Did you see what I did there?"

"Ha-ha, very funny," she said, trying to smother a smile. Thoughts of Diaz weren't far and sliced through Five's attempt to distract her. "Pity we can't track his ass," she muttered.

"Patience, babe. He'll be fine."

She wrung her hands instead of Five's neck. "I know that," she snapped. "I want this over with before Micky decides to take things into her own hands."

"Yup, that could be a problem. NOX says she's chomping at the bit." Five leaped out of the pilot seat to grab Selira's shoulders. "Listen here, honeybuns. You're in love, have a firebrand on the way, and a man-beast who adores you. Quit worrying, and trust that things will work out."

She released a breath on a whoosh. "You're always right, and you know I hate that." The tension eased a little. She cupped her belly and nodded. "Diaz will be fine. He's just swimming."

"Exactly." Five strode down the ramp but didn't disembark. "What do you think of this war?"

She joined him, appreciating the warmth coming off the beach. In the distance, massive shadows across the horizon marked the Okukuro's locations even as dragons swooped and burned.

"Both sides are getting nowhere. Don't see the point, to be honest." She raised her face to the beige sky with a bright sun and a weak one.

At their last meeting, she hadn't understood a word spoken, but the white-haired guy had seemed impressed with what Ober and Diaz had to say. Pappo staying behind was unexpected, but she didn't know what was agreed upon. Just that Diaz had to speak to this Da'Ager underwater.

"Seems like I'm going to have to learn to speak Gy'Ruxian." She winced, dreading learning a new language at her age. Well, if Diaz could master English, she could, at least, try for him and their son. "Going to take a while though. It's so guttural." She tossed a smile at Five. "I envy your ability to learn new skills and languages with a download."

"We can start with the basics," Five said. "A few words a day and soon, you'll be fluent."

She supposed that wasn't asking too much.

"About time," Five said and pointed at the bay where a dragon skimmed the surface.

She exhaled, shook her body to release more tension, and grinned, hoping to hide that she'd been worried. The dragon landed, throwing up sand. Diaz slid off. He scowled at a naked Ober who staggered to his feet, his smile taking the last of her fear.

"How did it go?" she asked when Diaz commanded his shuttle to unhide.

"Good. Da'Ager will support our cause." He stripped as he strode past her to the mirror. "It is a pity I cannot take you to the bottom of the bay. It is quite beautiful." He winked at her while the green beam ran over his glorious body.

She hummed, not planning to ever get tired of seeing him naked.

Within moments, Diaz was dressed in fresh pants, shirt, boots, and a coat. "Five, take us up. The first sunset draws near."

He ran his hand over his red fluff, crossed to her, and kissed her. She sank against him, relishing the solidity of his body beneath her touch.

"Thank you," Ober said, gesturing to his clothing she'd folded. "Has Mick landed yet?"

"No, thank the Lord," Selira said as Diaz sank into the pilot seat. "But she's becoming impatient."

"Ah, youth." Ober caught Selira by the elbow and tugged her away from the cockpit. "Five, to me," he said. "Diaz's about to call Hom'Garr with the news that he's captured me and is minutes away from the chambers."

Selira gasped. "You're the lure?" Warmth flooded her body at how considerate and brilliant her man was. Tears pressed to the back of her eyes, threatening to spill.

Ober's eyes widened.

She patted his arm. "Hormones make me cry. It's nothing you said." She sniffed.

Diaz spoke to a gruff-sounding man, their words in Gy'Ruxian.

Ober stiffened, clenched his jaw, and glowered. Whatever was being said wasn't nice, that she could guess. "It is as Da'Ager warned. Hom'Garr wants to meet me alone."

"Oh?" she asked. "To kill you without witnesses?"

"Indeed," Diaz said, abandoning his seat to join them. "Good thing the chambers have a view-room where anyone can observe in silence and secrecy. I am told few use it, though." He pulled her aside. "This is where you will wait, Selira. I do not want you or my sanno harmed."

Ober gestured to all of her. "And you're a curiosity best reserved for afterwards."

She glared at him for choosing sides. "Fine, but if the shit hits the fan, I'm coming in, guns blazing."

"Me too," Five said from the cockpit. "I assume I'm to fly you to the council chambers?"

"Please." Diaz kept his gaze on Selira. "Weapons are not permitted in the hall, but in the view-room, there is no law stating that. You may bring the bioblade. I do beg of you not to rush in unless I ask you to."

"How are you going to do that?" She smiled. "With a safe word?"

He frowned. "I do not know the meaning of this."

She leaned in to whisper, heat scorching her cheeks, "When in the middle of…mating, if either of us want to stop, we speak the chosen word."

He laughed and gathered her close to bury his nose in her hair. "We will never need such a word, but for today, I will let you decide."

"Hungry," she said, sliding her hands around him for a squeeze. "It's easy to slip that into the conversation."

He stilled, his gaze darkening with concern. "Speaking of which—"

"I'm too tense to eat, my love," she said, giving his cheek a kiss. "I assume we meet with Hom'Garr now?"

"Yes, when Five lands the camis on the platform. He will guard you in the view-room—"

"To make sure you don't do something silly," he said from the cockpit.

She scowled. "Name once I did anything stupid?"

"Fall down a hole? Rip your leg off? Bang your head on a ladder?" He laughed. "So many to choose from."

"I'll pull your plug, you rust bucket." She waved a fist at him.

"If you love me and you know it, clap your hands," he sang.

Diaz shook his head and sank onto his bench beside Ober. "Ready for this?" he asked.

Selira climbed onto his lap. "You're welcome to stay with us, Ober, whatever happens in there." She studied his face from the bold blue of his eyes to his dimpled chin. "I mean, I can get a bigger ship."

Ober chuckled. "And listen to you two kissy-kissy? Not to mention with a baby on the way? I'm going to give that a hard pass. Besides, I haven't been home for a while. If I can stay, I'd like to. For a bit."

"Fair enough." She patted his hand gripping his knee. "The offer stands for whenever you change your mind."

Up they flew, past where they stopped to chat to Johah. She caught a glimpse through the windshield at the narrow ledge Five had to land on. Intricate patterns marked the bridge to massive doors built into the side of the mountain. She'd never seen the like.

"That's where we're going?" she asked.

"Yes." A pulse ticked at Diaz's jaw. "I was last here when I was exiled. Never did I believe I would ever return." He dipped his gaze to her and smiled. "Nor did I think I would find you."

"You're going to make me cry," she sniffed.

"And we don't want that," Ober said, standing to face the ramp. "Come, let's hide you two before Hom'Garr arrives."

She grabbed the bioblade from Diaz's satchel and slid it into the back of her waistband. It offered little comfort when she might have to use it. If needed, she would. She lifted her chin, admitting she'd protect Diaz with as much fierceness as she would Micky or Five.

The wind whipped at her, threatening to topple her off the edge. She latched onto Diaz's hand, using his body as a buffer. Fear coiled in her stomach: no doubt from the height *and* from the impending confrontation. This was it. This was the moment that mattered the most to Diaz, to finally be vindicated. To see justice done. For Ober too. But there was danger ahead: if their newly made allies betrayed them, or if this Hom'Garr had a weapon.

"Where's Micky?" she yelled at Five when they reached the doors.

"Still in orbit the last time I checked," he said, nudging her behind him when they strolled through a smaller side entrance.

"Good," she muttered. *Oh, Lord, please keep her away. Until much later.*

A vast hall opened up, in grays and blacks with carved blocks of stone mounted to walls, stained glass windows up high, and mosaic tiles on the floor. Two long horns like didgeridoos sat to one side. The space was empty, echoing their footsteps when Diaz led them to a staircase on the left. Curving upward was an iron balustrade with shapes and details her fingers itched to explore. The steps were smooth, polished, and easy to climb. In a dark room overlooking the hall below, a hard bench squatted before a perforated stone wall. Space between the lettering and patterns formed a latticework of sorts, giving her a pixelated view.

"Sound travels well, so try not to speak." Diaz gathered her hands in his. "I love you, Selira. Whatever happens, know you have my hearts."

Pain tightened around the coils of fear. His words sounded like goodbye. "As you have mine," she said. "Whatever happens, Diaz, we can handle it."

He crushed her in a hug. "Five, guard her, please."

"Of course."

Then Diaz was gone, taking Ober with him. Their footsteps marked their progress down. Across from her, movement or a play of light caught her attention. No doubt there was another observation room on the opposite side. Maybe the other councilors were there to witness the scene unfold and hopefully Hom'Garr would reveal his duplicitousness.

She sank onto the bench, clasped her hands over the bioblade balanced on her lap, and suppressed a shiver. Why did everything have to be so damn cold? Johah's home had been the most inviting. That man was a stunner. He wore his age and authority well, and his voice held that deep resonating strength that a man in power should have. She'd trusted him without understanding a word he said.

Her instant belief in him had put her on the backfoot. Until this played out, no one other than Diaz's father was on their side. Ober stood on the dais, facing the doors at the rear. Diaz had one foot on the step, smiling at him.

"So, this is the chamber," Ober sniffed down his nose. "I expected it to be more impressive. I mean, we grew up on tales of this hall." He swept out a hand. "Not the look I would've gone for."

Selira stilled, her mouth falling open. "What are they saying, Five?"

"I expected this to happen. Here." He offered her an earpiece. "This will do until you have learned the language."

"You made an interpreter?" She smiled at her NOXV. "You know I love you, right?"

"Sure do, honeybuns." He blew her a kiss.

She hurried to place the piece in her ear and waited, hoping Ober or Diaz would say something so she could test it.

"Oh?" Diaz gestured to Ober. "With the way you dress, I am too afraid to ask what you would change with the decor."

Ober jerked back. "What's wrong with my clothes?"

"You are humanlike now. What are those trousers?" Diaz pinched the blue fabric.

"Jeans."

She chuckled. "We'll get Diaz into a pair at the first way station we dock at," she whispered to Five.

"Why would you when you like him without pants?" Five muttered.

"True," she hummed.

One of the double doors at the back creaked open. Through it strolled an older Gy'Ruxian in an opulent robe. No, not old, ancient when his wrinkles dug into his skin, his eyes almost sunken. She'd have to hazard a guess he was an aqua dragon. The fading sunlight caught a glimmer of indigo on his braids. The deeper the color the more power a Gy'Ruxian had? That's what Diaz had said about Tieren's yellow eyes—a griffin without the ability to spew fire. Did that mean Ober with his arctic-blue eyes was a weakling? It would explain why he was a soldier, but she wasn't sure. Perhaps the potency didn't matter when applying to become a justisaar, but a specific psychology did?

"I expected you to die out there in the wastelands. You, a mere soldier, survived the slavery I sold you into?" Hom'Garr shoved his face into Ober's, uncaring that the younger man towered inches above him. "Exiled Justisaar Diaz, kill this traitor."

"For what crime?" Diaz folded his arms across his chest. "Or will you make them up like you did for your danno?"

Hom'Garr's face darkened. He spluttered, "How dare you mention my Pyia. It was you who misjudged her."

"As a danno of such impeccable lineage, why was she a servant on the battlegrounds?"

Ober gasped. "Is that where you found her?"

"When I called her name, only innocence lay in her expression. Curiosity followed. There was no guilt and no fear of judgment." Fury poured off Diaz. "I was too arrogant to see it, how trapped she was, how the pappo she had once loved betrayed her. Nor did I for a moment think I was being played."

"What is this?" Hom'Garr demanded. "Why did you bring Ober if not to judge him?"

"He has a right to see justice done."

"What rights does a slave have?" Hom'Garr spat then spun in a circle with his arms wide. "What happens here is just, according to our laws, and sanctioned by our father, *Remyi.*"

Diaz rubbed his thumb from jaw to chin. "If it is like you say, then his captors were documented in the archives?"

"And Pyia's crimes stated alongside her name, lineage, and manner of death?" Ober waved a data crystal. "I have evidence of your deceit."

"What nonsense is this?" Hom'Garr tried to reach for the crystal.

Instead of raising it higher, Ober offered it to him.

The councilor snatched it and chuckled. "This is all you have?" He dropped it to the floor and crushed it under his boot heel. "That is what I think of your so-called evidence." He swerved around Ober to grab a ceremonial sword mounted to the front of a plinth. "If you will not do as commanded, I shall kill you both."

Diaz laughed. "Why would either of us need to die? Surely a new trial presented to the councilors would resolve this."

"And waste our precious time over this farce?" Hom'Garr faced them, his shoulders back, his feet planted in a fighting stance. Yet the tip of the sword dipped to the floor.

Ober huffed, crossed to the man, and took the weapon away from him with barely a struggle. "I have kept to my training schedule." He waved the sword. "You have not." He tossed it aside, not glancing when it slid to a stop.

"I, Diaz Rowfallak of the Opato clan, an exiled justisaar, will now judge you."

"You cannot," Hom'Garr cried out. "You have no authority."

"Do I not?" Diaz hummed. "Regardless, let us play this game. One: you kidnapped a male and sold him to a passing slaver. Two: you earned tokens for that transaction, did you not? Did you declare the blood price?" For each accusation, Diaz inched toward Hom'Garr, forcing the man to retreat. "Three: you manipulated the judgment records, fabricating crimes for your own danno. Four: you had me judge her so that I would be exiled. Why me? In what way had I offended you?"

"Five: you killed my heartsmate." Ober stood beside Diaz, their shoulders touching.

"And six: you failed to record any of this in the archives." Diaz peered down his nose at the councilor. "How do you plead?"

"Guilty," Johah called, stepping out from the shadows.

"Guilty," another councilor said, his red hair like Diaz's.

"Guilty." A man with blue braids dipped his gaze. "I suspected but could not prove it, blood mate. Why?" He lifted his chin. "Why would you do any of this? Your legacy would have stood the test of time, and yet, you threw it away for what? Another half-century as a councilor?"

"I need not explain myself to you," Hom'Garr snarled.

"How about to me, as Diaz's pappo?" Esha stood in the doorway Hom'Garr had come through.

Hom'Garr scanned the room, his body tense. With a roar, he lunged for Ober, knocking Diaz aside.

Blinding flashes like mini explosions tore through the chamber. When she dared to open her eyes, dragons in a multitude of colors filled the space, more than the number of men who'd passed judgment on Hom'Garr. She didn't know how they all fit.

And yet, Diaz hadn't transformed. He stood beside Ober, his gaze unwavering. "Throw yourself on the mercy of the council. Accept your sentences with dignity."

Hom'Garr swept out a wing, probably hoping to catch Diaz and Ober.

Instead, it collided with a massive dragon with red eyes. Movements blurred amid wings, teeth, flames, and rumbles. Selira struggled to follow, asking Five every few minutes to tell her what was happening. The two dragons grappled until, at last, the bigger one pinned the skinnier one to the floor.

"Accept judgment," Diaz said into the chaos. He nodded at the victorious dragon, who released Hom'Garr to lunge back, changing in a flash to Diaz's pappo.

Hom'Garr leapt to his feet, his nails clicking on the floor. When he charged at Diaz this time, other dragons knocked him back until he stood in a circle of black-winged beasts.

"Blood mate," a naked man said, snatching Hom'Garr's attention. "Please. If you continue to fight, you are courting death."

"Death it is," Hom'Garr said, a second after he emerged from the flash of light. Gy'Ruxian once more, he bolted into a run, scooped up the discarded sword, and thrust it into Ober. "For stealing my danno's love," he roared.

Diaz cried out, catching Ober, who fell back, clutching the blade sticking into his abdomen.

"Ass shit, that hurts," he said, then chuckled, purple blood dribbling onto the floor.

Cries for a medic filled the hall, with some dragons changing into their Gy'Ruxian selves. Pop by pop, naked men appeared. A few dragged Hom'Garr away. Then the crowd split when someone rushed in with a P.M. in hand. Silence fell with only Hom'Garr struggling in the background.

"He will live," the medic said.

The chamber exploded into cheers.

Like they juggled a hot potato, Hom'Garr was passed forward until he stood once more in the center, now surrounded by at least a hundred men.

"By the law, as decreed by the High Gy'Rux Council, to mete out justice falls on Ober Pontak. Exile or death?" Johah swept his gaze across the hall. "What say you, fellow justisaars?"

"A life for a life," a man shouted.

"Exile," another called out.

"For the death of his danno, for the erroneous exile of a justisaar we revere, and for the destruction of a sanctioned heartsmate? Exile is insufficient." A man stepped into the circle then faced his peers.

"Send him to negotiate peace with the Okukuro," Diaz's pappo said. "Let his glib tongue work for us. And should they not like what he says, let them decide his fate."

"If he succeeds, then we exile him," a blue-haired councilor said.

Hom'Garr's face paled to the color of ash. "Da'Ager, why would you—"

"I warned you about the greed within. I could not make you listen. Look at what you have done, my blood mate. *Look* at how you have destroyed what you held most dear." Sadness slumped his shoulders. "I do not know you anymore."

"Take him away and prepare him for the journey to the southern death grounds." Johah faced Diaz while a sobbing Hom'Garr was carried out. "Of course, your status is reinstated. Ober, you are free to return to your weyr and to resume your duties."

Selira stiffened. Fear tightened its hold on her stomach. This was it. This was what she'd feared would happen. As righteous as Diaz was, he might have to stay, leaving her to travel the universe alone…with their son.

"My thanks, for the honor this returns to both our weyrs, but I will remain with my heartsmate."

Relief flooded her, threatening to make her sob. She wanted to race down the steps and throw herself into his arms.

"Ah." Johah nodded. "Where is your pale female?"

"You did not mention this, Diaz," Da'Ager said. "That *Remyi* has blessed you so further proves your worth to Gy'Rux."

"Selira." Diaz raised his chin, his gaze on the observation room.

She bolted, skipping down the stairs to reach him. Again the crowd parted, letting her through, with Five on her six. She didn't run no matter how much she wanted to. With her head high, she strolled like a queen. No way would she embarrass Diaz with unladylike behavior. But when he held out his hand to her, she caught it and let him drag her into his arms.

"Selira, meet Councilor Da'Ager."

"Five, translate for me. A pleasure to meet you, Councilor." She smiled at Da'Ager then winced when Five used her voice.

"What species is your heartsmate, and what manner of machine is this?" The man addressed Diaz, his gaze expectant.

"She is human, and I am an A.I. in a metallic suit. My designation is NOXV." Five settled beside her.

A boom filled the hall like the cracking in half of an ancient tree. The gigantic doors parted, flooding beige light into the dark interior. In strode her daughter, as confident as she was. Gasps filled the air, cries of alarm and shock Selira didn't need an interpreter to explain to her.

"Diaz, am I too late? What did I miss?" Micky marched across the dais to Diaz, gazing at the men gathered around him.

"This is the Shikari," he said in Gy'Ruxian. "And her Greeven *kekaseea*, Prince Tieren."

Few must've heard of Micky and her abilities, which was what Selira preferred, for they dismissed her as yet another human. Tieren's presence, however, garnered a greater reaction, the men hurrying to greet him from where he guarded Micky's back.

His glower didn't deter them.

"A celebration is in order," Johah called. "We shall gather in the banquet hall."

Diaz hesitated, slicing glances between him and Selira. She smiled, stole a kiss, and whispered, "Now, I shall meet your mammo and sasso while you have fun with your friends." She tapped her ear with the earpiece nice and snug. "I'm taking Five though. I can understand Gy'Ruxian but can't speak it yet."

"Come, babe, I know the way." Five nudged her shoulder.

"How?" Diaz scowled. "You knew where the chambers were, too."

"I studied the schematics," Five said in a 'how else' tone.

"I shall escort you," Diaz's dad said to her, shoving Diaz toward the men.

"Thank you." Selira smiled at his father. "What would you like me to call you?" She huffed when Five had yet to translate. "What do I pay you for?"

"Hold your horses," he muttered then repeated what she said to Diaz's dad.

"Oh," the man laughed, laugh lines crinkling around his eyes and mouth. "Esha or Pappo is fine."

Using 'Pappo' felt wrong, having not spoken a similar word in years, not since she lost her dad. But Esha would do.

"I'm Selira," she said, looping her arm through his while Five mimicked her words in a monotonous tone. She glared at him and hissed, "Behave."

"It is a beautiful name." Esha ushered her out the room and down a long winding road carved into the mountain like a mining tunnel. Torches high up added some light, but it was dark and gloomy for the most part.

He didn't say much, but considering that he was her new family, sort of, she could endure.

"Mom," echoed off the rock walls.

Selira halted and faced Micky running toward her. "I thought you wanted to stay."

"Nope, no thanks." She bowed her head at Esha.

"Where's NOX?" Five asked, then bolted with, "I'll find you later."

"But..." *Frig*. Selira glanced at Esha and slumped.

There went her translator.

Epilogue

SINCE ESHA HADN'T SPOKEN, neither had she and Micky. So Five calling Selira's name was loud in the somber silence. He'd caught up to them when they reached the bottom of the mountain. NOX trailed him, looking humanlike in his skin. Perhaps she was mean to withhold that from Five? Just because she once had an issue with her leg didn't mean she had to pass her embarrassment onto him. She'd talk to him next time they had a moment.

They strolled on, stepping into the semi-night air. Stars dotted the brown-tinted sky with the weak sun still shining. There was no moon to be seen...yet.

Five offered Micky an earpiece to replace one of her others. "To understand Gy'Ruxian."

She laughed. "But I don't need it. NOX just slides the language into my brain."

"What?" Selira gasped and bulged her eyes at Five. "That's possible?"

Five's rubbery eyebrows arched high. "I didn't know this." He scowled at NOX.

"What?" the A.I. shrugged. "You didn't find that bit of knowledge while digging through my data files?"

"Sure, and vice versa," Micky said while the two NOXs argued in hushed voices. "It's how Tier speaks English so well." She clicked her fingers in NOX's line of vision. "NOX, do it."

"Hang on." Five threw up a hand. "Are you sure it's safe for the baby?"

Micky paled. "You're right. Okay, scan Diaz's dad and see if you can't—"

"On it," NOX said.

"What is the matter?" Esha asked, his gaze whipping between them. "My home is not far from here."

"We are attempting to breach the language barrier," Five said to him.

Esha jerked back. "How?"

"By giving you Selira's English." NOX gripped his shoulder and met his gaze. "The pain is minimal. May I?"

He hesitated, studied Selira's face, then nodded. His brow knitted, and he flinched.

"Done," NOX said in English. "I usually take it slow, but since you are so, well, healthy, I risked it. Tell me, how do you feel?"

"Good. You were correct. The pain was slight." Esha froze, opened and closed his mouth, and staggered back. "This is not my maiden tongue."

"It is mine," Selira said, offering a smile in commiseration.

"I understand you," Esha said, beaming. "Come, my Rifa must meet you and your...friends."

"This is my daughter, Micky." Selira grabbed Micky by the arm and dragged her closer.

"Daughter, as in danno?" Tears glistened in Esha's eyes. "I have a granddanno?"

"Hi," Micky said, giving him a wave.

"This has been an excellent day," he said, snatching poor Micky into a crushing hug. "Rifa and Vasaa will not believe me." He meandered along roads wide enough for a dragon and paused in front of a stone door. "Rifa, I am home."

Selira squared her shoulders, hoping with every ounce of her soul that Diaz's family would like her. They mattered to him, and she didn't want him torn between loyalties.

Esha moved the door aside as if it weighed nothing. "Come, *purlievo*, meet our new danno and granddanno."

"What nonsense do you speak, Esha?" a woman asked.

That was Selira's cue. She slipped through the door into a narrow room, a 'dining area' in the front, and a kitchen of sorts at the back. Doorways led to other rooms, their purpose unknown. The walls were solid rock, the same color as the council chambers, no doubt carved out of the mountain like an anthill.

And it was cold. *Frig*. Next time, she'd pack a jacket.

Before her stood a feminine version of Diaz, down to the shape of her eyes and his wide mouth. She gaped at Selira's then frowned at Esha. "Who is this?"

"Selira is Diaz's heartsmate." Esha grinned, his eyes twinkling.

Rifa's cheeks paled. "Diaz is home?"

"Yes, and his honor restored, but I fear he will not be staying long." Esha turned Rifa to face the kitchen. "Come, we need to feast, to celebrate. I have much to tell you."

Rifa took a step, pinched her brow, then swiveled, her gaze on Selira. "How many am I feeding? And what do you eat?"

"I'm pregnant, and until I know whether it is safe to eat your food, I'll skip the meal for now." She glanced over her shoulder at Five, expecting him to translate.

"Pregnant?" Rifa mimicked. "I know not this word—" Her eyes widened. "What am I saying? Have I gone mad?"

"NOX," Micky snapped. "Ask first. I thought you learned your lesson after the last time."

"Sorry," NOX called, waving at Rifa. "I taught you how to speak Selira's language without asking. My bad."

Selira inched into the room, granting everyone a chance to enter since she was blocking the door.

"She is with ruxling," Esha said in Gy'Ruxian.

"Oh," Rifa gasped, then started to cry. She grasped Selira's hands, drawing her deeper into their home. "Come, sit, my danno."

"And this is Micky, our granddanno." Esha captured Micky's arm and ushered her to the bench beside Selira. Five settled behind her with NOX next to him.

Rifa sniffed, flicking tears aside while she gathered platters and loaded them with what looked like a variety of fruits.

"They're fruitarians," Selira said to Micky.

"Wow," she said. "How did Diaz get that big?"

Selira chuckled. "Exactly what I want to know."

"Vasaa," Rifa roared, startling a yelp out of Selira. "Come meet your sasso."

"My what?" a woman called, thundering down the stairs before bursting into the room. "Oh, we have...strange guests." In leggings and a tight tank top, she towered over them. As beautiful as her mother, Vasaa still had too much of Diaz in her appearance, especially in the angle of her jaw.

"This is Selira, Diaz's heartsmate," Rifa said. "And she is with ruxling."

Vasaa stared at Selira for a while. "Does that mean Diaz's is back?" She glanced at her father expectantly.

"He is, for now." Esha still wore his grin. "And this is Micky, Selira's danno."

"Pappo," Vasaa snapped. "What of Diaz's exile?"

"Do not be rude, sasso," Diaz said from the doorway.

Vasaa squealed and threw herself at him. He caught her, his laughter tumbling free. Next was his mother for a hug and hurried words. Amid tears, she cupped his face and urged him to bend for a kiss to his temple.

A flurry of questions followed, and for the duration, Selira was happy to listen in. She shifted up to let Diaz sit beside her, while Tieren rested a hand on Micky's shoulder.

"Why didn't you stay for the celebrations?" Selira asked Diaz when Vasaa paused in her million questions to stare at Tieren.

"I am more content when I am with you." Diaz stole a kiss, clasped her hand, and smiled at his family.

"What do you mean I am speaking a new language?" Vasaa demanded, her fists on her hips. In her agitation, her unbound red hair swirled around her like a flickering flame.

"NOX," Micky whined.

Selira laughed, happier than she'd been in a while. This was her new life, and for once, she didn't consider herself undeserving. When Diaz stroked her belly, she layered her hand over his.

Whatever the universe threw at them, they would handle it.

About the Author

Sevannah Storm is a fiction writer who immerses herself in fantastical worlds both magical and science fiction. She has a flare for the creative, having studied art and interior architecture, and spends her time drawing, oil painting, and writing. An avid reader from an early age, Sevannah finds her inspiration from various sources: games, novels, music, and the land of make-believe. The unique versus the practical has brought on numerous debates.

In her spare time, she does Pilates and rereads novels that snatch her breath away. Having embraced the social media world, you can find her on most platforms.

Her home is a land south of Wakanda, where animals roam free. Born in Zimbabwe, she grew up in South Africa. The crisp blue skies with cotton-candy sunsets expand her heart and soul, encapsulating a sense of freedom.

Words she lives by: "Know your pothole and dodge it. Don't work in a pencil factory if you're a vampire."

Sevannah loves to hear from her readers. You can find and connect with her at the links below.

Website/Newsletter:

https://www.sevannahstorm.com/

Facebook:

https://www.facebook.com/sevannah.storm

Instagram:

https://www.instagram.com/sevannah.storm/

Twitter:

https://twitter.com/sevannah_storm

Thank you for taking the time to read *The Justisaar*. If you enjoyed the story, please tell your friends and leave a review. Reviews support authors and ensure they continue to bring readers books to love and enjoy.

Stay tuned for sample chapters.

THE SHIKARI

SPACE HUNTER CHRONICLES #1

Chapter One

The Bite

Year: 2358

Uncharted planet in the Leo I constellation (K2-18.)

MICK SPLAYED HER GLOVED fingers and pinned herself to the glistening stone wall. She slowed her heavy breathing behind the mask. The luminescent pink and yellow flowers hanging like droplets on the orange trees burned spots into her retinae. She squeezed her eyes shut while the drums thumped, reverberating through the soles of her magno-boots. Semi-naked tribesmen chanted and hummed, facing a dais. The chieftain or high priest, with the white plumage and black stripes painted across his torso, danced to the front. When he ululated, she winced, wishing she could cup her ears. Behind him towered a gold-carved deity—a three-man high statue with plump breasts, a hefty belly, and a penis resembling a thick snake.

Beside the chieftain sat her target.

Trusting the exo-suit to camouflage her, she wove through the kneeling humanoids to the altar at the center of the dais.

On the smooth rock squeaked a hokou male—so named for the swirling patterns of stars on their skin. Dad had been creative when he'd named his discoveries. She planned to steal this one since these unclassified humanoids would kill it as a sacrifice to their statue. Flicking a glance at the god's eyes embedded with precious gems, she wrapped her fingers around the hokou's pale elongated torso.

It chirped in panic.

The chanting ceased.

She swallowed a chuckle at the spectacle of a male hokou hovering in mid-air while she, invisible, carried it.

The closest she could compare it to an animal on Prime Earth would be an albino monkey. Except a hokou had three tails, three-fingered hands and feet, and razor-sharp teeth. It scratched her gloves, twisting to do so. Her exo-suit sparked under the abuse, and just like that, she uncloaked amid the worshipping humanoids. Silence reigned until she clutched the hokou to her chest and ran. War cries and bellows trailed her mad dash through the jungle. She retraced her steps to the shuttle at breakneck speed. Ducking as befeathered spears whizzed past her, she scrambled in her haste, sprinting up the ramp. As she dived onto the metallic flooring, she yelled at NOX to get her the hell out of there. At the same time, the hokou sank its teeth into her shoulder.

She screamed. Its teeth sank so deep, the bite numbed her arm. Blood flowed, plastering the suit to her body as she struggled to tear the creature off her. Each yank had more fire burning along her veins and nerves. She sobbed. In desperation, she punched it in the face. It unclenched its jaw for a second. She caught it by a tail and tossed it into a cage before ripping her mask off.

After a stagger and a tumble into the pilot seat, she gripped and released the console, drawing in deep calming breaths. Trembles gripped her, shuddering her limbs. The pain blazed through her, spasming her muscles.

"NOX, I'm wounded." She coughed and blinked at the crimson droplets on the fore vids. The metallic taste of blood registered. "Prep the pod."

"Your pain markers *are* elevated," he hummed.

Elevated? Her eyes stung too hard for an eye roll, but she was tempted.

On auto-pilot, the shuttle breached the atmosphere. She didn't admire the planet's beauty or the dark embrace of a cold expansive universe. Instead, she squeezed her eyes shut and focused on breathing.

When she'd scanned the planet in passing, she hadn't expected to find the hokou's homeworld. Thinking to have a mating pair, she'd observed the capture, chant, and slaughter that formed the humanoids' religious ritual. Not once had the male hokou killed or bitten a local. Not once had she suspected they drugged it.

The shuttle tucked into Dad's research ship, the *Jinsei,* and landed. Time ticked by as she waited for the bay door to close.

"Air pressure restored," NOX said. "Pod powered up and open."

Climbing the ladder to the raised walkway took forever, one hand above the other. Sweat dripped off her chin when she reached the top. There she hesitated, bending over to gasp in ragged breaths. Straightening, she stumbled forward, trailing a hand along the passage wall, needing the cool surface and its stability. She clung to the medbay doorway. Dizziness, dripping sweat, and the lack of sensation in her limbs had her fighting for air. Her chest tightened. Pain followed the crushing weight pressing behind her sternum.

She crawled into the white pod sitting centerstage of the stark-white medbay. Rolling over drained her remaining strength. The transparent lid closed, entombing her, and holographic stats flickered on its surface. Normally, she read the scan results but not today. The colorful lettering had nausea tightening her stomach until tamping down the vomit rising up her throat became a priority.

Drifting in and out of consciousness, she caught a few of NOX's words, a stat here and there before darkness dragged her into its merciful depths. Time slowed. When the lid opened, releasing her, cool airbrushed along her skin, raised the hairs on her arms, and drew a shiver.

"Results," she rasped as she pulled herself into a sitting position. She raised her arm, flexing her fingers to test them. The bite had shredded the suit and along the edges of the tears, blood had hardened the soft nano-bio fabric. With a groan, she climbed out of the pod, calculating how much a new exo-suit would cost.

"You are at peak capacity."

She arched a brow at the bulkhead. "But?"

"I am glad you caught that, Mick. I have been working on my human inflection."

"But?" she asked again, striding along the passage to the small loading bay she had used that now housed a pissed-off male hokou.

"The bite has infected your blood." NOX, her Nano Omnipresent X-class A.I, paused for effect; something he was working on too. She hoped he didn't master it.

"Why didn't the pod cleanse it?" While she studied the sleeping creature, she gripped and rolled her shoulder with no hindrance in movement.

"No record of such a conversion exists. The effects occurred before you entered the pod. It could only address the conditions it recognized."

"I'm dying?" She sat, leaning an elbow on the workbench to drop her face into a palm.

"No, quite the opposite. You have never been this healthy."

"What? I was unhealthy before?" She stiffened. The surprises kept coming.

"Space travel affects human bones, muscles, tendons even with artificial gravity. You no longer exhibit that deterioration."

"Huh." Grabbing the handle, she carried the cage to the lower levels where the *Jinsei* housed Dad's menagerie. There were fewer creatures, almost as if they died from grief, sensing he wasn't with them anymore. It was why retrieving a male hokou had been important to her.

On a bench under UV light waited a caged female hokou her father had bought on some backward docking station. Mick slid the male's cage alongside it. "Emma, what do you think?" She waited, but Emma did nothing but blink at her.

Dad could spend hours down here, and they'd interacted with him. She had teased him about being the universe's xeno whisperer, something she was not. Why she thought she could follow in his footsteps, she'd never know.

She had to find something she could do to keep his legacy alive. What did other xeno-zoologists do? Not once had she met another in this field. They couldn't all be lab-bound, right?

She paused, staring at the hokou male. Bagging this one had been easy, well, except for the bite. What if... She grinned. Tagging would be easier. Just sample data to send to scientific research companies might be lucrative enough. She tilted her head and studied the metallic walls of Dad's barely space-worthy bread tin.

"NOX?" She chuckled. "Investigate whether there's a demand for blood and tissue samples from alien creatures. If so, document which companies and who to contact."

"On it, Mick."

Spinning, she leaned over the workbench to note what type of guns and gadgets she might need. Dad had a rifle. She'd start with that, maybe add modified bullets or extractors. After all, killing the creatures wasn't the intention. She tapped her foot, excitement sparking along her nerve endings and thrumming in her ears.

A tick-tick came from the rear of the bay. It grew louder until it engulfed her thoughts.

"NOX, check out that racket, will ya?"

"What noise, Mick?"

She hitched a thumb behind her, expecting him to watch from one of the many hidden cams.

"Oh." He whirred in thought. "Um, Mick, I have prepped the pod again."

She straightened and glared at the ceiling. "Why?"

"It seems you are hearing minute sounds originating from the engines."

She scoffed. "Those are bays behind us, NOX."

"Exactly."

Ice spilled down her spine, raising the hairs on her skin. She exploded into action, bolting along the passage, only to bump into the sides.

"Preternatural speed too." He sighed, grinding bolts to mimic the sound. "Do hurry."

Gripping the railings, she hoisted herself up the ladder and ignored the crumpled metal beneath her hands. With a shuddering breath, she sprinted the final distance and dove into the opened med-pod seconds later. *Unnatural speed and strength? What next?*

While the pod scanned her, she sifted through what a xeno-hunter might need in the field. Red text on the glass caught her attention. Not that she understood the medical jargon. She waited for NOX to elaborate, but he remained silent.

"And?" She huffed.

"Fortified and mutated muscles could explain your speed and strength. But the creation of an abundance of nerves could be why you have sensitive hearing."

"And touch," she muttered. "Will these fade with time?"

"I cannot say."

So, no help at all. She gritted her teeth and ran a hand up and down her arm. The texture of her skin and flesh beneath felt normal. The pod slid open, and she hopped out. Now wasn't the time to deal with this when she couldn't control whatever *this* was. She had a new career to plan, a way to save Dad's legacy, and she was going to grab onto it with both hands, mutations or not.

She headed to the menagerie and carried Emma's cage to the playpen Dad had built. As soon as the tiny door slid open, Emma scampered out and climbed the fake tree. Motion triggered the UV lights set into the bulkheads, bathing the terrarium with warmth.

Mick clipped the male hokou's cage in place and flicked the door. He didn't leave as quickly. She supposed she should name him.

"Hey, Horatio." She grinned at her creativity. *Yup, that will do.*

The food dispenser hummed as it spat rehydrated fruit into a tray. He peeked out of his cage, then crept into the terrarium. Emma dropped from the branch to swipe a piece of fruit. Startled, Horatio leaped aside. In a blink, he lunged at Emma. She squealed, deafening Mick. Instead of cupping her ears, Mick yanked open the access door and shoved Horatio off Emma. He leaped onto her arm. Fire burned along her veins from where he'd sunk his teeth into her forearm, again. She swung her arm, sending him flying to the rear of the terrarium. Pain radiated, pulsed, rose, and fell like a tidal wave while blood dribbled to her elbow. She couldn't focus on this now, fearing a worsening of the mutation.

Glaring at a sprawled Horatio to make sure he didn't attack again, she gently scooped up Emma. Blood matted the fur at her throat. Her limp body said it all. The air in Mick's lungs froze. She couldn't breathe. *No, no, no. Not Emma.* A tear slipped off her chin and faded into Emma's fur.

"NOX, prep the pod." Mick croaked, spun on a heel, and slammed the terrarium door behind her, ignoring her own blood speckling the metallic floor.

"She's dead, Mick. There's no pulse."

"No," she gasped, cradling the little body against her chest. The tears flowed while anger and sorrow engulfed her.

"The male's dying too. His abnormal behavior has to be a side effect of whatever the natives fed him."

"What?" she squeaked. "I...did all this for nothing?" She slid Emma into a biodegradable capsule, taking care with her tiny hands and feet, even tucking her tail in with the gentlest of touches. "How long does Horatio have?"

A whimper from the terrarium snagged her gaze. Slumped in the corner lay the male hokou. Grief weakened her knees. Perhaps Horatio had been dying all along, and her "rescue" had doomed him to an excruciating death. She sniffed and flicked tears aside with her wrist.

"Could the pod—?"

"You can try." NOX sounded doubtful.

When she picked him up, he didn't resist. His sad gaze rested on her, and each breath shuddered his chest.

"Prep the pod." She carried Horatio, speed walking while trying not to jar him.

"Done," NOX said.

She lowered him onto the pod's bed she'd recently vacated. When she stepped back, the capsule sealed. The red writing flickered like birthday lights—sad and hopeless. It didn't bode well. She splayed her fingers on the glass and waited.

"Internal organ failure, too many to heal. As soon as the pod heals one, another collapses. Something in the hokou's blood—"

"That makes no sense. Why would his bite grant *me* healing but not him?"

"A mutation, Mick."

"Perhaps this is my fate too," she muttered. "Because *I* did this. I...couldn't save him...*them*."

With trembling fingers, she ordered the pod to euthanize, sure to grant Horatio a sweet death. Everything within her couldn't let him suffer, not a moment more. In an instant, his labored breathing ceased. A last breath rasped out of him, his lifeless gaze on her.

Opening the glass, she gathered his limp body. "I'm so sorry, little guy." Crying, she carried him to the menagerie. She placed him into the capsule with Emma, clipped it shut, and rolled it into the tube. "Fly past the closest sun, NOX, and launch tube one." Spinning the lock in place washer final task in Dad's empty and deathly still menagerie.

She scanned the cages once filled with exotic and colorful creatures.

"NOX, deactivate all feeding programs. Freeze the power and life support to this area." She slumped and left the room, jogging to her father's quarters. Only when she slapped her palm on the keylock did she notice the dried blood. Unblemished skin remained where Horatio had bitten her. She should have the pod reassess her, but that could wait. If she was dying, finding out tomorrow was good enough.

She staggered inside when the door opened.

On his desk sat a bottle of alcohol. She dared not look anywhere else. Not once had she stepped foot inside his room, not since the funeral. Dad's things were as he left them. She hadn't the heart to move into the captain's cabin nor had she sifted through it. Like a tomb, it would go down with the *Jinsei* as is.

Grabbing the bottle and bolting, she paused in the passage, her breathing ragged. She waited, listening for the door to seal.

Up the ladder to the upper level, which had once been the viewing deck, she slapped the keylock and entered her room. As shuddering sob escaped her. She uncorked the bottle with her teeth and raised it to her lips. The fiery sweetness of port hit her tongue and burned her throat and belly. As she drank, something slithered along the glass bottle to nestle against her cheek. She pulled the bottle away and blinked at the amulet hanging around the neck. Catching it in her palm, she studied the hieroglyphs on its edges and an embossed bird at its center. Her tears dribbled into its grooves. She ran her thumb along its hooked nose, smearing blood across the amulet's white gold. Dad had worn this every day, but the funeral parlor couldn't incinerate it. She vaguely recalled slipping it onto the bottle.

"Dad... I miss you so much," she whispered and crumpled to the cold metal floor. She looped the amulet around her neck and raised the bottle amid the tears streaming down her cheeks. Never had she felt more abandoned than at that moment. And she was isolated, in a metal tin, flying through space with no destination in mind. On this ship, she would live and die...alone.

www.ingramcontent.com/pod-product-compliance
Lightning Source LLC
Chambersburg PA
CBHW070607120726
47909CB00007B/2475